Lost Men

Rajorshi Chakraborti is the author of four previous novels – *Or the Day Seizes You, Derangements, Balloonists* and *Mumbai Rollercoaster* – two of which have been shortlisted in different categories of the Crossword Book Award. He was born in Kolkata in 1977, and grew up there and in Mumbai, and presently lives and works in Wellington, New Zealand.

You can find out more about him and his work at www.rajorshichakraborti.com

Praise for Rajorshi Chakraborti

'Chakraborti possesses the gift of good storytelling.'

The Telegraph, Kolkata

'Ambitious and challenging metafiction; [...] will fascinate readers who enjoy Haruki Murakami.'

Booklist, USA

'The images, descriptions are cinematic. [...] The language in Rajorshi's books glides smoothly, the twists and turns between reality and a fictional dream-like haze. [...] Rajorshi talks of exile, of journeys, that everyone is haunted by a past, "losses and scars [...] struggling to survive until they can come home".'

The Hindu

'Chakraborti is among the most interesting writers now operating in Indian fiction. He deals with dark and subversive ideas un-selfconsciously and shows the willingness to stay away from safety nets.'

Tehelka

'Chakraborti [is] an ambitious writer, bravely traversing vast spaces, literal and metaphysical, committed to developing original structures and ideas.'

Edinburgh Review, U.K.

Lost Men

Rajorshi Chakraborti

First published in 2013 by Hachette India
(Registered name: Hachette Book Publishing India Pvt. Ltd)
An Hachette UK company
www.hachetteindia.com

SRD

ISBN 978-93-5009-512-6

Hachette Book Publishing India Pvt. Ltd
4th/5th Floors, Corporate Centre,
Sector 44, Gurgaon 122003, India

Typeset in Adobe Garamond 11.5/13.8
by InoSoft Systems Noida

Printed and bound in India by
Manipal Technologies Limited, Manipal

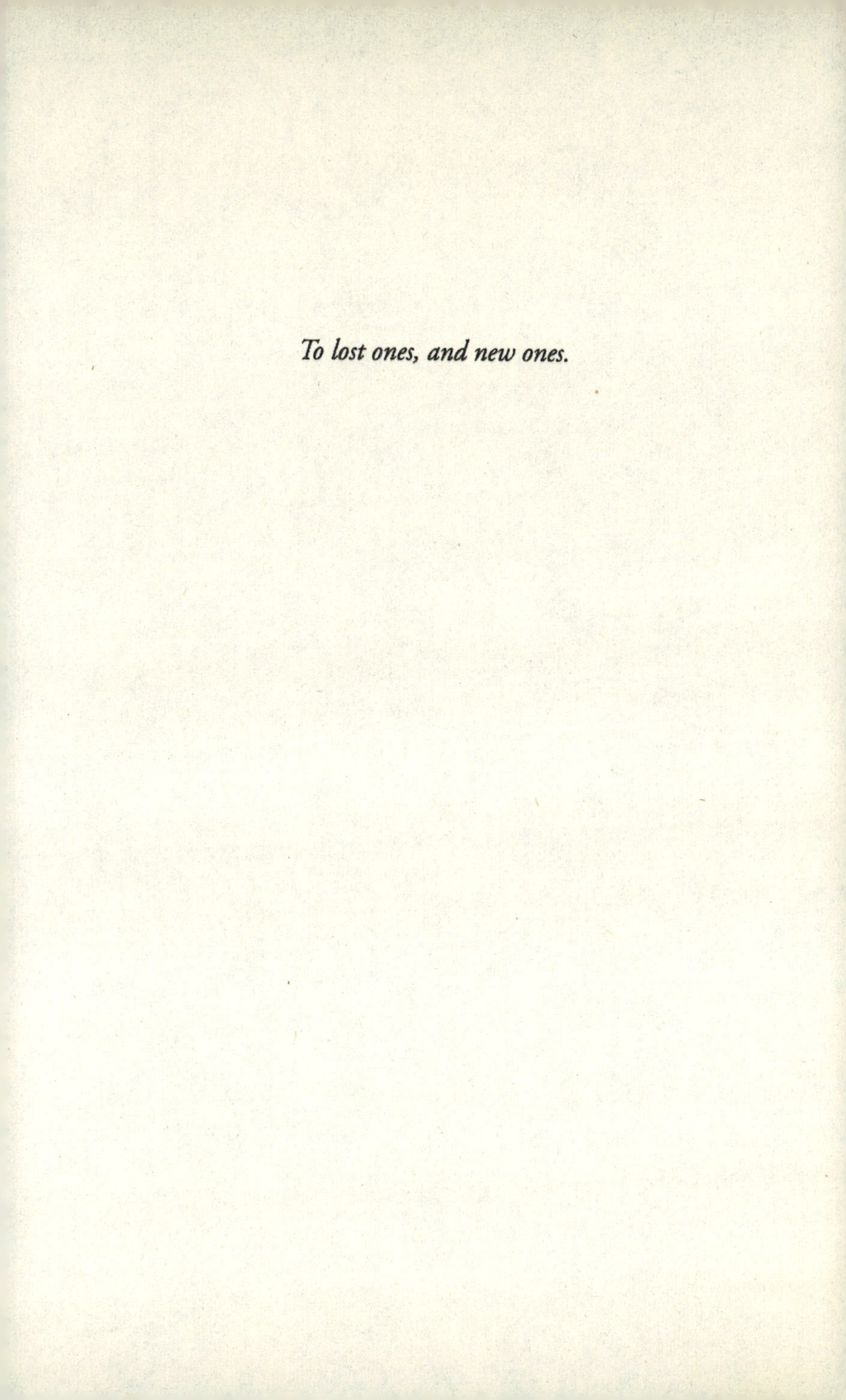

To lost ones, and new ones.

Contents

Knock, Knock

1

I'm reading the paper with my first cup of coffee when Mona comes in to say it was the bank that just called – there's one more form to do with our new account that we need to sign. I don't even look up as I reply: 'Typical. Nothing here can be accomplished in one day, even though we were there for two whole hours.'

Then I add, looking towards her, 'We'll drop by first thing in the morning sometime next week. You leave with me, and afterwards I'll drive you to your office.'

She remains standing as she speaks. 'This guy was very keen that we sign right away, so that the account is up and running as soon as possible. He said with these signatures it can be operational from today itself.'

This time I put the paper down on the dining table. 'So what are we supposed to do, rush over there right now? It's a Saturday, for God's sake. If they were so keen for the account to be operational, why did they forget to give us this form along with the ten thousand others?'

It might be my imagination, but Mona seems slightly nervous as she replies. 'He was willing to take the trouble to come and meet us with the form. He wanted to know where we would be this afternoon.'

Now I'm upset. 'And you told him?'

'He was very persuasive. He claimed there were benefits to signing the form today rather than next week, because Monday is the 1st of the month. If the account is opened right away, there are apparently some tax rebates we qualify for. He said he'd meet us on Camac Street, outside Westside.'

I cannot believe she has told him where we are going this afternoon, nor that she hasn't seen through his bullshit cover story. 'It's got nothing to do with benefiting us. It must be some commission *he* gets for booking new accounts. For some reason, he wants us recorded as part of this month's earnings rather than next month's.'

Then, because I still can't believe how naïve she has been, I scold her a little. 'How could you tell him where we were going? Don't you see how unusual that is, for an employee of a government bank to call up and agree to meet you outside his office? Only the most desperate salesmen do that, or someone angling for a bribe. Did you think he was just being selfless? Have you *ever* had a government employee repeatedly beg to be helpful to you, no matter where you are?'

But after saying all that I stop, even though I find the whole thing ridiculous. I can see I'm making her uncomfortable. She is standing there like a student being sounded out by an angry headmaster.

'I'm sorry. I didn't mean to yell. It's not a big deal. He'll be there. We'll sign the form, and carry on with our shopping.'

2

We have easily taken over two hours, because I know I tried on at least four pairs of jeans (before putting off the purchase for another time), and then afterwards we had a leisurely buffet lunch at the restaurant on the top floor, but when I bring the car out to the front of the shopping complex from the underground parking lot, there he is, standing beside my wife, the bank guy who'd brought the form out for us. We'd signed it on the way in as promised: surely there cannot be yet another thing he had forgotten.

Mona has that same odd, slightly ashamed look I had noticed earlier that morning; it isn't normal at all. When I pull up beside the two of them, ready to give this joker a piece of my mind, she quickly walks around the front, gets in, and starts speaking before I can park further to the left and call the guy over myself. He remains there on the raised platform – thin, in his early thirties, unfamiliar. Shorter than me, and quite relaxed.

Yes, I forgot to say, when we arrived at Westside and he walked over, he certainly had a form pertaining to our new account, but he wasn't one of the three people who'd been present the Tuesday before when we'd gone into the branch to set it all up. This was a new guy neither of us recognised. He'd said by way of explanation that this stage of processing new accounts was part of his domain.

There is something definitely the matter with Mona, because she is speaking far more rapidly than usual. She seems flushed, excited, but also embarrassed, as if she is about to seek a big favour on behalf of a friend. This is precisely the formulation that comes to my mind at that moment, as I move the car to the left to get out of the exit lane.

'He has another customer to see this afternoon, who lives right near us. He knew our address from the form, so he decided to wait in case we were returning home and could give him a lift.'

Can *you* believe what I am hearing? Is he mad, is naturally my first response. Next I am about to ask how *she* is feeling.

'Well, we are going home anyway, aren't we?' is Mona's strange reply.

'You told him that?'

To which she says nothing, instead glancing past me quickly as if to check if the fool has heard me.

'He waited two hours to get a lift. He could have gone to our area and returned to his branch by now.'

'Please, I beg you, don't make a scene. What's the harm if he comes with us?'

'Is everyone crazy, or am I losing my mind? How could you tell him we were going home? You want him in this car with us? Did you forget why he called us today in the first place, so that the account would be up and running as of this afternoon. Weren't those his exact words to you? Well, take a look at the time; it's almost four. His working day will soon be over. He's not going to return to the office after getting this other signature. What was the point of all this hassle if he was going to process our form on Monday anyway?'

'Achcha, he's waiting right there. What should I tell him?'

'Tell him to go fuck himself. I don't care. I don't see why we have to tell him anything. You're in the car, right. Let's just leave. In fact, if it's true that opening the account today would have earned us a tax rebate, that bastard has just cost me good money by waiting there like a moron. If you like you can warn him that I'm going to complain about him to his branch manager first thing on Monday morning. That way the new month will begin auspiciously for both of us.'

'It's my money too, don't forget. It's a joint account,' is Mona's next mystifying statement, after which – are you still with me – she waves the man over.

3

I haven't said a single word to the idiot in the back seat throughout the ride. He's sitting behind Mona, so I cannot see him in the rear-view mirror, but I know he's got his right arm raised and relaxed along the top of the seat, as if I'm his fucking chauffeur. He also hasn't spoken since getting into the car: instead he seems quite happy to gaze out the window as we drive, which for some reason infuriates me even more.

We're across the road from Purna cinema, a couple of minutes from where we live, when I ask Mona in English to find out from his Highness where he wishes to be dropped off. I'm certainly not going a single step out of my way for this bastard.

'You can just drop me off outside your house. That'll be fine,' is his reply in Bengali to Mona.

At this my rage boils over. I am driving alongside the central divider on S P Mukherjee Road, yet, without fully checking to see what is behind or beside me, I cut across to the left and pull over, double-parking next to a taxi.

'This is as far as we can take you. Please get off right now,' I speak to him directly in Bengali, although I'm still facing forward.

'But your house is a lot more convenient for me,' he says without even changing his position, which means he's telling me where to go in my own car, with his arm still draped atop *my* back seat. Just then, when I finally turn around to make my feelings crystal-clear, I also realise he has a permanent half-smile playing on his lips. I had noticed it before, but had semi-consciously dismissed it as arising from a typical clerk-like urge to curry favour. Now I see it in a different light: this fucker is just arrogant to an improbable degree.

'Look, I've already wasted a lot of time with you, so don't try my patience any further. I'm not going to drive you to our house, so please get off right now.' As I speak, I can hear a car behind us honking loudly to be allowed out, which is why I restrain myself and don't really fly off the handle.

Obviously he can hear the horn too, but he just remains

seated, without speaking or following my order. Instead, this is what changes in his demeanour – he cocks his head to the left, and looks away from me towards Mona, as if leaving her to be the final judge of things. The little smile stays in place: he looks like he is indulging a tantrum of mine.

Mona too isn't oblivious to the insistent honking, and perhaps says what she does in an effort to make peace.

'Let's not argue in the middle of the main road. It's just another two minutes: why don't we drop him outside our house?'

'But what if I don't want to go home? What if I wish to go for a walk around the Maidan instead?'

'The Maidan is that way. You should have said so earlier,' our new family friend pipes up to remind me.

By now, I can hear the driver behind us yelling, and am aware that I'm also holding up an entire lane of traffic. Which is why I decide just for the moment to suspend this quarrel and get off the main road. There's a crossing up ahead, and I turn left, but although our home is a few hundred metres along I pull over and park as soon as I have turned.

'We'll walk from here,' I say to Mona as I switch off the ignition. For once thankfully, she doesn't undermine me in front of this asshole. Instead she gets out onto the pavement and begins walking homewards without another word. I'm pleased to note the bastard finally realises the game is up and also leaves the car without protest. I lock up and move along, still on the road, to the right of the parked cars. I'm probably shaking my head in disbelief at the events of the day so far. I mean to sit Mona down as soon as we get home and ask her what exactly had come over her today. She's behaved all morning as though she were under some sort of spell.

The first stone is a small one and strikes me in the back, but it still definitely hurts. I turn around in shock (I might even have cried out), and realise the bank guy, who is about the length of a cricket pitch away, has picked up a handful of stones from a pile gathered outside a building site behind my car, and – get this – is *bowling* them at me! In fact, by the time I fully understand what is going on, because it actually takes me a while to look in his direction and trace the stone back to him (at first I turned towards the buildings on the opposite side of the road, expecting to see some kids fooling around, or even a car driving by that had run over a pebble and sent it flying), he has delivered the second stone, again with a full, accomplished over-arm bowling action, but no run-up, directly at me. It is all I can do to fend it away with my arm – that's how long it takes me to react to what is happening; this man is bowling high speed stones at me, with incredible accuracy, while standing in the middle of the road – but this is a bigger piece, and it strikes my forearm bone very smartly.

Then, while I'm doubled over and clutching my right arm, he does something even stranger. I look up and can make out the ever-present smile widen slightly (yes, despite what he is doing, so far there hasn't been any trace of anger on his face; in fact, just now, he looks positively playful), as he lobs a couple of stones in my direction. These aren't bowled or thrown hard – no, they are lobbed quite gently and land near my feet. I suddenly understand he wants me to 'join the fun', pick them up and bowl them back at him.

Of course I don't touch them. Of course, unlike him, I am furious. My first impulse is to run towards him, and despite my painful arm, I set off with a loud curse, heedless of how this might look to passersby at twenty past four on a Saturday afternoon. But instead of dropping his stones and taking off in fear when he sees I'm not willing to 'play' with him, he bowls a third stone at me just as I've narrowed the gap between us to about six metres. This one hits me in the forehead, because I'm running totally unguarded, and instantly I'm blinded by salty blood and intense pain.

But I'm still thinking clearly enough, for the moment, to change plans in mid-stride, and dash to my right onto the pavement through a narrow space between two parked cars. Only it doesn't dissuade this psycho at all, and his fourth stone, once more delivered with an on-the-spot hop and a Harbhajan Singh-like action (except this guy sends them down much faster), thuds into the rear windscreen of the car behind which I'm sheltering. I'm not sure if he is bowling them quicker, or the stones are getting bigger, but with each 'ball' he seems to be causing more damage. The blood is now dripping down my face. I'm wearing a half-sleeved T-shirt, and carrying no handkerchief or tissues.

Within these last moments my feelings about the matter have changed completely. I have no desire now for retribution, neither to confront the man nor to strike back at him. I wish I knew at what point he would stop, whether he hasn't seen that I'm bleeding, how much more damage he wants to cause.

I also wish I could raise my head just a little, to see if a crowd has gathered that will help me. Where will I run to next, if he decides to move to his left and target me from the pavement?

Amid all the pain, I quickly assess my options. I could come out from behind the car with my arms raised as a gesture of peace, but that would mean leaving myself vulnerable to further attack. Besides, what did surrender mean when neither of us had ever declared war, when, on the contrary, the aggressor himself appeared to believe that he was merely playing?

No, walking out defencelessly would be stupid. Very soon, I must either shout for help as loudly as I can, hoping other people will realise what this madman is doing, or else shout the one person's name that can help me. The one person who seems to be able to communicate with the psycho, and understand what makes him tick. In fact, where did she get to after she left the car? Wouldn't she have turned around when she heard me cry out after the first or the second stone? Surely she hadn't just carried on home by herself without looking back for me even once.

I have already made my choice and yelled out Mona's name when the stone hits me exactly between my right eye and ear.

The Last Time I Tried to Leave Home…

… I ASKED TO BE DROPPED off at one of the bus stops where the city-to-airport coach picked people up; it would save everyone the hassle of making their way back from the airport during what would be the evening rush hour. I have plenty of time, I argued, six whole hours, so the speed of the coach would be fine for me, and this way everyone else gets the afternoon to themselves. When they realised I was serious, my folks agreed quite easily to my proposal (and right they were to), because it was on the whole a saving of at least three hours for them, and several more if they were thinking they'd have to wait, for the sake of form, until my flight departed.

Six hours, I had six whole hours, and even factoring in the usual hold-ups due to traffic, the coach couldn't take longer than two. So I decided not to take the one that was due to arrive in five minutes, but to give myself an extra hour to wander around this bit of town. After all, this was my home city and I didn't know when I'd be back, so I was going to seize my final chance to look around and soak it in. The weight of my suitcase was just about manageable, and there was a bus to the airport every half-hour.

Within a couple of minutes of walking, I knew which way I should head. It was too inviting to ignore – our first family home was about ten minutes away (ten minutes with me pulling my suitcase). And today of all days, when I was leaving my birthplace to start a new life, it seemed right that I should return to say goodbye to the house where it all began, where I'd spent the first seven, extremely happy years of my life.

Since we'd moved, we didn't pass through this neighbourhood much, so I was surprised to find that the house, while still standing, looked in terrible shape, as though it hadn't been painted in over a decade and was now in a state of terminal neglect – suggesting that the landlord had finally got rid all of his tenants and the building was going to be pulled down very soon.

As indeed so many other houses in the area already had been: one in three of the present buildings looked like they had come up in the last ten years, nondescript blocks of flats four or five storeys high that had replaced the old family homes on generous grounds which once dominated the street. And I didn't really (even) have the leisure to stand and contemplate the decline of the house I'd once been so sad to leave – with its small balcony outside the front door on which I remembered numerous welcomes and goodbyes, and my ayah and me watching the life of the street go by round four o' clock each afternoon before ourselves setting off for my daily walk and play – because directly opposite it, demanding my attention and awe, and expecting me and my suitcase to either keep moving or get out of the way of a constant two-way trickle of shoppers, was the gigantic re-development that crowned all the other changes to the street: the main entrance to a shopping centre that had replaced an entire block of homes. It was now clear why our one-time landlord was happy to let his building fall to pieces – there would be many developers eager to put up flats right opposite such a shiny mall, or even just a multi-storeyed car park.

I entered the mall in search of a drink (because despite the relatively pleasant mid-monsoon temperature, lugging that suitcase around for fifteen minutes had been hard work) as well as to take a look around. I also had some idea of trying to find a vantage point on one of the higher floors from which to view our old home more fully. Yes, I remember, it was our terrace I especially wanted to see, that had been the site of innumerable thrilling games of hide-and-seek and chor-police, with its pipes and ideal-for-concealment water-tanks, and the dangerous, strictly-off-limits, spiral wrought-iron stairway that winded down the left side of the building, which we defiantly used all the time despite ourselves being terrified of falling through one of the large gaps between the steps. But when I got to the fourth floor, from where I would have had an ideal view of the terrace opposite, I realised all the glass panels were heavily tinted, and besides, there was hardly anywhere one could get close enough to the glass to try and look through it without leaning over merchandise or attracting the attention of one of the sales assistants nearby.

On my way to the food and drink section of the department store I had entered, I noticed there was a big CD and DVD sale on, and stopped to take a look. Within just a minute's browsing, I'd spotted heavily discounted box-sets of *Seinfeld* Season 6 and *Curb Your Enthusiasm* Season 2, so I picked these up and moved quickly on, afraid to look any further, because I had neither the time nor the space in my hand-luggage to go on any kind of buying binge right then. Instead, I efficiently located the drinks fridge, picked up a bottle of pomegranate juice, and looked around for the nearest till.

Just then an announcement came over the PA system that owing to a sudden computer problem, the store unfortunately could not process any sales just now and would have to close for thirty minutes, therefore would all shoppers kindly make their way to the nearest exit? I however still kept walking towards the sales assistant I had spotted, but he claimed to be unable to help me, since all the tills were down.

'Please come back in half an hour, Sir. It'll be fixed by then.'

'I can't come back. Can't you see I have a suitcase? From here I go straight to the airport.'

The guy apologised again, then asked me where I was going. I ignored the question.

'Look, I really want these DVDs and this drink. How about I pay *you*, in cash, and you hand-write me a receipt, and later when the system is back on, you record it in the till?'

He asked my forgiveness a third time, and said that my plan wouldn't work because the sensors at the exit would go off if the items hadn't been scanned correctly.

'But you said the system is down. Then the sensors won't go off.'

'No Sir, only the payment system is not working. Everything else is fine. It's not a power-cut. Look, the lights and the air-conditioning are on.'

'So you're telling me that I want to buy these items, I have the money ready for them, I'm leaving the country in a few hours, but you still can't sell them to me because of some stupid glitch in your system.'

'That's right, Sir. It's very unfortunate that you don't have a little more time. You're going abroad? For higher studies or for job?'

Without aggravating myself any further on such an auspicious day, I planted the DVDs and the bottle of juice on the counter, and marched out. I got my drink from the small paan-shop right around the corner from the mall (although this guy didn't have pomegranate juice, he also thankfully didn't have a computerised payment system), and made it comfortably onto the 1 o' clock airport bus, on which I was one of only eleven passengers. And everything else about the afternoon proceeded smoothly, so much so that even though, to my surprise, the coach took the old route through the middle of town rather than the ring-road around the outskirts, we still arrived at the final leg of the journey (where we would connect with the highway and reach the airport within twenty minutes) by 1.40, leaving me with over four hours to kill. Which was why, on a whim, I pressed the 'stop' button on the nearest handrail, picked up my suitcase from the luggage rack and asked to be let off at the last stop just before we got onto the highway. There was this new architecture college coming up to our left whose much-lauded campus had opened four months before, and I'd decided to quickly take a peek rather than waste the time hanging around the airport.

There were some students chatting in the bus shelter, and I asked them to suggest some architectural highlights of their campus that I should particularly look out for. I also mentioned that I only had about twenty minutes because I wanted to be back in time for the airport bus at 2.30. Unfortunately though, I had happened upon a group of rather unfriendly, unhelpful students, one of whom replied cursorily that everything was plain to see right from the campus gate itself, and that all I needed to do was stay on the main path in the centre and glance to my left and right.

I was disappointed: I guess I had expected a little more enthusiasm from these people for the discipline they were supposedly studying. The guard at the gate took me, with my suitcase, for a new student, and pointed out the first-year hostel to me; I thought better of correcting his impression in case he then forbade me entry. Once I was inside, I realised that in a sense, the boy at the bus stop hadn't been wrong – several, extremely innovative buildings, many in red sandstone, were immediately visible from the gate itself. My first thought was that the architect had attempted a modern interpretation of the Jantar Mantar.

I had walked for a few metres, and was wondering whether or not it was worth the trouble to fish out my camera from my backpack, or even just my phone from my pocket, when a student who was sitting on a bench with an open laptop asked me if I was lost. I said no, I'm just looking around, as if he was a shop assistant trying to foist help on me, but then decided to repeat my earlier question to this more helpful-seeming guy. Could he point a visitor towards the one or two buildings he would deem most architecturally noteworthy on campus?

'Tell you what, I'll show you,' he said, shutting his laptop. 'I'm Karan.'

'Hey Karan, don't take the trouble. I'm happy to just wander.'

'No trouble. It's a great campus. You *should* get a tour. How long do you have?' and with that Karan did exactly what I'd been hoping for: within the next fifteen minutes he'd walked me briskly through the main administration building, the library foyer, the pool and gym entrance, and a glimpse of his first-year dormitory at the other end of the football field. In each case, this phenomenal student – who also had time to tell me about all the architecture-related software that was available to students these days, much of which he had already downloaded onto his laptop – had the necessary breadth of knowledge, and interest, to be able to name the various architects, eras and styles that had been referenced in this or that building or design detail. At the end of our tour, I was left feeling secretly embarrassed about how shallow and incorrect my initial association with the Jantar Mantar had been, grateful that I hadn't mentioned this idiotic idea to Karan, as well as profoundly impressed at the point Karan was trying to illustrate through each of the examples on our walk – that the campus itself had been designed as a three-dimensional textbook, encompassing centuries and diverse traditions of planning and design for the students to live in, notice, and absorb.

At the end of our tour, I was also left feeling thirsty, so when Karan said that we were passing by the canteen and could stop for a drink, I took a quick look at my phone and said sure. Truth be told, taking the 2.30 bus would have been over-cautious on my part; I was a twenty-minute highway ride away from the airport. If I arrived at 3.20, that would still leave me with two hours and forty minutes in hand for my flight. This way, I wouldn't have to cut short Karan's stream of enthusiasm for his subject, and indeed, for his college campus; and also, standing him some refreshments would be a small way of showing my appreciation both for his intellectual keenness as well as his even rarer qualities of instant openness and warmth. This encounter was truly a wonderful note on which to leave my home-city, an outstanding example of energy and freshness to take abroad as a keepsake. In fact, I suddenly realised, my travels amongst the exciting and unfamiliar had already begun, and I hadn't even got to the airport! All in all, this experience had completely wiped away any lingering sadness I might have felt about the transformation of my childhood street and the derelict condition of our former house, as well as any small measure of irritation against that sales assistant who couldn't help me grab the great bargain that had already been in my hands. It probably wasn't his fault: I guess he *couldn't* let me go without scanning the DVDs properly.

At some point, while munching on an especially delicious fish cutlet and taking a sip of my Mountain Dew, I realised I had been lost in these thoughts and had failed to hear Karan asking where I was going. He repeated his question, and I was about to answer him when it occurred to me that it might be prudent to first check the time. It was 2.49, and I got up immediately because in my mental map of the campus, I was certain the bus stop was at least ten minutes away. Karan said, more like fifteen with a suitcase, but maybe I could make it if I ran. He still had quite a bit of food left on his plate, and clearly didn't want to abandon it, so I asked him for the absolute quickest route back to the front gate, which he assured me wasn't complicated at all – all I had to do was retrace our steps around the football field, continue past the admin building, and I would see the main path leading directly to the gate. At this point it was 2.51, so even my thanks were shouted out to him whilst I was already on the run.

At 2.54 (I was clutching my phone in my free hand as I ran, alternating it with the pull-out handle of the suitcase whenever I needed to rest an arm), I saw Shalu coming out of the administration building from about ten metres away, and couldn't help but call out her name. And yet, such was the nature of my emergency that I couldn't even stop and speak to the one person I had yearned to say goodbye to, but hadn't been able to persuade to meet me before I left. She herself was so surprised at the apparition running past her (someone she'd taken pains to avoid for over eight months) shouting her name and dragging a huge suitcase behind him that she could only follow my progress open-mouthedly without a word. To this day (it's been four years, and true to form, I still haven't managed to see her again, even though I know where she has studied this entire time), I can summon up clearly that gaping but lovely face as I sped past, moving from her left to her right: a slow-motion shot of a spectator at a tennis match.

Maybe I should have stopped and talked to her. Maybe then these past four years would have been different. It would have seemed a suitably heroic gesture – a future gambled away on the off chance of love – and who knows, might have swayed her heart back towards me. Besides, in any case, although I couldn't have known it at the time, the outcome of my mad dash that afternoon would still have been the same, so I might as well have given love one final shot, when it had cropped up so unexpectedly on the verge of my permanent departure.

I missed the three o' clock bus by five minutes. No matter. I could still have made my flight by arriving at the airport at ten to four. But it was at the moment of handing my fare to the driver on the 3.30 bus that I realised I wasn't wearing my jacket, in which I'd been carrying my passport. I had last placed it, owing to the sweat generated by an over-brisk campus tour, around the back of my chair in the canteen, planning to put it on again in five minutes right after I'd tackled that gorgeous-looking fish-cutlet. What a perfectly apt gastronomical note to go out on, I'd been thinking, at which point Karan had started talking, if I remember correctly, about features his college campus had in common with the city of Brasilia, which had also been constructed, apparently, out in the middle of nowhere. And right then, with Karan in the midst of articulating a complex idea, me two mouthfuls into my cutlet and half-wondering if there was such a thing as an evening class in architecture-appreciation, Baba had called to find out if I had already gone through security check. It would have been too much trouble to explain where I was just then, and why, so I'd simply promised to call back in a few minutes and hung up, and this had been another reason I'd forgotten about the jacket hanging behind me: later, while I waited at the bus stop for over twenty minutes for the half-three bus, my mind still awhirl with that sighting of Shalu, I had also been on the phone with my parents, giving them (each, separately) excited accounts of my afternoon adventures.

In case you're wondering, Karan was no crook. He'd simply not noticed the jacket for the first little while after I dashed off, preoccupied with his own meal. Then he – understandably – assumed that I had caught my three o' clock bus, and left the jacket with the canteen-wallahs, saying either a guy with a suitcase or a friend of his might come to ask for it.

The guy with the suitcase showed up at a quarter-to-four, managed to prove his case indubitably by asking the sceptic behind the counter to pull out his passport from the left-hand breast pocket, but couldn't make it back in time for the 4.00 p.m. bus. By now the commuter rush-hour had begun, and it took him fifteen minutes to get an empty taxi. When the guy with the suitcase, and the jacket, arrived at the airport at 5.10 (the highway during evening rush-hour was not the smooth twenty-minute journey he had anticipated), his plane to Frankfurt was still on the tarmac, but he simply was not allowed to board, despite his lamentable condition and his heart-rending pleas that his entire life could turn on this moment. Looking back, his lamentable condition – sweaty, desperate and out of breath – might actually have worsened his case.

Here's one thing that did work out for me later that week: I managed to return to the mall on the street of my childhood, and buy those *Seinfeld* and *Curb...* box-sets, as well as, on an afterthought, that appetising-looking bottle of pomegranate juice. I had also prepared for what would (inevitably) happen, and told the sales assistant when I ran into him that I was back from my business trip abroad, and that he could expect to see me quite regularly from now on.

Half an Hour

IMMEDIATELY AFTER LUNCH, Ma said that Uncle Vinay and Priya Aunty would be visiting in half an hour, and pressed the button for an attendant because she wanted the room tidied up. What she especially seemed to want was their bed re-made after its cover had been taken off and dusted, because Baba and I had eaten on it while watching the end of the movie.

When no one showed up after even the third buzz, I was dispatched to the end of the corridor where we knew the staff had a room of their own. Ma in fact handed me the bed-cover, so that one of them could give it a thorough dusting. She would convey her displeasure at being ignored when he or she returned with me, I was sure.

But when I looked through the little window in the door of the staff room, I could see there were three of them eating and chatting. They were right in the middle of their meal, and I didn't have the courage – or the heart, whichever it was – to go inside with our bed-cover, interrupt their lunch, ask one of them to wash his hands, and get to work for me right away.

Yet I also couldn't return to the room without a clean bedspread as well as a staff member in tow. I briefly stood beside the door hoping one of them would finish eating and come out, but when this didn't happen in the next three minutes, it struck me that I could go downstairs, get one of the bellhops who hung about in the main lobby to take the bed-cover out the back and give it a good shake (or I could ask the friendly receptionist we always greeted to summon one of them on my behalf), and afterwards come up to our room.

But there was no one downstairs just then apart from the receptionist, and it wasn't the man we smiled at every time we passed through the lobby. This was an unfamiliar woman, about Ma's age, working busily at her computer screen. I certainly couldn't expect her to step out from behind her desk and shake the bed-cover for me, nor did I feel I could ask her to call up one of the presently invisible bellhops. The only other option was the liftman who'd escorted me downstairs, and him I couldn't request to leave his post for an errand as petty as this.

It was then I realised that I myself could take the bed-cover outside, shake the crumbs off, and then, when I was back on our floor, check the staff-room once again to see if those fellows had finished their lunch.

The lobby opened directly onto the footpath of the main road, which was where I would have to carry out my vigorous shaking, in full view of the passing public. That couldn't be helped, I decided, but I unexpectedly found an ally right there – the doorman, who was only too happy to hold two corners of the queen-sized cover, so that together we could open it out and shake it extra-thoroughly. Yet I realised, as I counted aloud and we shook, that while we were getting the crumbs off, this was probably doing more harm than good because of the inevitable smoke and dust the bed-cover was picking up on a busy city road.

I'd just asked the doorman – an enthusiastic shaking partner – to stop for this reason, when a car drove past with what looked like a blind guy in the back seat, judging by the glasses he wore. But not just any blind guy, he resembled quite remarkably my classmate Abhinav from three years before, who certainly hadn't been blind then. What could have happened? Was it really him? The car had passed too quickly for me to be sure; wouldn't someone have written to me or mentioned it somewhere if he'd had such a serious accident?

But I still had a chance to find out, if I grabbed it right away. I asked my new friend the doorman to hold on to the bed-cover for me, maybe put it on one of the sofas in the lobby for me to pick up in a couple of minutes, while I just ran behind that car to confirm something.

And I would have made it too, if the car had encountered a red light at the next big crossing. Unfortunately it went straight through, and there was no way I could run across a giant five-way crossing – so big it also had a flyover spanning it – quickly enough to follow. I was standing there on the corner of the footpath regaining my breath in a space between a vendor of hairclips and another of socks and underwear, and wondering which of my old friends I could tactfully broach the subject with, when someone asked me where I wanted to go.

'Nowhere. I was just trying to catch up with that car, but it's gone now,' I said to the kind-looking woman who'd spoken to me, about thirty, in a sari, looking like she was waiting for a bus to take her to work.

'Which car?'

'The red Hyundai Accent. It just went that way, towards the market. My friend was in it.'

'Your friend the blind boy?' the woman said next and stunned me.

To my flabbergasted, and obvious, next query, she answered, quite nonchalantly, that she was often at that corner and knew most of the cars that regularly went past because they stopped at the lights. She'd often seen a boy in those special-looking dark glasses in the back seat of that car.

Then she added that she knew where he might have gone.

Five minutes later, I was following her down the middle of a footpath crowded with vegetable vendors to our left and small hardware stores on our right. It had seemed too extraordinary an opportunity to miss, that a stranger had appeared from nowhere and looked like she could lead me to the exact person I wanted to find, in the middle of this huge city.

And a minute after that, I knew where she was taking me, and asked her just to be sure – the J.C. Bhabha Junior College, right, coming up just over there on the right?

Ah, you know it?

I had to explain as we walked, now alongside one another, that I was actually from here. My parents had migrated to Australia three years before, and we were back on our first visit. So if that had been my friend, he would be in his first year of junior college.

She didn't seem so interested in my explanation. Perhaps she was a bit put out that I had undermined her big revelation, the conjuror's trick she had been about to pull off. I attempted to put things right.

But you have still been enormously helpful, because I wasn't even sure it was my friend. Now it makes perfect sense; he would be the right age. And I would have never thought of coming along to the college to check.

All she said was, you don't look any more as though you're from here, and kept walking.

At the college gate, she told me to go in and search for him, and I thanked her once more. As I was walking inside, I heard her calling out to me. She was pointing at something to my right – the red car parked under a tree. I shook my head in admiration and disbelief, waved at her, and kept walking.

There were dozens of students all around to choose from, and I asked a couple of girls ahead of me the way to the first-year classrooms. I had barely entered the building they directed me to, in the middle of a fair-sized throng, when two voices simultaneously called my name.

They were a couple of guys from VIII – B (I'd left while in VIII – C): I recognised them right away, but we hadn't been especially close. They were amazed to see me in college (one of them even asked if I'd moved back permanently), and also commented positively on my hairstyle and T-shirt. I corrected a misconception of theirs, that I now lived in Tasmania.

After these initial remarks, I felt the ice had been sufficiently chipped at to ask them about Abhinav. I didn't want them to leave for their class without knowing something definite: after all, I still wasn't sure it had been him. That was something the friendly woman obviously couldn't confirm. A blind stranger could resemble a classmate my age in hurriedly-glimpsed profile.

But it had been. They told me everything readily, in just a couple of sentences, before returning to their questions about what I was doing in Australia, what I was studying, what we drove. It had been a chemistry lab accident early last year, during a Class IX practical exam. They didn't know a lot more because they hadn't been in his class, but apparently he still had some sight in one eye.

I felt a tap on my arm: an unknown student was telling me that Tarabai was waiting. He had to say it twice more before I understood he was talking about the woman at the gate. She hadn't left, either because she thought I wouldn't know my way back to the big crossing, or perhaps she was waiting for a more substantial expression of gratitude.

I thanked the guys, excused myself and returned briskly to the main entrance, where Tarabai was indeed waiting on one side, although she was on the phone when I arrived. She cut her call short when she saw me, and I pulled my wallet out even as I assured her that I knew my way back to my hotel, and gave her a hundred-rupee note. She looked startled and self-conscious and did a quick check to see if anyone was watching us, but kept the money nevertheless. She actually seemed disappointed, and said she'd come all this way and waited, and here I was from foreign and dressed so well. I did have some more money on me, so I gave her another hundred, and then said I really had to go back inside and find my friend. I told her I was getting close but hadn't reached him yet.

You won't find him now, she said. Their classes have started. Next you'll see them at four, or some of them maybe three.

Why don't you come back with me? We'll make it an even five hundred. This was her, looking directly at me, so I could be certain of what she was proposing.

Finally I could reply knowing what I was replying to. I said thank you, I would walk back to my hotel if what she'd said about the class times was true, but I didn't want to go anywhere with her. In fact, my parents, and an aunt and uncle, were expecting me back a while ago. They would be wondering where I was, and were probably going to call any minute.

But my entire afternoon is now gone.

No, it's not, it's only 2.30. I am very grateful for your help, so I gave you some money to say thank you. Come, let's walk back together. I can return another time to see my friend.

You know, I can scream, and everyone here knows me. Then it will cost you much more.

But she said it with a mix of listlessness and humour and didn't scream, even though the gateman was avidly watching us. Instead, we did return together to the crossing, this time with her shuffling along behind me as if she was the newcomer to the area. I said goodbye at exactly the place where we'd first met, and told her I was now returning to my hotel. I thanked her yet again, and smiled.

Which hotel, she asked, as I turned away. I can come.

I wasn't going to answer that, I was going to say goodbye with something different, but just then, amid all the cacophony of the crossing, I heard my name very clearly shouted out, once and then once more. I didn't even have to turn around to confirm who it was.

I'm off, I replied to Tarabai. This whole thing was about putting a clean bed-cover on before they arrived, so I have to run right now, otherwise Ma will be very annoyed.

For the first time since we'd met it was she who looked at me uncomprehendingly, so before taking off I added, I might see you again. I'll go past here. I definitely want to try and meet my friend tomorrow.

The Good Boy

1

I MIGHT AS WELL begin here, because this story is about nothing else. And even after all this time, I haven't come up with anything that would explain or reconcile it in any way, nor can I think how it might be led up to gently.

Twenty years ago, last Wednesday, a friend of mine killed himself. He was supposed to be studying for his board exams that were four weeks away. So his door being shut, and the long period of silence, weren't noticed as especially unusual. But when his mother got no response to her repeated calls for lunch and then found the door to be padlocked from the inside, the building watchman had to be summoned to break it down. He was hanging from the fan, I've been told. This everyone knows. What very few found out however was that he had been dressed unusually, in a salwar suit belonging to his sister. When the police arrived, they authorised (in fact, the understanding inspector himself advised) a quick change of clothes, back into his jeans and T-shirt, before the body was removed. The watchman was threatened with scary consequences: any leak would be attributed by the police directly to him.

All this has been buzzing in my head especially loud the last few weeks, ever since I decided to pay his mother a visit for the first time since the tragedy. I had been kept away at the time because everyone in the family came up with excellent reasons for doing so, to spare me some of the trauma, and to shield me as much as possible from any inadvertent influence of the 'evil eye'. They reasoned that since we'd been so close in age and such good friends, his parents couldn't but resent on some level my continuing existence. Perhaps they'd also hold against me a failure to notice any signs of danger. Besides, it had been an especially auspicious time for *me*, incongruously so, because I was to fly out to the US on a full scholarship soon after those same board exams. I would be eighteen and alone, so far from home, all-too-vulnerable to any curse or ill-will. So, taking everything into account, I was kept from visiting their flat in the days after the death, and forbidden to attend the funeral.

2

Which make my last significant memories of Avinash those from the end-of-term excursion, where the 'condemned' – as we felt then, about to be placed before one firing squad after another (board exams, followed by engineering-college entrance exams, medical entrance exams, law exams: 'if law doesn't get you, dentistry must') – are encouraged to ignore what's looming, and somehow frolic without a care one last time. That's how we'd thought of it, but the simile seems in poor taste now. Still, another reason to live it up had been that we would never again gather under the banner of the class of '87, at least not as eighteen-year-olds.

What are the few images that remain from that trip? Walking around with loaded rucksacks stuffed with beer, and explaining to Mrs Sabarwal: 'Yes, Miss, we felt too much anxiety, so we decided to bring all our textbooks along in case we could squeeze in some time to study. I know, Miss, we'll do our best to have some fun, but it's the thought of our entire future at stake.' And then, on the way back to Bombay, the bus coming down the hill, and somehow ten of us ended up piled high in the aisle in a rugby-style scrum, with me somewhere near the top and Avinash even higher almost touching the roof, spilling into the driver's front cab, the view of the woods and winding road through the windshield taking on a spinning quality as if we were on a ride in an amusement park, until the driver had to stop and order us to disentangle, because he was presumably worried about the centre of gravity of the bus. Not that he would have phrased it quite so, but we assured him that everything would be perfectly safe, because *we* were looking after the physics of the situation, and that he might not be aware of it, but he was transporting a contingent of the country's finest future scientists.

Earlier that morning, I remember the last of the football games against the village boys, played unbelievably up and down that steep alley, ten feet wide, wall to one side, huts to another, shallow drain running through the middle. The key to winning was to score as often as possible during the half when you ran downhill; and the narrowness of the alley, the deft rebounds made possible by the walls and the huts, and the incredible fitness levels of our local rivals, made the matches addictive. We won two games out of five, played over three afternoons, and felt entirely satisfied with our overall away performance. We would put everything right on the plains if ever there was a rematch; there was no way their lungs could handle the enriched diet of carbon monoxide on our home turf.

After the scrum had reluctantly disbanded, but not before being treated to a wonderful solo performance of Marathi swearing from the hapless driver (original, never-encountered gems we would ourselves gleefully re-employ for months to come), I remember spending hours pacifying an inconsolable Vandana, whose dreams of a romantic getaway with Tariq lay smashed in the dirt. It didn't help that Tariq was five rows ahead of us, obliviously chatting up the brain-deficient but chest-compensated Neha. But then I too lost my patience after three hours, just as we approached the outskirts of Bombay. To listen on an endless loop to someone complaining about being neglected as you lean in with large eyes doing your best to convey sympathy, and not once have them grasp the obvious solution to their troubles that you're all but thrusting into their face: Screw Tariq, pick *me*, kiss *me*. So it rather took her by surprise when I got up and announced, 'Vandana, you're a moron, and you deserve everything that you got,' and never once spoke to her throughout the study-leave or the exams that followed.

And what is my last vivid memory of Avinash? At the 'rehearsal' exams a fortnight later (because apparently the sentenced must 'rehearse' their punishments), during the Physics paper, five minutes after it had been distributed, Avinash raised his hand and asked for permission to go to the toilet. 'You didn't think about that before you came in?' asked Mr Shahpurwala. 'Yes, I did, Sir,' he replied, 'in fact I went just ten minutes ago. But now these questions are making me need to go again.'

Two days later we dispersed to prepare for our finals. We were nominally on five weeks leave, but it was a period when most of us lived like monks under the totalitarian supervision of our parents, so I didn't see Avinash for the first few days. Then I was told he had died. The extra, troubling detail about his unusual attire I learnt from his younger brother, at school, on the afternoon of the first paper, behind the middle-school building, after everyone else had left. Shail sobbed throughout as he spoke. I explained why I hadn't been able to visit, but insisted that he tell me everything. He was aware of how close Avinash and I had been, so I had a right to know. He made me swear never to pass on what he had just confided.

He was only twelve, so I suppose in a way I bullied him, but I have kept my word until now – not even my mother knows any more than the official story.

3

I decided to visit on the Friday, because I reasoned they'd be inundated with visitors both the actual anniversary on Wednesday as well as during the weekend. After much thought I also elected a) not to call ahead, and b) not to wear all-white kurta and pyjamas. Instead I wore a regular brown shirt and jeans.

There was a large wide cushioned swing attached to the ceiling at the centre of the living room, and this was where Mrs Mehta sat (they'd given up the house I'd visited as a boy long before). The maid who'd opened the door had no idea who I was, but I asked her to say I was an old friend of Avinash and Shail's. She seemed disconcerted when I presented myself thus, and I regretted mentioning Avinash's name at all. I should have just gone with Shail.

I'd waited for the maid to return rather than follow her in directly. I wanted to give Mrs Mehta the option of refusing to see me. But this sixth-floor flat was as well-maintained as the other place, the drapes were drawn to keep the glare off the TV screen, and Mrs Mehta on the swing – who I now realised would have been much younger than my mother when she'd had her children – was dressed in a blue sari, and switched off the soap she and the maid on the floor had evidently been watching. She had jade eyes, a detail I instantly recalled had captivated me whenever we met, but somehow had not recurred to me in decades. The maid, who'd returned to her place in hope of not being interrupted for too long, now rose and shuffled off to fetch me water. She was young, probably not yet twenty.

All of what follows occurred in Hindi.

I explained that I was in town for two weeks, and remembering the occasion, I thought I'd come in to see them.

She said I'd done well.

I asked after Kavita and Shail.

'Kavita's soon going to have her third child, and Shail is a lawyer in Bangalore.'

'That's wonderful news. Where does Kavita live?'

'Worli.'

'And her other children?'

'Both girls. One is fifteen, and the other thirteen.'

'Is Shail also married?'

'Yeah, one son of five.'

'Wow, you must be busy grandparents when they come for Diwali.'

She asked if the maid should warm some food. I refused vigorously, insisting I'd already eaten. I added I wouldn't stay long.

'At least have tea.'

'It's too early for that. Don't worry about me. This water's enough.'

She said I'd become very 'formal'. This was a common observation about me among relatives of a certain age. It merely implied that I was abnormally obdurate about turning down offers (or extra helpings) of food. Then she asked me my news. The maid appeared and stood by the door waiting for instructions. Mrs Mehta sent her away saying this young man's stomach is full.

'I'm a professor in California, teaching physics.'

'You were mad about science even then,' she recalled.

'Well, at that time to be honest my parents were more keen on it. But now I enjoy it too.'

'And?' she began.

'And what?'

'Have you established a family?'

I trotted out – with the appearance of nonchalance – my standard response to this query over the last fifteen years, to everyone who asked at home, and any Indian encountered elsewhere.

'I spend so much time in the lab that I somehow forgot about all of that. But I'm still looking. Maybe I'll get lucky soon.'

To her credit, she was much less startled than I'd expected, and nowhere near as vehement as some others in her disapproval.

'So you haven't even got married. Do you live with someone? You can tell me.'

No, I half-smiled, attempting to remain serene. This is where all such conversations began to run into troughs and potholes.

'Shail had girlfriends in college. He knew his wife for three years before they decided to get married. Luckily she is Gujarati, but we had to give our blessing. And these days, everything is on TV anyway, so nothing can shock the parents.' Her rocking grew slightly more discernible, as she entered into the spirit of teasing me.

'No, no real girlfriends just now either. I guess I spend too much time at work.'

'But there must have been girlfriends while you've been there. While you were a student, after you started earning? What happened to them?'

She wasn't really smiling, so I couldn't be sure to what extent the baiting was innocent. The fan whirred and the swing creaked. I was glad the maid wasn't watching. But I got this line of grilling all the time, from grandparents, uncles, even strangers on planes and trains, and beyond a point, I lacked the patience. I decided to fold the visit.

'Is Mr Mehta home?'

'No, he still goes to the Kalbadevi office every day. He'll be back after six.'

'I should get going. I have a lot of people to see. I only have four more days.'

'You didn't eat anything.'

'Next time, I promise to come at a better time, and stay longer. Will you do me a favour? Can I take down Shail's cell number? I'd like to give him a call.'

Her phone was right beside her, behind one of the cushions. She expertly located and read off Shail's number, then asked if I'd like to speak to Kavita too. I said sure, if Mrs Mehta thought she would remember me. Then I asked for her number as well. I said I'd call before I flew off.

I wondered if I should touch her feet before leaving. In my indecision I made a hesitant move towards her and then drew back. Instead I joined my palms and left. Even I could agree that this was excessively formal.

4

The rest of the stay flew by doing the obligatory rounds of visits – seeing the ill, the dying, the old and the easily offended. There was no use my protesting, since Amma invariably reminded me this was all she asked once every three years. Besides, she griped, she didn't force me to go to the temple any more. At this point I hastily agreed, knowing well the next ace she would throw down: how, after my 'cruel' outburst during the last trip, she had even given up arranging matrimonial viewings without my approval, in her tireless quest to introduce me to potential brides.

In this way, for the final four days nearly every mealtime was booked in advance, and often impromptu slots had to be created on the spot for a second (even third) teatime or lunch. I was repeatedly vindicated in keeping only so much energy in reserve to deal with the marriage question whenever it arose. At such junctures, Amma would fix me with an accusing stare, and then turn away the moment I acknowledged her. It was her way of underlining that I could be merry and carefree in California, but *she* had to suffer the consequences of my callousness. It was *her* Achilles heel at every clan and community gathering.

I suppose none of the relatives could make up their minds about me: on the one hand, such unanimous approval of the career and its milestones, and yet, such a wilful waste of the same golden years. Perhaps they concluded – looking at my non-flammable idiot grin, my effort to grit my teeth and ride over the awkwardness with sheer amiability – I was slightly autistic.

For some reason, even after such sustained battering, I decided to keep my word and call Mrs Mehta before I left. To avoid interruption, I told everyone I needed to make a call to LA, and then made sure by bolting my door.

I'd picked the same hour as when I visited her, since I'd be likely to find her alone. She asked if I'd contacted Shail or Kavita yet. I said no, but they were on my list for that evening.

'I'm sorry if you were watching your show.'

'I watch it to keep Mala company. Anyway, the story never moves forward.'

'I wanted to say something that I couldn't the other day.'

She waited to hear me out.

'Mrs Mehta, it's always bothered me that I didn't visit you after Avinash passed away. I wanted to tell you that I still remember him as a close friend, on the day of his anniversary and at many other times.'

She must have put the programme on mute, disappointing Mala yet again. I couldn't hear a sound of affirmation.

'My parents decided it was best I shouldn't go, because the exams were so near,' I continued.

Silence followed. I didn't say any more. My piece was complete.

'Why didn't you say this the other day?'

'Somehow I couldn't. I still feel ashamed of it. I should have just gone to see you, no matter what my parents thought. They didn't need to know.

'Anyway, that's what I wanted to tell you. I'll go now,' I said after allowing for another longish pause.

'We found a letter for you.'

'Who?'

'I did. It was in the same exercise book he was supposed to be studying.'

'It was written to me?' This was genuinely unbelievable.

She remained silent, until I called out her name.

'He was begging you not to go to America.'

Her voice stayed even, although the silences were getting longer. 'But he gave up after a few lines, and tore the page in half and threw it into his drawer.'

'No one ever told me. The last time I spoke to him was after the rehearsal exams. But we didn't *fight*, and I promise, I never saw him that whole week.'

'But then you talked to Shail?'

At that moment, I cut the line. This woman held all the cards. It was I who was finding it difficult to breathe or to keep my voice down. And yet, I had set it all up. I visited her, asked for her number, called back to say goodbye.

Amma would choose this moment to hammer on the door and insist I hear out an uncle in Malaysia who wanted to say Happy Journey and reprimand me at the same time for not flying through KL, but for once, I gratefully surrendered.

Later of course I wondered if Mr Mehta knew, and what Shail or Kavita knew. But when I'd had a few minutes to absorb everything, set it all down in front of me and consider the likelihood one way or the other, I felt pretty sure she wouldn't have told many people, or there would have been repercussions. And I doubted she was going to begin now. She didn't think of what she knew as a 'card'.

And the more I turn things over in my mind, last night, later again on the plane to Hong Kong, and now while I wait at the airport to board my flight back home, the more certain I feel about this.

The Third Beside Us

'When I count there are only you and I together…
But who is that on the other side of you?'

– T.S. Eliot, *The Wasteland.*

A YEAR AFTER MY UNCLE DIED, this strange thing happened.

My uncle and my father knocked on my door to say they were ready to leave for the gallery if I was. It was something I had unthinkingly said yes to a long time before, as we often do when an event is far away in the future, but now the day had arrived and I couldn't back out, because, apparently, after the opening the gallery would be putting on a special lunch – and there was going to be a place for me. As late as yesterday, my uncle had confirmed to the organisers that all three of us were coming, and if I dropped out now, it would simply upset everyone concerned. Someone had cooked extra food thinking I would come; there might even be a printed place-setting at the table to mark the seat reserved for me.

Of course I went. Of course the show was extremely ordinary – lacklustre academic paintings out in an ill-planned suburb where my father knew I hated to go. Of course no one at the gallery cared in the least that I had come, although they seemed happy to see my uncle. Of course the pious speeches at the inaugural function went on for hours. In fact, so indifferent was everyone to the fact of my presence, and so bored was I by the time we were halfway through lunch (it was already four o' clock!), that I believe no one even noticed when I quietly pushed back my chair and walked out of the large upstairs dining room (there had been no printed place-setting, just for the record), hoping to join a cricket match in progress in a neighbouring driveway, which I had been following through a window behind me for some time.

Now that I had boldly taken charge of matters, my luck seemed to improve as well, for I was welcomed into the game and drafted immediately into the fielding team, that had a couple more overs to bowl. In the initial excitement of being part of a match scenario so suddenly, and after so many years away from the game, I, who'd been deputed to field midway down the pitch (with a boundary wall right behind me – anything that struck that wall after a bounce counted as a four), let a stoppable shot pass between my legs on the fourth ball of that penultimate over. There were some shouts of disappointment among the gathered crowd: yes, there were passersby who'd clustered on the footpath to watch from behind the closed gate, as well as several others all along the compound wall behind me watching avidly from the parking area of the adjacent building. I should perhaps add that although the driveway was both narrower and shorter than a full-sized cricket pitch, the (over-arm) bowling was ferocious, with no compromise made for the constricted space: it was this entertaining spectacle that the crowd had gathered to see, and their cheers and cries that had first drawn my attention during the lunch next door.

My team-mates, however, were forgiving of my error (recognising possibly that it was a difficult position I had been assigned – in a slog-over situation – requiring extremely practised reflexes), and I'm happy to be able to report I rewarded their confidence just three balls later by stopping with my left foot what would have been a certain four. In any case, despite my earlier flub, our opponents ended their innings on a modest 47, which sounded like a breeze for us in our seven overs.

During the brief interval, my teammates were courteous enough to ask me what role I specialised in, and I said truthfully that I had usually been a batsman. Imagine my surprise, honour, and delight when they consulted quickly amongst themselves and proceeded to ask if I would open – me, a complete stranger, who'd walked into their game from next door just two overs ago. Of course I agreed, pronto, and if there was a mild nervousness somewhere within about not having played in several years, it was far outweighed by the thrill of competition, and the fierce wish not to let down my new friends who'd shown such faith in me.

In hindsight of course I should just have gently demurred, stating the truth about my lack of practice and offering to bat much further down the order. These guys would have understood and even respected me for my candour. But what can I say – greed got the better of me: the chance of batting right away as opposed to later on, where they probably wouldn't even have needed me, so gettable was that target, and the prospect of getting some batting in before Baba and Kishoreda were ready to leave? Vanity must also have played its role, the glamorous vision of the stranger appearing out of nowhere and covering himself in glory in this unfamiliar neighbourhood before this decent-sized audience. And as so often happens when you act against your better judgement, everything turns to shit exactly as you feared it would, and then some.

Do you remember the infamous story of Sunil Gavaskar's 'crawl' in the World Cup match against England, when he couldn't score a run no matter how hard he tried, but worse, he couldn't even terminate his own agony and get out? So, over after over his torment continued, ball after ball blocked or missed, or hit directly to a fielder. Even now he claims he has no idea what malign spirit took possession of him during those tortuous hours. Well, whatever it was, it awoke again that afternoon. Of the first six balls I faced, I made contact (barely) with one. It was baffling: I was trying every focusing and calming technique I could remember – visualisation, deep breathing, watching the ball, inhabiting the moment – but each proved as ineffective as every other. With every delivery virtually the same thing happened: I had relaxed myself through deep breathing and was successfully watching the ball right from the moment the bowler began his run-up, and yet somehow I'd lose sight of it just during that crucial second when it actually travelled past my bat.

Before the second over, during our mid-pitch conference, trying to look oblivious to the jeers and catcalls coming in from over the front gate and the right-hand wall, I assured my partner – who, it must be emphasised, was solicitous and trusting to the last, clearly, in this case, to a fault – that I now had my eye in, and that he wasn't to worry; with the target we were chasing, the run rate was still eminently achievable with just a couple of boundaries every over. And the wall was only a few feet away, right, I mean how hard was it to send the ball between that guy's feet or just past him? All I had to do was take a mighty swing and he would immediately duck for cover: the ball would sail past him every time.

Unfortunately, tragically, one of us believed my nonchalant words. My partner took a confident single off the very first ball of the next over and returned the strike to me. Once again, I missed the next four balls. But then, to make matters worse, so delighted was I by the chance edge that I managed off the final delivery of the second over that I was off and running even though my partner yelled 'No', and then he simply had to run just out of the decency of his soul (I honestly believe, looking back, he was too sweet to even consider letting this fucking idiot run himself out), thus restoring the strike to me, so that I could waste another four balls of the third over.

Let me put everyone out of their misery. My prayers were finally answered on the fifth ball of the third over, and my off stump went down. At this point, the score was 2 for 1, I had made contact with precisely two balls out of fifteen, and the target now was a pretty steep 46 off 4.1 overs. I had single-handedly turned my team's walk-in-the-park into a breathless treadmill sprint. You can imagine the loud applause I walked off to – from the opposition players and supporters. I even heard a couple of taunts and reprimands directed at the bowler for doing something as foolish as getting me out. I chose not to look in any direction but downwards, handed the bat over in a daze to the incoming batsman and went and stood silently behind my teammates, who showed impossible restraint in not clubbing me with their bats. They just kept their eyes on the game and cheered on their friends in the middle, still hopeful of a win, still full of solidarity with one another.

But do you think that ended my nightmare? No, of course not, there was another sting in store for me, perhaps the most ignominious of all. Just three deliveries later, Baba and my uncle suddenly appeared beside the wall on our left to say they were ready to leave and I should make my way to the car. I did try to protest that we were in the middle of the game, and it still had another half-hour to go, but Baba was having none of it. Kishoreda has two other places to go after dropping us off, he said, and he needs to leave right now.

So, picture the situation. I barge in halfway through a match, am nevertheless invited in warmly and offered a chance to play a role right away – without having paid my dues in the field – because I misrepresent myself as a competent, practised batsman, proceed to wreck the game for my side and bore everyone watching beyond jeers to the point of leaving (oh yes, I omitted to say, the crowd had visibly thinned during my match-ruining innings); and then, as soon as my turn is up, without even the minimal courtesy of standing by my teammates to cheer them on through the extremely tough overs that would follow, I swan off to my waiting car as if I was some kind of visiting Cinderella. I'm amazed they let me go with my teeth intact that afternoon. The game actually stopped while I walked away. Everyone took note, too open-mouthed to even yell abuse: *who is* this jerk? Perhaps the only reason I escaped alive was the presence of my respectable-looking father and elderly uncle, and the gallery owner and his wife from next door who'd come down to see them off. I tried to show my contriteness in my face, and apologise through my expression and tone of voice as I explained, but I don't think anyone noticed or cared.

I didn't say a word during the ride home, not even to contest Baba's accusation of rudeness at having left the gallery mid-lunch. I didn't say goodbye to my uncle when we arrived at our place. He drove away, and Baba and I walked upstairs. I had taken my key with me, so I rushed up ahead, unlocked the front door, went straight to my room and shut myself in. After the fiasco of that afternoon, I didn't want to see anybody for a long time. And the worst of it was, I now clearly saw, every single stage had been so *avoidable* – I could have just stood my ground about not going to the gallery; I could have stayed put at the lunch; I could have been honest and not batted. Jesus, if I wanted to be part of the game so bad, I could have simply watched and cheered along with the rest of that lively crowd. How did I manage to ruin the afternoon for *so many people*, just with a few innocuous decisions?

And then it hit me, while I lay in the dark on my bed, so that I sat up too quickly and nearly fainted – what was *my uncle* doing with us, and how had I not noticed or remarked on it throughout the afternoon? Why had Baba not said anything either, or had he acted as though he was aware of the incredible, and it was me that had missed all his cues? What on earth had I been so wrapped up in for so many hours not to realise that my uncle had returned to see us?

I must rush out and ask Baba what he and Kishoreda talked about during lunch and in the car, if Kishoreda had said anything important, if he'd said when we might see him again, if he'd said anything meant for me.

Lost Men

1

I FINALLY DECIDED I had to get out of London after my mother-in-law walked in on me wanking. It was four days after Jane's memorial service, and Debbie had stayed on in the house because she wanted to be near her daughter's things a while longer. One afternoon I thought the bedroom door was closed when apparently it had been left ajar, and she entered assuming there was no one inside. I had the duvet off and the laptop open; she rushed back out with a loud cry; I followed shortly after (once I'd pulled up my tracksuit bottoms) and found her in her room where all I could think to say was to make clear that I had been looking solely at pictures of Jane. Which was true.

Jane had been operated on 'successfully' for the first tumour in her ovaries in late May, and was gone by the 14th of July. I knew that Debbie, who lived in Boston and had last seen Jane at Christmas, held it against me that I hadn't noticed her symptoms sooner. She'd said as much several times during Jane's final fortnight, in varying tones of voice. Even though Jane herself had had no idea until the second round of tests in June that the cancer was spreading so quickly, I too blamed myself for this.

A friend in Calcutta had said in a condolence email that I was welcome to come over if I wanted to get away. Now, when I wrote back asking if her offer had been serious, she replied immediately to say that for the price of a seminar with her students, she'd be happy to put me up for as long as I liked (she taught English at Jadavpur University). And, she added, if I wanted to travel elsewhere while I was in India, colleagues at other departments would be delighted to host me, with or without a similar consideration. When I mentioned all this, along with a brief account of the wanking incident, to my friend Jim, and said that I was thinking of leaving immediately, he thought for a while and replied that he'd be able to take a fortnight off in a month or so, and could meet me in Thailand if I liked. I could wander around India for a few weeks, then spend some time with him, and afterwards we would return home together.

2

The man beside me was scratching his balls, openly, brazenly, although he was sandwiched between two strangers, and numerous others were still moving down the aisle. His fly was wide open in the shape of an eye, and he was busy in there with all the bunched-up fingers of his right hand, face down, gaze focused. Yes, true, I hadn't been home in four years, which meant I probably needed reminding about the incredible degrees of Indian frankness regarding all bodily matters and discharges, but this surely wouldn't stupefy just me. I wasn't strolling along Dhakuria Lake on the bank adjacent to the railway line slums: we were in an aeroplane, on the tarmac at Muscat Airport, this fellow was an international passenger.

I fixed my stare towards the opposite seats until he had soothed his discomfort to full satisfaction. The chap by the window seemed equally oblivious, his head stuck in the duty-free brochure. Was it indeed me who had become so squeamish? Perhaps flights were the new buses, I reflected, as I looked up and down the aircraft to get a better idea of my co-passengers, and in the faint hope of a vacant seat, at least those that travelled to the Gulf, in the sense that this one seemed full of characters you would only ever see on buses before, especially rural ones.

What made things worse was that I'd run out of reading matter. As usual, I'd underestimated, believing like an idiot that I would spend a fair portion of either flight asleep, or at least a few of the movies would be bearable. But all my life, whether I was travelling alone or with company, I'd been a mile-high insomniac, and so there I was, desperately clutching onto the op-ed page of the *Herald Tribune*, determined to continue with business, sport and obituaries after that, anything to avoid conversing with Mr Itch-Guard until I could bolt immediately after take-off.

But here again I'd underrated the cunning and agility required to bend the law to your purposes in my native land, how briefly any opportunity lasts, how many competitors there are eyeing whatever it is you secretly desire. And besides, these were exceptional conditions: how could I compete with the eagle-eyed resolve and who-gives-a-fuck audacity of commuting champions who travelled usually on the tops of buses or hanging by their toes from suburban trains? No one could have accused me of being tardy in searching for another place as soon as the seat-belt signs were off, but within that legally mandatory pocket of time, all the empty rows I'd spotted in the rear and moved delightedly towards had been seized already, and their new occupants were stretched out full-length, armrests raised, apparently fast asleep to evade any argument. And what argument could there be, since their right to usurp empty seats was as valid as mine?

Things deteriorated upon my shamefaced return. I clung resolutely to the earlier strategy of devouring the *Tribune* as if I would be attending an IAS exam on current affairs directly after landing. But very soon, the fidgeter was up to something novel. He'd placed his cushion upon the armrest that I had readily surrendered just to avoid contact with the hand that had scratched the noodle, and was now employing his blanket vigorously to wipe his arm. The white cushion was already stained a light brown. With gravest misgivings I faced him finally as if to request an explanation, because this was simply too much, but instead of pointing downwards as I'd grit my teeth to expect, he gestured towards the seat-lights and the luggage bins. And this time I had to concede a misjudgement; I'd wronged him just this once. A fairly regular brown drip – that could have been diluted grease or dirty water, something I'd never seen before in an aircraft (though often enough on an Indian bus) – which originated near the console for switches and lights, was indeed falling upon the armrest between us, and had been staining the pillow and his shirt.

'Dekhun na Pepsi ki na?' he implored, as if it was odd of me not to have risen already.

It seemed distant enough from the door of the bin for it not to be leaking cola, but there was a slim possibility. Yet there was nothing that looked like a bottle visible among the bags. Everything was sealed and the drip clearly had another source.

'Aami air-hostess ke dakchhi, daran,' and I pressed the button to summon her.

Yet though she could neither solve nor explain the problem, she seemed entirely sanguine while considering the scenario that our mid-air pressurised cabin might have sprung a leak, and simply suggested, heels already turned around, that we shift seats, since it was a far-from-full flight.

Something wildly optimistic within me noted and capitalised upon my opportunity.

'She's right. Many seats empty behind us. You should move immediately. Look, it has stained your shirt.'

Why he didn't take to this suggestion beats me. He frowned and shook his head. Conversation stalled. I spent the next few minutes making sure I didn't re-occupy the armrest by mistake. I was wearing a warm-golden shirt that was now almost an heirloom, a Christmas present from Jane from three years ago.

Not half an hour had passed before my neighbour was at it again. So blatantly, as if he was squatting by the railway tracks, facing away from the overflowing trains. He unbuttoned himself, stuck in his hoof, felt his jewels cautiously, and then scratched as if there'd been a mosquito inside. Yes, yes, I know, but how could I not have noticed? In fact, since Itch-Guard was leaning forward, I actually looked across to see if the fellow by the window was as perturbed as I was. Perhaps together, egging each other on through eye contact, one of us could broach the unspeakable subject.

But he was already fast asleep, and since he was evidently from the same class as Mr Minor Sexual Misdemeanour, I imagined he would have been tranquil even if he'd witnessed everything, twice. I want to clarify, vis-à-vis my countrymen, I was no prude. Eleven years away cannot soften a shell acquired over a lifetime. I was hardened to the projectile spitting, the copious clearing of noses and other orifice-exploring, the non-alcoholic belching and the preparatory hawking, the tubercular fits of coughing. But this weed had lowered the bar.

Finally I felt compelled to draw attention to the matter, however obliquely.

'Do you want to visit the bathroom?'

'No, it's no use,' he replied. 'It doesn't go away. In fact, I feel worse when I return.'

A mystifying response: I momentarily forgot I was supposed to be annoyed.

'Aren't you well?'

'No, I had an accident. Since then I'm in constant pain. To sit still is an agony, I can't walk far any more, and in the toilet it burns even worse.'

'What happened?' I asked, facing him for the first time, looking upward from what I realised had been a near-constant stare in the direction of his groin. He must have found *me* odd. He was ordinary to look at, perhaps thirty, not unpleasant or hostile, rendered slightly pitiful in light of his predicament. I wasn't angry any more, not after I heard the word 'accident'.

'You know how we have two balls each?' he explained without a flicker in his expression, calling them seeds, which is the colloquial Bengali term. 'A crane pierced my bag and damaged one of them. It took twenty-three stitches to join. They were removed day before yesterday, but it hasn't healed well.'

'A forklift crane?' was all I could think of asking by way of continuation, as if it was vital to be sure! My face must have creased in horror as he spoke, factually and without overt self-pity.

He nodded. I turned away in shock, and perhaps to work up a better response. I wanted to hear more, where he worked, what the hospitals were like, what he was going home to.

It was he who resumed with a non sequitur. 'Please excuse my Bengali. You know, I'm a full-fledged Bengali. But living there, you speak so many languages, Hindi, English, even the occasional Arabic where you have to, so suddenly it's hard to switch back. But I speak Bengali perfectly. You don't mind, do you?'

'The same thing happens to me,' I replied bemusedly. 'It also takes me a while to get used to Bangla. Don't worry, after a day or so, it'll all flow back. So you picked up some Arabic while you were there?'

'Yes, a few expressions. Some people don't speak English so well. And if I'd known some more, it would have been useful at the hospital to explain my problems. I couldn't really tell them in English.'

'Are the hospitals free? Was the treatment alright?'

'Yes, they're free, but I think cat and dog hospitals are in better condition. They did the basic dressing and stitches, but that's why I'm going home. The pain has increased, because they didn't have time to understand what I was saying.'

'It'll be better at home. You'll have a familiar doctor to whom you can explain your symptoms, and you can recover in your own house with loved ones to look after you.'

'I had no other option. I can't lift anything so I haven't been able to work since the accident. And the company would only provide a ticket home by way of compensation, so this is all I could do.'

After a while he spoke again. 'You might form the wrong impression from my clothes.' He wasn't wearing exceptional clothes, just a cotton shirt and trousers, socks and 'duplicate' white Reebok trainers, which reminded me momentarily of Jerry Seinfeld. 'And this watch,' he held out a fake Casio digital, 'is a fake. You have to wear something special for those who'll come to the airport, after you've been away for a year and a half. But I'm returning empty-handed. I had to borrow money from friends even to buy a few things. Some cosmetics for my family from the airport, and a few utensils. Nothing more.'

It was slightly later, when he used the expression again to inform me that his 'family' was completing a teacher-training certificate to qualify for a job in a school, that I recognised he meant his wife. 'But surely they'll understand the situation, in what circumstances you were forced to return. There's always time later for presents. First priority is your health.'

'I haven't confided in anyone yet. With what face shall I tell them? I borrowed a lakh and a half just to pay the agent to go to Dubai, and now I'm home after only eighteen months, empty-handed, having thrown away my job. Even today I won't be able to say a word. They will have rented a car to come all the way from the village; we'll return to a big lunch; neighbours will visit; everyone will ask questions. Maybe tomorrow, when I have some time alone with my family.'

Two unworthy thoughts passed through my head at this point, at differing rates: one was light-hearted and sped through, and the other lingered and assumed a more definite shape. Surely his 'family' would find out within the first few minutes they were alone, that he was for the moment an 'oddball'. (Appalling, I know). And then I wondered if he was a practised swindler, and this was an elaborate routine. I decided to be on my guard for a while, perhaps slightly stand-offish once more. But what an accomplished artist, if he was indeed a trickster. He'd added fine details to the routine, even donating the lamb and the mishti from his meal to his other neighbour – because he claimed to have no appetite and to be eating simply for sustenance – who through all this had been a remarkable study in avoidance. (Accomplices?) He appeared not to have registered a word of our exchange. Oh, and Santosh Biswas, that was his name, had also re-buttoned his fly.

And yet, the shifting in the seat, the periodic winces of discomfort: what if they were genuine? How much money was I obliged to offer, in the event of his sincerity? Because then it wasn't a matter of his asking; rather I myself should step forward. But what kind of sum could *begin* to tide him over his troubles? A token gesture would be next to useless. He had personal debts, loans to human traffickers, and for starters, presents to pick up hastily at the Calcutta airport duty-free. Jesus!

Should my offer of help merely cover the gifts? Would that be generous enough?

However, once the trays were removed, Santosh shifted the conversation to other matters, reminding me first not to use the armrest, even by mistake. He told me about taking the taxi to the supermarket to buy his weekly provisions, which brought to his mind the insane speeds at which people drove on the highways of Dubai. There seemed to be no rules or limits. He warned me, in the event of my visiting, that I was asking to be killed if I ever slowed down or stopped without ample warning: the cars behind would have no way of braking in time and would slam headlong into mine. Such incidents invariably culminated in a gigantic fireball, it seemed. In a year and a half, he'd witnessed four.

At this point, his discomfort became unbearable, and he departed for the toilet. I returned to my seat and continued trying to make up my mind about him, about which of the roads in the forest to choose: the path of credulity or that of cynicism.

When he returned I asked him to describe the accident. In fact, to cloak my real motive (the testing of his back-story), I asked him more generally about work conditions on construction sites.

'I have been very lucky before. In fact, I should already be dead. Last year I was high up on the scaffolding near the twenty-first floor of a tower, carrying some large window panes, when one of those huge gusts of wind that are common at such heights nearly blew me off my feet. I was at a corner, so I couldn't move, nor could I rest my load. God knows how I held on.'

'You mean there's no requirement to wear safety harnesses?'

He shook his head briskly as if to swat off the bleeding obvious, and continued. 'And yet this time, my feet were firmly planted on the ground. In fact, I was working inside a pit on a small masonry job. The forklift driver insisted afterwards he couldn't see me down there. Another inch and he would have ripped out my scrotum.' He called it his 'whole thing'.

To change the subject I asked about his housing situation. He claimed to be a teetotaller, but revealed that the primary cause which drove most of his friends to drink excessively in the evenings was the ordeal of calling home. 'The only thing anyone is interested in: when and how much are you sending? And an unending list of emergencies and demands. No one asks how we manage there, what we do, about *our* ups and downs. They have their fixed image of life in Dubai, fast cars, gold, electronics and air-conditioned luxury. This constant pressure leads to all the drinking.

'But they're good boys. Three of them helped me out with two thousand dirhams after the accident. Somehow I have to return, because they lent the money on trust. I don't want them to believe I tricked them.'

At this point I grew silent to gather my thoughts. My doubts had vanished: I just couldn't absorb so much detail while listening. I still didn't know how to spontaneously extend a hand beyond repeating what I'd said already, that I was a great believer in Providence (now who was dissembling?), and that this trip home had been the right choice. He could recover with the care of his family, and return healthy and restored. God had averted a much worse disaster, though of course, I could not ask if he knew how bad the internal damage was. But the extent of his worries truly awed me, dwarfing at that moment even my own: his health, his debts, his family, his future as a worker and as a man. I was fleeing the aftermath of a catastrophe; he was arriving into the next phase of one.

Yet I had been en route for fifteen hours straight, and it was only the plane touching down at Dum Dum that awoke me from the snooze into which I'd inadvertently slumped. I noticed he was awake and looking forward without any particular expression. There wasn't much to say before leaving the aircraft, and the next thing I had to do was hurriedly fill out my landing card while waiting in the queue at immigration. That was when he approached me once more, with a request to fill up his form, because he said his hands were too shaky. I showed him where he had to sign, and noted that the date of birth in his passport was dubious. Come on, Santosh had been twenty-six well into the previous millennium.

Before passing through customs with my bags, I pushed my trolley towards him to shake his hand. He had an unusual favour to ask. Nothing to do with money: he wanted me to sign a small pocket book as a memento, as if I was a celebrity he'd encountered.

I don't know what prompted me to include my sister's address in Hazaribagh along with my 'autograph'. I honestly cannot account for it, because soon afterwards, when I spotted Sharmistha outside the airport and launched into an account of Jane's final few weeks, I forgot for the time being all about Santosh's story.

3

I didn't ask Sharmistha before my seminar with her students whether she had told them about Jane's death. The hour itself passed quickly, and for most of the second half we discussed just one story of mine, about which a girl had asked a question. She wanted to know what the narrator's decision to refuse to be a father at the end of *The Open Sea* implied.

'It implies exactly the things he worries about in the story,' I said. 'The more he thinks about how many variables there will be beyond his control from the moment of the child's birth, or even inside the womb, the more he realizes how vulnerable he will always feel, precisely because of his great love for him or her. He feels that the burden of such a love would be intolerable for him to bear.'

'Sir, then why doesn't he say this to his wife instead of making her so unhappy?'

'Because he feels he won't be able to explain it in words. He thinks he'll sound stupid for only focusing on the risks of love. But the risks of loving a little child are what keep him up at night, even before they have tried again to conceive. He decides he can't go through all that a second time. At first there are the chromosomes that could go wrong, congenital illnesses and defects, then the actual pregnancy, followed by the chances of hurting oneself as a toddler, falling on concrete and hitting one's head, then the dangers of crossing the road, learning to drive, moving abroad to study, learning to surf with reckless friends in a faraway country. He feels he will die from all that anxiety.'

This had led another student in the back to ask *his* fourth question of the hour: 'But Sir, no one would have any children if they all thought like that.'

'You're quite right. Thankfully only the character of a single seven-page story of mine thinks like that.'

Although I had then asked for another question on a different topic, the persistent smart-alec in the back had refused to let go.

'But isn't that a very selfish position, Sir? Love means risk. He shouldn't have got married if he didn't want to face the risks of being a parent.'

Sharmistha did me the favour of pointing out that the couple in the story had tried to be parents before, and how the narrator had been quite willing the first time round. In response to her demand for a new question, the boy in the back, whose name was Saikat, asked why I never wrote about anyone going through the 'happy phase of love'. Apparently I only showed people 'after they have lost or wasted their chance for love'.

I replied to him that it wasn't news to me that there were many things my work didn't cover, that no matter what I wrote or how much I wrote, there always seemed to be a vast underside just below or beyond it, which had once more inevitably eluded me. A kind of dark side to the moon, which often made me feel like I only wrote about well-behaved figures doing mundane things in sunlit parks and making sure to be in bed by nine.

Who writes about that other side, Sir, asked Saikat, who wasn't really a bad sort. I thought a bit and said films go there a lot, just to cite an obvious example, because the violence there is very attractive to show on a superficial level, but it's the exceptional foray that actually sheds some light on it. I asked them to see what they thought of Bolaño, who in my opinion frequently set off by night for uncharted waters, and at a certain moment in the journey, was quite willing to let the reader's hand go, so that he, the reader, and the story, were each suddenly alone, without knowing where they were in the dark.

On the way home from the seminar (we were walking, as Sharmistha lived close by in Jodhpur Park), I told her that one of the last normal evenings that Jane and I had had together, before her first serious bout of illness in May, we'd finally watched a couple of hours of season one of *Mad Men*, three or four years after everyone else, after I'd brought home a box-set from the library. We were like that with TV shows: for example, we'd only ever watched a few episodes of *The Wire*, again, years after everybody else, and so far remained complete strangers to many names we'd heard from friends or students or seen in the papers – *The Sopranos, Six Feet Under, Boardwalk Empire. True Blood.*

The *Mad Men* box-set was the last thing I'd noticed just before leaving the house for Heathrow. I thought briefly of asking Debbie if she'd drop it off at Hammersmith library for me, and I'd pay the fine later, but then forgot to text her about it before taking off.

I also told Sharmistha about a dream I'd had during my first night at her place a few days before, after I'd asked her for some Calmpose to help tide over the time difference. I was driving along High St Ken when Jane, who was having coffee by herself at a table on the pavement on the opposite side, spotted me, and signalled to me to turn around and come over. I waved back to show her I'd understood, made a U-turn up ahead and headed back towards her. Yet she was so happy to see me that she'd left her table and was running towards me, laughing, running first along the pavement and then onto the road. My attention too was on her, and on looking for a space to park, which was why I didn't notice that a 4x4 had cut into my lane from the right trying to bypass someone ahead of it. In front of my eyes, Jane darted out from between two parked cars, and was knocked down promptly by the 4×4; yet what I did next was to quickly change lanes myself, move over to the right, accelerate past the accident and keep going until I could turn right into a quieter residential street, as if *I* was the hit-and-run driver making a getaway.

But despite the unhappy nature of this particular dream, I said to Sharmistha, I love the nights when I fall asleep and Jane shows up, saying or doing stuff that I haven't seen before. Surprisingly, autonomously.

Strangely, I added, it doesn't happen that often.

4

There was a photograph in my mother's room in Hazaribagh that had hung in our house throughout my childhood, a large portrait of my great-grandfather from his brief phase as master of the family estates. My father had never met his grandfather, since one morning when he was thirty-five, in their ancestral village near Bardhaman, he'd sat his five sons down one behind another on the floor beside his huge four-poster bed to tell them that he'd earmarked two thousand rupees for each of them to receive when they came of age (my grandfather was his youngest son and had just begun sitting up straight at the time, in the version I heard from my grandmother, who died in 1999).

My great-grandfather had no particular advice for his sons about what to do with the money, but he did suggest Calcutta as a place of good prospects, and counselled them to avoid fraudsters and temptation. The next morning he left for 'the mountains' and nothing was ever heard from him again.

Five years later his first son – my grandfather's oldest brother – disappeared one day without warning. He was slow-witted, according to family lore. When telling the story, my grandmother would insist this brother-in-law of hers, whom she'd never met, had left in search of his father, and she would tell of how her mother-in-law waited for her son to come home all the way to her dying breath. Three years after his disappearance, a postcard had arrived signed by him stating simply that he felt exhausted and would now like to be brought home; but with a tragic omission – he didn't put down his address. Not the local postman, nor the police inspector, nor the authorities at the Calcutta GPO a few days later, could decipher the blurred postmark. My great-uncle never wrote again.

As a teenager, I once asked my grandmother if anyone ever learnt what had happened to her father-in-law. She recounted an odd story that my grandfather once shared with her. During his first months in Calcutta a friend took him along to a kotha, and there was a man sitting upon cushions behind a money chest with a warm, well-born manner, dealing cheerfully with customers, and acting very gentle with the girls as though they were his daughters. He had smiled at the two boys and asked them what they studied. His presence at the top of the stairs made the place feel cleaner and safer, and therefore falser, than it was. Apparently, my grandfather had had a strange sensation, unsupported then or later by any evidence, that his father could be doing exactly this work in any old, large city of India.

I had come to Hazaribagh half-intending to ask my mother if she would come and stay with me in London, at least for a few months; Ma even brought it up herself, suggesting she should come because she worried for me, but within a couple of days I had abandoned the idea, because I had seen how much her grandchildren – my sister's son and daughter, aged six and four respectively – loved having her around. She was the one they both sought out as soon as they were home from school, and, while my sister and her husband were away at their nursing home until seven or eight most evenings, the three of them were one another's world for much of every day and week. I had last seen my nephew shortly after he'd started talking, and this was my first meeting outside of Skype with my niece. Alok, my nephew, asked why his Jane Aunty – whom he'd only ever talked to via webcam, but they'd got on very well, and caught up with each other regularly during my calls home – hadn't come, and for some reason, instead of telling him the truth, I said only one of us could take a holiday at a time. The other had to stay back and keep going to work.

During the mornings, after my sister and brother-in-law had left and Alok and Shreya had been dispatched to school, Ma and I would talk at the dining table or in the drawing room. One of those days I pointed out that Jane hadn't even had a chance to use the ovaries that had killed her. One minute they were pristine and unused, then they suddenly went bad and took her down with them. I added that you realise how absurdly wasteful it is for an entire person to be extinguished when one single bit of their body goes wrong, when you take a look around their room afterwards at the evidence of everything they were, everything they worked to be, everything so rich and fine and varied and subtle that is now gone. There were all of Jane's books waiting to be dipped into many, many more times, there were all her CDs that still demanded playing, the diaries full of this great range of thoughts and impressions, countless unexplored leads that only she could have followed down.

Another morning I said to Ma that this visit reminded me of earlier trips when I'd been back alone and had yearned for Jane (all the way back to my first return home as an undergraduate), but with one crucial difference. Until now, during any separation, each night apart had also brought us one day closer to the moment of our reunion: I would go to bed thinking I'd served out another day of my sentence. Now the sentence had no limits; you were never brought any closer to the day of your release. You just kept falling further away.

In short, there was never a journey I would take again that would have her waiting for me at the other end. So what was the point of any journey at all?

One of the things that made me fall in love anew with my mother during this visit was that she didn't rebuke me (or us) for not having taken the chance, in the near-decade-and-a-half we'd had together, to use those ovaries even once, not even when I myself spoke those specific words. She'd mentioned this wish of hers (to both of us) on several earlier occasions, but not once on this trip. It was all I could do on my last day not to break my promise to myself, and beg her to come to London for me.

5

I had seen Peter on the paths around the NEHU campus, on the verandah of the guest house further along from my room, and in the dining room several times before we talked. He was often smoking, and always alone, and we'd begun acknowledging one another with nods. We spoke for the first time during breakfast on my fourth morning: Professor Sharma, my host, had an early class, so I was eating alone. Peter was already at the big table when I arrived, there was no one else in the dining room, and it would have seemed odd if I had sought out a small table in a corner for myself. So I introduced myself and sat down opposite him.

He started by asking if I had come there from Delhi.

'No.'

'Bombay?'

'We could do this for a while,' I said with a smile.

'I'm sorry, why don't you just tell me?' Peter said, and then continued when he heard, 'Oh, really? I'll be passing through Calcutta too. You guessed I'm half-Indian myself, right?'

If he hadn't mentioned it, I might not have guessed. He was pale with light-brown eyes and hair, and nothing besides America in his accent.

'Yeah, my dad,' he continued. 'My full name is Peter Mangalam.'

He was going to spend the next six months in Shillong as the lacrosse coach at the university. He said the international federation was promoting the sport in virgin areas, and that he'd had a stint in Samoa previously, coaching for six months.

'Oh, wow, so have you brought all the equipment with you?'

'No, it's coming by ship, and should arrive up here by the end of next week. I came early to get my bearings and meet some of the staff and students.'

There was a pause, then my pot of coffee arrived, along with Peter's breakfast. I greeted the waiter and ordered my usual fried egg and toast. When he'd gone, I asked Peter, 'So your father went over to the States?'

'Yeah, in the sixties, for university.'

As he buttered his toast and poured milk over his corn flakes, I thought to myself that he looked the part of a sports coach, compact and toned, with a wide bullish neck.

'You know something funny? Whenever I tell someone I'm a lacrosse coach spreading the game to new places, they assume straightaway I am a CIA agent. I can see it in their eyes.'

'Really? Have people said that to you?'

'Oh, yeah, dozens of times. It's often like that with far-flung Americans. Peace Corps workers get the same grief. The mood can turn ugly very fast. You could be having a beer among friends, someone starts up a conversation about some world-affairs shit, and before you know it, you're very aware of being the only American in the bar.'

He said all this casually, while stirring his cereal, and then unwrapping the paper napkin around his cutlery. I took my first sip of coffee.

'So what do you tell them? Do you ask them to come and watch you play lacrosse?'

'I don't mind what they think. In fact, I tell them about my FBI file back home. Then I sit back to enjoy their reaction.'

'You know what's in your FBI file?'

'Sure, I requested to see a copy when applying for my Samoan work-permit. Why, you want to know?'

'Only if it's a funny story, where it turns out at the end to be a huge misunderstanding.' This earned a grin from Peter.

'The first time was when I was eighteen. We were in training outside San Francisco: I was on the way to being a Marine. One day a bunch of my dorm-mates were discussing amongst themselves what it would be like to go visit the Soviet embassy. They fooled around with daring each other for a bit, then dropped the subject, but somehow the idea stuck in my mind. It didn't seem like much of a challenge, so I went over there and started chatting to the guards at the gate. One afternoon, without telling anyone, just for the heck of it. This is 1984, mind you. Anyway, back then the rule was, if you'd had any kind of contact with a Russian, anything at all, you had to report it to a superior officer within 24 hours. I kind of forgot about that. I didn't think this counted. So two days later, two guys in suits show up and interrogate me for an entire day. And that's one of the two things on my record.'

I wondered at this point if he was toying with me, if he was in fact a spy just spicing up a boring breakfast. Or else he'd decided to make me think he might be a spy, in order to spice up a boring breakfast.

'Wow, that's some story. Is that when you left the army? I mean, I take it you're a civilian now?' After I'd said this, it briefly crossed my mind that Peter might be building up to a 'gotcha' moment.

'No, but soon after, for an unrelated reason. I decided barracks life wasn't for me.'

After a pause, he asked, 'Hey, you want to hear about the second count?'

'Only if you don't mind talking about it.'

'To me it's another story, a little silly, a little funny. So you know the movie *Taxi-Driver*, with De Niro?'

I nodded.

'You remember that scene where he shows up at a political rally, wearing a big jacket, and he's clearly got something hidden under it?'

'Not too clearly, but go on.'

'Anyway, we were watching that one night at college, and this was during the Bush campaign in '88, and a couple of us got to talking about how that would be a fun stunt to pull, because Bush was actually due to visit a town near us the following weekend. Once again, I listened to that little voice inside of me and volunteered. So we got down to shaving my head until I had a Mohawk just like Travis, and then we looked for the perfect jacket. This is southern California in August, no one needs a jacket of any description, but we figured it'd be even better, make me appear more suspicious. Then we debated a while over what to pick that would bulge prominently inside the jacket. My friends wanted to get a stuffed toy, but I suggested a camera with the biggest lens we could find. That way, with the Mohawk, and the long bulge underneath the unnecessary jacket, I'd be sure to get stopped by the Secret Service guys.'

My food arrived, but I didn't want to interrupt his flow.

'Wow, you were taking a huge risk. They could have done anything, thrown you into prison, or just shot first without asking questions.'

'They wouldn't risk unprovoked shooting at a crowded rally. But I knew they'd confront me sooner or later, which they did, and I was going to take my time about unzipping the jacket, which I did. I read them the 'Last time I checked, this was America' line, reminded them I was free to wear whatever I liked no matter what season it was. And besides, what exactly were they accusing me of?'

'So did you finally show them the camera?'

'Yeah, eventually, when five of them had encircled me. I'd taken my time roaming around the place, deliberately standing right beside them, to make sure they noticed me. Once I got into an argument with one of them, the others showed up pretty quickly. Then they stood back, pulled out their weapons, and insisted I put my hands up while one of them pulled down the jacket. They took apart my camera, while I stood there making a scene. By now, three of my friends had also joined me, and we were threatening them with complaints and lawsuits and stuff like that.'

'And that's on your FBI file now? Under what charge?'

'Nothing specific. It's just been noted for future reference. Watch out for this troublemaker, I guess.'

'But it's great that you're free to move around the world,' I said, without meaning anything further by my remark. Yet, for some reason, Peter seemed to want to scrutinise it.

'That's an interesting assumption. What makes you say I'm free to move around?'

'I just meant the obvious. You said you were in the South Pacific, which implies you got your visa despite what they found in the FBI files. Now you're here in Shillong. Looks like freedom to me.'

Peter remained unsmiling, and seemed to be choosing his next words. I had no idea what had set him off, and decided to be more cautious about what I said to this guy.

'I wouldn't have brought it up if you hadn't made that remark about freedom. But it's a topic I think about a lot myself. Let me do something, let me present some of the evidence as I see it before you, and you can offer your opinion on how free I am. What do you say?'

'Well, we've only just met, so I doubt I'll be much use.' I had begun eating by this point, hoping the awkward moment would pass.

'But you're unbiased. You can offer an impartial perspective. I'll tell you a story. I was involved in an accident a few years ago. I was driving with my daughters down an empty road, two lanes but very little traffic, when suddenly a car showed up from the other direction and braked without warning right in front of us. Obviously it skidded across our lane, so we had to collide. It was an old couple, and they apologised over and over saying they'd lost control, and couldn't make us out because the sun had been in their eyes.

'Everyone was lucky not to be seriously injured but one of my daughters sprained her wrist. And that was the excuse my wife seized on to take both of them and walk out on me. I was an unfit father who couldn't even drive them home safely from school.

'As you can imagine, I've replayed this incident a million times in my head, because of the tremendous consequences that followed. And over time, it's become more and more unlikely to me that it could have been an accident. I mean, the chances were next to nothing. It was an empty road, mid-afternoon, the sun wasn't that low in the sky – even someone of moderate driving experience could easily have swerved the other way, onto the side, instead of entering my lane. There was no pressure on him; neither of us was speeding. There's no accounting for it. Unless, of course, you admit the possibility it wasn't an accident.'

Despite my earlier warning to myself, I looked up. 'Meaning what?'

'Well, look how convenient it proved for my wife. It gave her the pretext she was looking for. And then it struck me, what if that old couple weren't regular Joes after all? Because it takes a lot of skill to *fake* an accident, especially to fine-tune it to the exact degree where the collision is mild and therefore no one is seriously injured.'

'I have to say I don't see the connection,' I replied, knowing I was risking Peter's wrath.

This time he remained calm. 'Maybe I should continue for some of the links to become clear. A few weeks later my wife, again without any notice, moved with my daughters to the East Coast. She knew I couldn't follow them, because I was out of work and had no savings. A couple of *days* after this, I'm in a diner where I usually go for lunch to get out of the condo, and who walks in but my college lacrosse coach. I've been eating there for years, but I never saw him before. And guess what, turns out I was just the fellow he wanted to meet, because apparently he had an offer for me, exciting, well paid, and with the opportunity for travel around the world. He wanted me to consider coaching lacrosse in exotic destinations. And that's how I am here today, having this conversation with you.'

'Isn't that simply a fortunate coincidence? I mean, fortunate in the sense it provided you an occupation out of the blue and a chance to recover yourself?'

'Look, this lacrosse coach of mine used to deal drugs, ok? We were actually close in college, and he kind of trusted me. Back then, one day he'd seemed really stressed. He confided in me he was in it up to his neck. And because certain important people knew what he did on the side, they had him on a short leash. He was bound to obey them whenever they sent for him, and carry out any task they might assign. That was the price of his freedom. And what were *my* options, after my wife moved back east? How come something shows up, right on cue, as if someone was listening at the door, an offer I can't refuse that has the convenient side-effect of distancing me from my kids?'

'So you think your wife planned this? She let the coach know where you hang out in order to get you out of the way?'

'Of course not. She'd never met him. We got together after college, long after my lacrosse-playing days were over.'

I knew it was risky, but I felt I had to ask Peter one question.

'Have you ever seen that movie, *The Truman Show*, where the guy's whole life turns out to be a TV show?'

'Yeah, I know what that feels like.'

'So if it's not your wife, who do you think is manipulating this? Who ordered the old couple to crash into you, and sent the coach into that diner? And why?'

'Why? Because I'm one of those rare people who don't mind following through on an idea when someone dares me. Most people wonder briefly about doing crazy shit and then forget about it, but I actually enjoy seeing where it might lead. Those who keep track of me are well aware of this. I mean, it's in my FBI files. They can't predict what I'll do next, which makes me potentially dangerous, so they make sure they control *where* I'll be, far away from trouble in Samoa and Shillong. There's another whole story I haven't told you, of how I found myself playing lacrosse in the first place. I mean, I hadn't even heard of it when I left the Marines and entered college.

'Plus this is the United States we're talking about, where certain powerful elements have never forgiven the crime of my parents in crossing the race divide, in a small town in Massachusetts in the early sixties. I mean, I have evidence they started fucking up my mom while I was still in her womb. And they succeeded. They managed to break up my parents before I was three. That's when my dad moved to London.'

'When you say 'they' do you mean the local town elders, or do you mean the government, the military, or the FBI?'

Peter treated my question as deadly serious, which was probably safer for me. 'Do you think there's a difference? They have the same agenda. They tried to straighten me out, to get me to fall in line. They destroyed my home and screwed up my mom. They arranged it so I'd have no option but to join the Marines. When that didn't work out, they brought me under control at college.'

'Through lacrosse, you mean?' I asked, still without daring to smile. He didn't register my interruption.

'But they could never let me be. They had to step right into my home and break it up. They even endangered the lives of my kids.'

I decided to stop teasing him. 'Look, I'm only asking this as an outside observer, and because you chose to open up to me, so don't take it the wrong way. But surely your marriage was in trouble even before the faked accident?'

Peter shook his head. 'There's lots of ways of fucking up a couple. You can cut off the money supply, keep the guy from finding a decent job, show him up to be a loser and a fool.'

Then, leaning forward over our breakfast dishes, speaking to someone he'd met about thirty-five minutes before, Peter Mangalam uttered the following desires. 'You know, sometimes the rage climbs inside me, and I want to kill a whole bunch of people, and force them to share my pain. I want to drive to a high-concentration area of those controlling assholes, and just open fire. I don't care about guilty or innocent. There'll probably be some selfless hero who rushes up to try and stop me. He's the motherfucker I'll make sure to shoot in the head.'

'Do you mean like a corporate HQ or a government building?'

Peter ignored my need for specifics. 'But who's innocent? Is my lacrosse coach innocent? Is my wife innocent, after what I know about her? Are the assholes in my hometown who made my mom feel like shit even though she was raised there, are they innocent? Who is truly selfless in the world? Show me one person. Are fat people innocent? They fucking wear their greed and selfishness all over their disgusting bodies.'

I decided it was time to calm him down a little.

'Peter, if you're looking for innocence in that pure state, I doubt you'll find it anywhere. But what do all these people have to do with your life?'

'I have a dream of buying a motorbike and taking it from Shillong all the way to Bangalore, where I have an uncle, once I'm done with the coaching. That might make me happy again. I was looking at the pictures my relatives took in England, on the way here, when they were showing me the sights. It's plain to see: the pictures tell me I'm not happy. I can't run right now because of an old injury. I'm due back in LA for surgery in January. If my leg heals I'll be happy. I can go running. And if I find a pretty girlfriend, or my wife calls again and wants me back, but I warn you I'll consider it only if she really loves me. She'll have to prove that to me first.

'But if the surgery fails, and it turns out I have a bum leg, and I can't afford to see my children…'

I felt this small sign of hope and optimism needed immediate boosting.

'Look Peter, what would be the point of rendering yourself

irrelevant by killing all these people? You'd be in the papers for all the wrong reasons, and that too for just a week. Suppose you were right about being manipulated and controlled, no one would believe a word of it. No one would have any time for your story if you did something like that. They'd be able to dismiss you as another psycho. And those forces that destroy lives in this fashion could go on doing it to other people. This is what they want, right? They want to wipe you out with no trace. They want everyone to think you're insane.

'You want to know what I think? I believe you should stick around and be a pain in their arses. Write a book, expose them. Show them up, bring their practices into the light. Go on TV. Talk about it. Encourage all the others who feel this way and think they're alone to come forward. By sticking around you'll be fighting back in a far more effective way than by disappearing in a storm of bullets.'

It was just as well we were the only guests in the dining room, and the lone waiter too had returned to the kitchen, because this entire conversation was taking place at normal volume.

Peter shook his head. Clearly this thought had occurred to him. 'I could write two books, one that would be all about hugging and learning, the sort of self-healing story that gets you straight onto Oprah. And then there'd be the ugly truth. But what's the point? That won't make me happy. I'd still be alone and injured and far from my kids.'

Then suddenly he leaned forward to confront me. 'So what do you really think about everything I've told you? What's your take on it?'

I tried to mask my surprise at being put on the spot. 'Well, Peter, I doubt my opinion will be of much use. I mean, we've just met, and what can I really say that would be of any interest? But I can assure you I'm spellbound, everything you've said so far has really stirred me up.'

'So then give me an opinion,' Peter persisted, still looking directly at me.

'Look, I agree entirely with your basic idea that our lives are lived out in the grip of immense forces we aren't even aware of. Take advertising for example, or CCTV, or all the propaganda on the news.'

I had thought I was offering up a very reasonable concession, but this was all far too bland for Peter.

'I'm sorry, but you're an actor, Mister. You're a fucking diplomat. You think you're humouring me? Why're you being so fucking blah? Tell the truth, man. At least acknowledge your own experience. Because I can tell from the stuff you've said that none of this is new to you. You've obviously thought about this shit before. No one comes up with those questions on the spot.'

This encounter had just stopped being (wholly) funny, so I took a bit longer to reply, and spoke slowly.

'Look, Peter, maybe the reason I don't feel these forces controlling me in a specific way is because I'm too ordinary for them to worry about. I'm just an English lecturer at a university in London. You spoke yourself of the majority of people, who discuss crazy things sometimes but would never dream of actually doing anything risky. I guess my life so far has pretty much been like that, which is why I've been left alone. I mean sure, do I feel entirely un-manipulated in all my thoughts and influences? No, of course not. But you must believe me when I insist I cannot recall ever having felt specifically picked on, not the way you're describing, by great invisible forces.

'The reason I was interested in what you chose to share with me is that you've had your whole adult life to think through these things. So if this version of events rings true for you, I'm willing to listen seriously, without always being able to enter into your experiences.'

I deliberately omitted to mention that I was also a writer.

Peter might feel resentful, or spied upon, if he thought he was going to be written about later.

Shortly afterwards, I excused myself saying I had a lecture to deliver in an hour, which was true. I had only two more mornings in Shillong, and didn't find myself alone again with Peter in the dining room. I saw him a few more times on the paths near the guest-house, and once or twice smoking outside his room, but I'd had enough of the craziness for just now. Before I left, I debated long and hard whether I should let my colleagues know they were going to share a campus for the next six months with someone seriously unstable, but in the end decided to take the risk of saying nothing. Peter had indicated he wanted to return to LA to have his surgery and give his life there another go, see if he could get through to his wife or even meet someone new. I decided to bet he wouldn't unleash any madness just yet, although I did wonder if his anger was specifically bound up with hating his fellow-Americans, or the rest of humanity in general.

6

The friendly boy who usually brought us breakfast and lunch at our favoured beachside place was sitting with his back to us at a table away to our left. Jim noticed him first, and surmised that we might be witnessing a holiday romance. To be sure, he looked very cosy seated hand in hand with a beautiful dark-haired girl his age (probably seventeen, max). She seemed Italian to me, and equally amorous; she wore a sarong and a bikini top. The only unusual element in the scene was the presence of what looked like the girl's Mamma, who sat across from them, sometimes speaking to them (with no apparent awkwardness), sometimes looking away.

'There's a nice liberal parent for you,' said Jim.

'True. Or perhaps this is the ultimate rebellion, being conducted in open defiance, which is cool too.'

'But I'm happy for our man,' I added, and I was. We'd really grown to like him during our four days there. He'd already told us about two secluded beaches, and a great hill walk that went past his village three miles down the coast.

We drank and watched them for a while longer. It was three in the afternoon, we were seated under a large beach umbrella, drinking beers on an empty stomach. This was a place a couple of hundred metres down the beach from where the boy worked, and where we usually had lunch. His name (for us) was Andy, and he was a surfer.

The girl seemed genuinely affectionate, and murmured a lot while Andy drew closer and listened. The mother, who wasn't unattractive herself, occasionally exchanged words with her daughter in what was (now) clearly Italian, and then would look away, usually to her right. She was sitting with her back to the sea, having something like a Mojito. The young couple would continue talking while holding each other's hands, and nuzzle sometimes. If the mother seemed at all uncomfortable, it was in the usual way of being too close to a case of PDA (especially when one of the displayers is your daughter), and not wanting to seem either disapproving or nosey.

I started making up a story that the woman was some super-successful editor or journalist or even the owner of an Italian media group, taking a brief but expensive business-class holiday with her daughter, who's always felt harshly judged and closely watched by her Mamma. Hence the holiday affair being conducted like this in the open.

'And then, when they're back in Milan, then what?'

'She seems sweet, so let's say she keeps in touch with Andy, and returns here next chance she gets, during her Christmas holidays, and stays longer. Our Andy is a cool guy with, let's face it, one heck of a body, so they fall in love and get married right here next time round. She then has to return to Italy, but helps him dutifully with all the visa formalities of moving there to join her, and because her mum is so influential it even works out. Andy moves to Milan. They get a flat together and she starts university. He goes five times a week for Italian classes, but doesn't get a job, say at a Thai restaurant, in the meantime, because this is Milan, everyone knows Signora Moretti, how would it look if her son-in-law was working as a waiter somewhere?'

Jim takes up the thread. The fucker's a pessimist. 'Either he starts seeing someone from the Italian classes, and of course, since this is Milan, where everyone knows the Morettis and especially that the only daughter has gone and married a Thai waiter, Andy is spotted with the other woman immediately in some café and word gets round to her mother, who finally has the big confrontation with her daughter to ask if she's done with her stupid rebellion.'

'Our Andy would never do that. Look at him, he's kissing her fingertips.' He was also stroking her leg under the table with his foot. Once more, I must clarify, there was nothing in the mother's expression as she spoke to her daughter to suggest a disapproving, haughty media magnate.

'Ok, then Annabella meets someone at university. With Andy the sex is fantastic, and of course they are in love, but she has much more in common with this fellow first-year politics student. He's grown up there, hates Berlusconi just like her; they sit in and demonstrate against the debt crisis together. In the beginning they're friends, but one day she gets home really late, and confesses the truth when Andy confronts her. She loves Andy of course, but this new guy is more than just a friend. Our Andy is so proud he leaves the flat immediately, sleeps rough the first night, then gets a job in one of the Thai restaurants he used to visit to eat and chat with his compatriots. But he is actually shellshocked, and can't bring himself to tell the folks back home, nor can he reason with Annabella.'

I didn't really like the turn the story had taken in Jim's hands, so I asked him what he thought Andy's actual name might be (Jim was a Thailand regular: this was his fifth visit). But he ignored my question and continued spinning his mournful tale.

'Who calls him several times, begs him to return to the flat, tells him she still loves him and let's see what happens. All she needs is a bit of time, everything has happened so fast. But, she promises him, even if they do split up, Andy can continue to live with her, right until his Italian residency is confirmed. He has nothing to worry about. So will Andy go back home, will he try and stay with a co-worker from the Thai restaurant, or will he do something stupid in his sorrow, like steal some money from the till at the restaurant one day in a bid to leave Milan?'

I shook my head. 'Andy wouldn't steal. And besides, Annabella would be so guilty she'd give him any amount he asked for.'

There our soap ran out of steam. The storyline that had occurred to me, but I didn't say, was that Andy and Annabella, no matter what their initial obstacles – immigration, Mamma, first-year politics students – overcome everything and remain together. They find they were after all kindred spirits who'd managed to recognize one another in a miraculously fortunate way. They have several happy years through their twenties, both of them going to university and supporting themselves with part-time jobs, travelling around the world, growing up together to the point where Annabella has completely left behind her mother's shadow. Then one day, the doctors find an abnormal cyst in Annabella's ovary, and she is dead of cancer within two months.

That night I'm being tit-wanked by the girl from two nights before when there's a knock on the door followed by Jim calling for me. He's with someone new tonight, taller than usual, certainly not yet twenty. I put on my underwear and open the door; he wants his camera, which apparently is in my bag. He says this is an ass he has to film from behind. The thought of him fucking and filming the girl next door turns me on as well, and I'm harder than usual for the remainder of the hour. These are the only two nights we spend with girls in Thailand. Jim shows me the footage afterwards: he has her from behind, but also sitting up and facing him, and doing a slow dance for him at a distance, naked.

7

He wanted a story from me (for once) about the 'happy phase of love', so this one's for you, Saikat, from Sharmistha's Creative Writing seminar.

It's from a holiday seven years ago: Jane and I are in our hotel room in Fort Cochin. We've just woken up, and I've reached for the remote and switched on the TV, to postpone getting out of bed for a few minutes. I flip past the news channels and the South Indian channels before pausing at a Hindi movie that's about to start.

Vinod Mehra is a cop who's just stopped Kader Khan's (left-hand-drive) sedan at a checkpoint, for smuggling contraband. Yet, even as he crows righteously while slipping the handcuffs onto KK's wrist, KK steps on the gas and the car lurches forward, although they're still joined by the cuffs. VM refuses to panic or let go however, and a deadly-seeming (although not terribly speedy) struggle ensues, which culminates in the tenacious Inspector, who has also been shot at several times, being dragged along behind the car like a water-skier on its luggage rack.

From this distinctly unpromising position, an indomitable VM finds a way to open the boot, scramble back on board, and then slither through the cavity behind the back-rest of the rear seat to emerge behind KK, gun poised at his temple, compelling him to halt and surrender, even as he swears through gritted teeth to one day turn the tables. Somehow, although they're on a country road distant from any habitation, it also happens to be the precise spot where, slightly further ahead, one of KK's henchmen was waiting to meet the boss, and therefore witnesses both the arrest and the vow of vengeance.

In a fit of inspiration rare among sidekicks, he divines what must have transpired straightaway, and the next shot finds him at the house of old A K Hangal, whom he has correctly fingered as a police informer. Despite the impassioned entreaties of his young daughter, Hangal is shot without mercy, although the thug does display some merit by refraining from 'looting the honour' of the newly orphaned lass. It is directly upon his leaving that VM arrives, too late to defend his source under some threadbare witness-protection programme that clearly needs looking at, but just in time to hear AKH's dying regret about not having arranged his daughter's future before he departed this world. Remorseful *and* upright as he is, VM promptly steps up above and beyond the call of duty, and does his bit to plug the major shortfall in government funding mentioned above by promising the expiring father that he would make the grieving but winsome maiden the pride and light of his own home.

Not five minutes have elapsed since the film began with the dramatic car chase. Meanwhile I am shaking Jane awake (she's dozed off once more), and filling her in breathlessly on what's happened so far, because this really is something she must watch. It isn't subtitled, and I'm going to have to translate, but I even reach over and hand her her glasses from the bedside table so that she doesn't miss another moment of this extraordinary passage of cinematic storytelling. Next shot finds us in VM's family mansion, where he and his new bride have arrived to seek the blessings of his clearly loaded dad. Om Prakash however is infuriated by his son's disregard for all social norms and filial obligations, and it takes him less than a minute to disown him and write him out of his life once and forever.

Moving swiftly on, we cut straight to a few years ahead, when VM and his wife are already the proud parents of a five or six-year-old girl, and in a renewed effort to win his father's approval through the unsubtle emotional deployment of the adorable grand-child, they set off in their car, driven by Pran. I quickly clarify to Jane that it's not yet easy to tell what Pran's true colours are today, whether he'll shortly turn out to be a KK plant, or if he's playing one of his excessively honourable roles, in which he will go down displaying friendship and loyalty until his final breath.

For some reason, the journey to Om Prakash's house *within the same city* involves a long drive along a desolate mountain road, where a false detour sign leads them onto a grassy plateau and straight into the clutches of a freshly-released KK. Naturally, taking full advantage of these favourable circumstances, he promises to make good his earlier pledge, and shoots both VM and his wife as they step out of the car in a vain attempt to flee. The valiant but doomed inspector's last words to his driver are to escape and save at least his daughter from the same fate. I remind Jane to watch closely: this is the moment when Pran's true nature will be revealed. He steps on the gas, and dashes off in the car, straight towards the edge of the plateau. But at the last moment, just before the car hurtles to its fireball end, Pran leaps out, girl in arms, and then rolls down the well-padded slope, protecting his ward in a foetal embrace. The goons make a half-hearted effort to chase and shoot, and fire twice in his general direction, but they give up for the time-being, satisfied with a morning's work well done, and determined to finish them off later on.

Less than ten minutes after the film began, Pran arrives breathless and harassed at Om Prakash's mansion to implore him to reconsider his decision in what after all are vastly altered circumstances. Proud old OP refuses even to look at the face of his grandchild, lying limply in Pran's arms. Pran begins to walk away, although in a fit of pique he adds, that sure, he'll raise the little girl as though she were his own, but OP shouldn't forget that he is only an ordinary driver, and so if one day despite his best efforts, she is to be found dancing in some bordello or bar, and people point to her and ask one another if she isn't the abandoned grand-daughter of one of the city's most renowned families, OP should neither be surprised nor shocked. It is an inspired touch. Within seconds, OP has seized the child from him, and is clutching her to his bosom and weeping copiously, promising to forget his pride and his grief in the raising of her, the only living trace of his ruined home. Pran walks away, and even manages to resist a wink at the camera.

Ten-and-a-half minutes, but Pran has another surprise in store. With the onerous burden of guardianship off his shoulders, he now breaks into KK's house, determined to wipe out the entire family in an act of reckless retribution. Yet when he sees another little girl, the same age as VM's daughter, peacefully asleep, he cannot go through with smothering her with the pillow as he had originally planned. Instead she is awakened and begins a right racket, which he is compelled to cut short by picking her up and escaping through the window.

But KK's henchman isn't far behind. Pran arrives at what looks like the entrance to the Red Fort, or perhaps it is a temple, and glancing around him desperately, spots a trio of women, apparently together, leaving the complex. With pleas of fleeing extreme danger, he convinces Sushma Sethi to take charge of the child in his arms, while he gives his pursuer the slip. Soon the goon has arrived, and SS retreats into a corner, shielding the child with her body. Yet, a few minutes later, when Pran, having managed to elude recognition and capture, returns to pick up his abductee, the other women inform him that SS wasn't one of their group, and that she disappeared with the child soon after. So on the one hand, we have KK's distraught wife begging him to retrieve the blameless girl, and yet – we're only too aware of the irony – not even her kidnapper now knows where she is.

It is at this juncture that, almost as an afterthought, the credits appear, along with, for the first time, the title of the film. The whole sequence has taken not fifteen minutes. It is a masterpiece of editing and compression, and the two of us, hypnotised by happiness, our sides hurting from laughter, are utterly spellbound.

8

What else is there to say? Such were the first thirty-six days after Jane died. I kept moving around, met a few diverting people.

Then Jim and I were back at Heathrow.

A Good Dry-Cleaner is Worth a Story

IN MY DEFENCE, it all happened so fast.

I was driving down to pick up some dry-cleaning and had just entered the high street when I noticed S at a café table on the opposite pavement. She saw my car about two seconds later and waved vigorously, looking really pleased to see me. Although I hadn't counted on her spotting me I thought to myself, what the hell, I can stop for a few minutes and say hello. So I raised my hand to indicate to her that I was turning around and kept driving until I reached a gap in the road divider, where I made a smooth U-turn and headed back in her direction.

She could see that I was approaching her, she would surely have guessed that I intended to stop, but for some reason she chose to leave her table and come running towards me, and in her excitement, she ran right onto the road. I could see her smiling, I felt pleased myself that she seemed so enthusiastic about seeing me after what had been more than a while without any communication, and like her, I too didn't notice that another car, in the lane to my right, had decided to suddenly switch lanes and move in front of me, perhaps attempting to bypass a slowcoach ahead of him. He had his eyes on the slowcoach, I had my eye on S, and she had eyes only for me.

Of course he came to a stop immediately after the collision, but I didn't. In those few seconds, acting I know not from what impulse, and although I was only a few metres behind him and had seen, even heard, everything, I recklessly switched lanes, moved to my right and just kept driving. The traffic came to a halt directly behind me, but I managed to make a left turn, entered a residential street and soon resumed driving in the direction of the dry cleaner's.

I could imagine the other driver's testimony – she just ran onto the road without looking. She seemed to be running towards another car. It was so sudden I had no time to react.

All her friends and acquaintances would be asked the same question, but no one would know who S had been running towards – if she died. If on the other hand she was only injured, as was most likely because the car that hit her hadn't been going very fast, she would soon come to and clear up the mystery. And then I would be blamed for something I had no part in, something that happened entirely because of another person's carelessness and flawed choices. Flawed personality, if you ask me, always jumping the gun and over-reacting to everything. In fact, *that* was why the relationship, such as it was, hadn't worked out between us. You simply could not trust somebody like that to be discreet. It was fun the first couple of times with a personality of that sort, but afterwards it would have just got exhausting, and then, plain dangerous.

I thought all this on the way to the dry-cleaner's, but I still had to decide how to react. It was obviously too late to turn around and return to the scene of the accident. Should I just appear at the hospital and try and retrieve the situation there? But that would only exacerbate everything. How the hell did I find out S had had an accident?

There was of course the chance that S, even in the confusion of coming to, would remember to be considerate about naming who she'd seen that had made her run onto the road. Because if I was fair, that was another side to her character: yes, irrepressible and spontaneous as she often could be, she'd also been very good at respecting boundaries, both during and after our thingummy. Truth be told, she'd never made any trouble for me, even though I'd remained on tenterhooks for months after it was over, wondering what reckless thing she might think to do.

By this time, I'd found a park and was a couple of minutes' walk from the dry cleaner's, where I had to pick up a suit and a party dress of Tilly's. That last thought had actually fortified me, and I was even feeling somewhat cheerful. The accident definitely couldn't have been serious, she would be fine in a couple of months at most, and there was a more-than-fair chance that she wouldn't blurt out my name, except perhaps in private to a couple of her closest friends.

And full redemption arrived for me while Kevin the dry cleaner had gone into the back of the store in search of our things. If I paid her a hospital visit very early into her recovery, shortly after she'd regained consciousness, and emphatically told her with the most natural of expressions that of course I had stayed right beside her after the accident, but surely she would understand why I couldn't accompany the ambulance to the hospital or let my name be entered into the record alongside hers, who else had been present who knew us both and could contradict my story? S would have been knocked unconscious: I was pretty sure of that. Whatever I said about the few minutes after that would be the unchallenged truth. All I had to do was get in there early with my story, have that one visit alone with her.

Kevin had as usual done a fantastic job with our clothes: they were so pristine and unwrinkled it always seemed a shame afterwards to wear them. I told him the party we were going to wasn't far from here, just behind the Albert Hall in fact, after a recital that evening. He asked me what I thought of the 8-2 drubbing at the hands of United a few days before: it was one of our regular topics of lament, although this week had been even more painful than usual.

'In a way, I feel a perverse satisfaction,' I said to him. 'When a man who's way past his sell-by date, who has nothing to offer to the club any more, just refuses to recognise that and leave, this is the kind of shit that will happen.'

And as I left after paying and thanking Kevin, I felt pleased with myself for having finally got that off my chest. I had wanted to say that out loud about Wenger for a long time now, especially to a fellow supporter. This last season, every single thing about him – his accent, his expressions, even his suits and his hair – had just brought out the venom in me.

Viju's Version

Part I: Miss Bose

1

THIS IS MISS BOSE'S *only* memory of him from school. He was in the principal's office, sweating much more copiously than he could remember to dab away, frequently scratching his head, and appearing as anguished by his mother's desperate, high-pitched efforts to defend him, as he was by Mr Sen's stony silence and the focused, hostile disapproval of the rest of the 'Senior Disciplinary Affairs Committee', of which she, at twenty-seven, had been the junior-most member. It was only her third year on the job, and her first time on that panel. Which was why, in deference to her older colleagues, she hadn't said a word throughout Viju's interrogation: she'd felt guilty about this afterwards, but found out much later that Viju had taken her silence to be a form of tacit support, in that room full of people so eager to condemn and expel him. Eventually he begged his Ma, trying hard not to raise his voice, to let *him* tell the story. It was clearly not doing him any good for her to insist in between loud sobs that the whole thing was her fault: after all, the committee couldn't punish a student's mother, and that was just one reason why blaming her and acquitting Viju would have been an extremely unsatisfying outcome. So, while Mrs Sinha subsided into further hanky-muffled bursts of maternal weeping, this is the gist of what he had to say in his defence.

2

No one could have been more aware than him of the significance of the occasion: two of Calcutta's best-known writers had agreed to speak at the school's 125th Founder's Day celebrations, and he, Viju, of Class XII B, had been placed in charge of looking after these esteemed guests. Yet the duties attached to this extraordinary privilege had been simple: all he had to do was meet the driver of the principal's car at ten in the morning, and the two of them would pick up the writers from their respective homes, and make sure they arrived back at Mr Sen's office at least half an hour before the function began (that is, by 11.30 a.m.). Then he was to remain available throughout the afternoon to attend to any needs or questions the guests may have, and afterwards, following the customary Founder's Day staff lunch in the faculty common room (during which he was to wait outside), Viju had been supposed to lead his charges back to the principal's car and escort them safely home, or wherever they wished to be dropped off.

Had Viju been picked for the job because of its incredible logistical difficulties? No, because there weren't any: the driver had been given the writers' addresses, and had handled the pick-ups impeccably. Had he been asked to show any initiative beyond following these clear instructions? Not that anyone remembered. Why, oh why then, was Vijay Sinha, out of the 120 students in his year, assigned what should have been on the one hand a very straightforward set of tasks, but also an opportunity that (the staff had felt) *he* in particular would cherish for years to come? It was only because he had consistently earned – right through his school career – the highest marks in English (both Language and Literature) in his batch, culminating the previous month in his winning the Kedleston Memorial Essay Competition, which was one of the school's most venerated contests for its senior students (anyone only had to glance at the list of previous winners – painted on a board placed prominently beside the main entrance to the auditorium – to see how many of them were now renowned names in diverse fields). Naturally the teachers had felt they were picking the student best qualified to host these stellar literary guests, the one who would benefit the most from spending time in their presence, and, needless to add, the one who, by his mature and thoughtful questions and remarks, would also reflect his schooling in the most desirable light. What no one had realised, before it was catastrophically late, was that being a halfway decent writer also logically implied that in the simplest practical matters, Viju would prove to be a clueless fool.

Because here is what had happened, in Viju's telling of it, the sequence of events that led to the school's 125th anniversary celebrations falling off a cliff, in full view of the large audience of current students and their parents, dozens of enthusiastic alumni and their families, several other well-known personalities in the front rows from various walks of life, as well as a large group of reporters and photographers who had of course (with what now seemed to be the bitterest of ironies) been *specifically invited* to ensure that the occasion obtained maximum media coverage. And coverage it had received with a vengeance: the city had not collectively had a laugh like this over something for a long time. You could feel the envy and the malice rippling through every article, so many columnists and letter-writers palpably ecstatic that one of the city's most august institutions had fallen hard on its face like this, and had actually invited the world to come along and witness the moment.

Of course, after what they had been put through, one would have expected the two great writers involved to go public about their awful experience in the sharpest terms (and they had, before the week was out, without even calling first to consult Mr Sen). Yet the most pathetic aspect of it all, as he had sharply pointed out in a letter of his own to *The Statesman*, was that several of the gloaters, if or when they had sons of their own, would have given an arm and a leg to have them admitted to the very school they were mocking with such unseemly relish. The jibe that had hurt Mr Sen the most, the one he'd cut out and saved and had now placed on the table for Viju to consider – on this, the day the Senior Disciplinary Affairs Committee was meeting to decide on whether expulsion would be the most appropriate punishment for him, even though it was the year of his final board exams – was the op-ed cartoon in *The Telegraph* with the tagline, 'The coffee that broke the camel's back?' It was a heavy-handed reference to the events leading up to the Founder's Day fiasco (a bank manager is shown denying Mr Sen a loan to buy his chief guests two cups of coffee: 'No, Mr Sen, no, *coffee* on top of everything else??'), but unfortunately the theme had caught on, and a rash of shrill jokes in a similar vein, about St George's supposed 'birthday-party budget crisis', had followed throughout the previous week.

And this calamity, that just wouldn't go away because the school itself had invited the entire city to watch while they offended two prickly writers and scuttled their own gala celebrations, had been caused by one seventeen-year-old, and apparently, a pair of crumpled trousers.

Because in Viju's version of that disastrous morning, his mother had switched his trousers while he was in the shower. She'd walked into his room to hurry him along and remind him breakfast was on the table, noticed his uniform laid out on the bed, and decided unilaterally right there and then that the trousers he'd picked out weren't pressed perfectly enough for such an important occasion. So she'd taken them away, and left a freshly ironed pair for him to wear instead.

Of course, Viju had been too excited and focused on being punctual when he rushed out of the shower and got dressed to notice the switch, and if he'd actually stopped for even a bite of breakfast (as his mother repeatedly requested), she might have mentioned the matter to him, in which case everything would have been remembered at the right time, and the rest of the day, according to Viju, would have turned out just fine. Because, contrary to Mr Sen's impression of him being a bungling incompetent, the pick-up of both the guests had gone absolutely smoothly, and they were heading back to school well ahead of schedule at 10.50, forty minutes before they were expected in his office.

Which was the only reason why Viju had decided to go through with his idea, of them stopping for a quick coffee before they arrived at the school. It had occurred to him the previous evening, as a wonderful opportunity to steal an invaluable half-hour with these luminaries, perhaps pick their brains a little, as well as add a personal touch to the day's formal events; but only if there was time, either in the morning or later on, while dropping them back home. Of course, it was going to be his treat, no question about it, he'd set aside money for this the night before as soon as he had the idea, but we'll get to that soon enough.

So, when he noticed they had forty minutes in hand, and were less than a minute away from the perfect café, right then, as they cut across Park Street, without wasting a moment Viju asked the driver to pull over, and turned around and checked with his guests if they'd like a brief stop for some refreshments.

They had been chattering along amiably, and had loved the idea, and Viju had told the driver they would be back in less than half an hour, with plenty of time in hand to make it to school by 11.30.

But the driver had demurred, saying his instructions were to drive everyone back directly to Mr Sen's office, and despite Viju's reassurances that they were well ahead of schedule, as well as additional support from both the distinguished guests, he simply refused to park and wait.

At this point, Viju had accepted that the plan had been scuttled, and was about to ask the mule of a driver to carry on, when suddenly both writers spoke almost in unison to suggest that they stop anyway, and continue to the school after coffee by cab. And so, it was only because he felt understandably elated by this show of support for his idea, this evident keenness to have a cup of coffee in his company, that Viju jumped out of the car, opened the left-hand back door for his guests, and then simply and crisply informed the driver they would see him back at school.

In the café as well, all the omens were good: at five to eleven on a Monday morning, they had their pick of tables in the house. Viju, with his prior knowledge of the various beverages on offer (this was a place he visited with his friends whenever they had enough pocket-money saved up), asked his guests (yes, *his* guests at this moment, not the school's) what they would like, made suggestions and recommendations, and presently went up to the counter. It was *after* he'd already ordered coffees for everyone as well as a selection of his favourite pastries, that he realised there was no money in the pockets of these trousers. He would learn why only that evening, from his mother once he was back home, but right then, as he patted and dug into every pocket with increasing panic, all he could figure was that the hundred and fifty rupees he'd specifically put into his right trouser pocket last night in the hope of such an opportunity must have fallen out somewhere, perhaps down the back of the front car seat a little while before.

(At this point, Mr Sen had curtly asked him why he didn't carry a wallet, like any other civilised near-adult male. That way, he would always know whether it was on him or not. Viju's sheepish reply was that his pocket had been picked in a minibus only a month before, and he was saving up to buy himself a new wallet. He added that if there hadn't been any time for coffees, those hundred and fifty rupees would have been transferred into the wallet fund.)

You can imagine the embarrassment that followed, even though Viju managed to get the cashier to cancel his own coffee and pastry right away. He had to return to the table and somehow find the words to ask these impossibly distinguished guests, whom *he* had invited for refreshments (and a cab-ride back to school, although that next problem hadn't even occurred to Viju just then), to pay for their own coffees. At this point in his disciplinary committee hearing, Viju insisted repeatedly that it was far and away the worst moment of his life, which was probably not a great idea, since it would have motivated at least a few members on the panel to raise the bar that afternoon.

One of the writers paid readily enough for both of them, but with an unsmiling face, and from that moment on there was a complete transformation in both their attitudes towards Viju. As he turned around to return to the counter after repeating his gratitude at least a dozen times, he heard one of them remark in a normal voice, apparently indifferent to the possibility of being overheard, about how such behaviour was 'typical, of this kind of boy from *this* background, who are also admitted to such schools these days'. There was also no offer made – then or slightly later, when their drinks and cakes arrived –

to order Viju something as well, not even after they realised he was only having a glass of water. In fact, they managed a remarkable impression of pretending to be two friends out on a coffee date, and talked non-stop about acquaintances they had in common, most of whom Viju had never heard of. The young aspiring writer, who had gone to the trouble of actually buying books – one each – by these giants in preparation for this morning, had suddenly become invisible to his guests.

After ten minutes of being ignored, Viju had decided to test, on a perverse whim, what would happen if he were to suddenly get up and walk away, whether such an action would even be acknowledged. And he did, he left the table without a word, before regretting his rudeness barely five steps later and returning to ask if they wanted some water, as if that was the errand he'd intended to perform. Neither of them looked at him long enough to answer, the slightest of nods sufficed to convey their disdain. That was when Viju, who was nearly in tears by now, remembered finally he had another huge challenge coming up in just a few minutes, bigger than any catastrophe that had occurred until then. Either he had to call the principal's secretary, whose number he didn't have, to ask her to send back the school car as soon as possible to Park Street (while explaining to her – and perhaps even being put through to Mr Sen himself – everything that had happened in the first place to cause them to send the car away and then to request it again shortly after); or else more realistically, but even more horrifyingly, because it would be in person, he was going to have to break the news to these two pillars of Indian literature that they would have to fork out their own cab-fare to the school, and as a kind favour, carry him along as well.

To put it simply, Viju found he couldn't do it. He wasn't up to the task. The best he could manage was to sidle up to the table, his eyes burning from drops of sweat even though the café was air-conditioned, and say – through repeated gulps and hesitations – that if they didn't mind setting off a bit early and walking for about fifteen minutes, he knew a short-cut back to school through some back-lanes and side-streets, and they could still be there in time for the function.

At this point, the two geniuses had shaken their heads at each other in shared disbelief, momentarily deprived of their habitual eloquence. Viju had stunned two legendary speakers (because they *were*, quite apart from their mastery of the written word) into silence. After a few seconds, during which he hadn't dared to look at anything but his perfectly polished shoes and the knife-like crease in his trousers (though the mystery of what had happened didn't therefore clear up for him: he failed to notice the vital clue, not that it would have achieved anything), the younger legend finally managed to ask a question.

'You want us to follow you in this heat down lanes and alleys, and then speak at the function?'

'Sir, it's fifteen minutes maximum, I promise,' Viju had reassured them, in his telling of it. But they simply lapsed again into shocked head-shaking and eye-rolling, before the senior legend responded very briefly to Viju (how irrevocably this relationship had shattered, when Viju thought back to their interaction just twenty minutes before in the car).

'Why can't the car pick us up?'

'Sir, because I don't know the phone number to the principal's office,' Viju had managed to reply, although his courage didn't extend to being able to face them.

It fell to the younger luminary to deal with the scoundrel again. He did so with his distaste evident in every word.

'You run through the gullies and tell your principal we are coming. We'll take a taxi when we've finished our coffee.'

At the time, despite the dispiriting levels of disgust he'd felt emanating from his idols, this had seemed like such an impossibly easy and practicable solution to Viju that he had actually smiled at them in gratitude through his tears. What a godsend of an idea: this is why these guys were considered geniuses. Yes, it didn't matter that he would have to run through jam-packed lanes as fast as possible in the midday heat to be outside the main gate to meet them before they went inside to see Mr Sen; it didn't matter that they wouldn't offer him a ride in the cab and he'd probably never get another minute alone with them *in his life*: all that was important right then about this direct and uncluttered plan was that it meant – even if they left ten minutes after he did and factoring in an average amount of traffic for this time of day going in that direction – they would get to the school latest by 11.45, at least fifteen minutes before the function started. And the most important part of the day would proceed smoothly from there on.

In his testimony to the committee, Viju claimed to have no idea what demon-like energy possessed him as soon as he'd managed to back out of that café (after profusely thanking his heroes – newly restored, and raised, in his esteem for their no-nonsense practicality – at least fifteen times, although they'd appeared not to take the slightest notice), and propelled him down crowded pavements and through a maze of ever narrower and more congested lanes and alleys under the fierce heat of a June morning, so that he was back outside school by 11.35, fifteen minutes after he'd started running. (Yes, he admitted that his estimate of how long it would have taken the three of them to *walk* here from Park Street had been extremely optimistic, but what else could he have said?) He didn't even have a hanky to wipe his face as he rushed through the gate to check whether the taxi had arrived already, but no, it looked like he had narrowly beaten them after all. The principal's driver was standing outside his vehicle, parked next to the porch of the church, and he asked where the chief guests were, because

Mr Sen was waiting for them in his office. Viju confirmed from him that no taxi had come in within the last ten minutes, then informed him they were on their way, and that he was going to receive them outside the gate.

The short of it is that Viju waited for five minutes, anxiously scanning the faces of the dozens of parents and other invited guests who were arriving by now in droves and making their way towards the church, after which the driver came to fetch him on a summons from the principal. Five minutes later, an infuriated Mr Sen had asked him to save his explanations for the Senior Disciplinary Affairs Committee, and rush out immediately in the school car to see if the guests were still at the café. If they arrived in the meantime by cab, the function could begin right away. But Viju should also keep his eyes peeled whilst on the road, in case he spotted them en route in the other direction.

Yet there were no writers to be found again that day, either in the café, or in a cab on their way to the school. There was only a much-delayed 125th anniversary celebration that had to proceed eventually without either of its advertised chief guests (at the last minute, a city-councillor parent of a current student and a successful mineral-water-bottling alumnus gladly filled the vacant seats of honour on the podium). And if it was possible, things got worse two days later when the entire city learned from the horses' mouths – in a co-signed open letter to *The Telegraph* – that both chief guests hadn't in fact been taken ill by an awful coincidence, as Mr Sen had announced to the audience at the Founder's Day function. Instead, they had been led under false pretences by a St George's student to a coffee shop on Park Street, where they were asked to pay for their own refreshments before being unceremoniously told to make their way to the school by cab. If this was St George's idea of hospitality towards its guests of honour, they had decided to drink up and withdraw entirely from the event, making a joint decision to register an emphatic protest.

3

The second time Viju surfaced in Miss Bose's consciousness, she of course had no chance to hear his version of events at all. It was fifteen years later, around June or July 2003, and all she ever learnt about the incident was what everyone else saw in the papers. Of course, those in the staff room who remembered Viju marvelled that he'd managed to land himself a teaching job in another school in Calcutta (even though this was some place way out near Dum Dum), after the ignominious conclusion to his career as a St George's student. How had he managed to keep that out of the record? The suspension had fallen just short, on compassionate grounds, of outright expulsion – primarily because his mother had howled so much at the disciplinary hearing. Viju had been barred by Mr Sen from attending the last few months of classes. He could only show up for school exams, then sit his ISCs, and disappear forever after: no appeals, no second chances, and certainly no question of any future references, unless he didn't object to the Founder's Day incident being comprehensively described as well.

This new stink he'd caused just went to show, all his former teachers agreed, that boy still spends half his life talking himself into trouble, and the other half trying to get himself out of it.

Except, from the performance Miss Bose had witnessed, and also this latest evidence, he didn't seem to be all that skilled at the self-extrication part. Once again, he looked decisively buried under a disaster of his own making. The media had clearly (and collectively) decided to make an example out of this particular scandal: each paper drew out the story detail by detail on a daily basis for at least a fortnight, as a shocking insight into the level of sleaze that had permeated every aspect of school life and the 'education system', in which children were used as opportunities for personal gain in the most brazen of ways.

Apparently, there was a boy in Class 9 in Viju's Dum Dum school who had been in grave danger of failing his half-yearly English exams; failing regularly in English would also have meant he would go on to fail the year. Viju was his English teacher (although not his private tutor: clearly, the papers had decided, this was Mr Sinha's grudge against the boy to begin with, and the reason he was failing his exams), and had contacted his father to offer the boy an advance look at the upcoming question papers in exchange for a new laptop computer. After a few days, the father had responded to say he could only afford a second-hand desktop. Viju had agreed to this, on condition that the boy joined his tuition classes for the rest of the year. Everything had gone well after that, and the boy duly passed his half-yearly exams with a 65% mark.

About four months later, a few weeks before the final exams, Viju had sent an email to the boy's father to say the desktop had turned out to be an almighty clunker, erasing files and freezing on him all the time, and that he wanted a brand-new replacement. The father this time had stood his ground, arguing that second-hand computers didn't come with warranties, and besides he honestly couldn't afford to gift Viju a new machine. At most he could try and get the desktop repaired. Viju had apparently agreed to send the computer away as long as the boy's father paid for the repairs.

Then the boy failed his English exams, and by such a big margin that he failed on his overall average. He would have to repeat the year. At first his father seemed to have accepted this outcome, but right about the time the summer holidays ended, he'd gone to visit the principal, and told him he believed his son had been victimised because of his refusal to pay up on a bribe. When the principal had said there was nothing to be done since the new academic year was about to begin, the father had gone directly to a newspaper with copies of the emails exchanged between him and Viju, all the way back to his first counter-offer of a desktop computer.

Which is why, as Viju was sacked and led away to a few days in prison (after his second sustained stint in the media spotlight), the consensus among everyone who remembered him at St George's was that once again, fifteen years on, he had proven to be a kid not quite smart enough to pull off the schemes he came up with. He always got one crucial thing fatally wrong.

4

Miss Bose was just about to climb onto a rickshaw outside Gariahat market when she heard someone calling her by her name. Of course, she was used to being recognised in the street by ex-students, as well as being unable to return the compliment. As she told herself (and sometimes reminded her former students when she sensed a trace of disappointment or accusation in their voices), they had one Miss Bose to remember, whereas she had to pick them out from amidst twenty-five years of teaching, and literally thousands of faces. She'd even, she would say, had her first few experiences of teaching boys whose fathers had been her students. Besides, the two frank truths one could never utter aloud, although she sometimes smiled to herself afterwards about them, were that for young men mostly in their twenties and thirties, several of her ex-students had rather let themselves go, and secondly (perhaps this one was even harsher), not all students are equally memorable.

Sometimes she was stopped by college-going kids she remembered having taught one or two years before: those were the easy ones. But when a man in his forties – who had lost his hair but picked up a French beard, along with forty extra kilos and a family of three – appeared out of the blue to greet her outside a Puja pandal or in Pantaloon's or the Gariahat mall, she often asked candidly for a few helpful clues. Only as they continued to speak would she notice traces of a distantly familiar face, and gradually situate them within their batch and likely classroom, the cluster of people they had sat among, whether they had submitted any memorably brilliant or terrible exam-scripts, or had had especially overbearing parents who insisted she take them on for private tuitions (and refused to believe it when she tried to assure them she never taught anyone at home), and so on.

These encounters had a pattern. The boys (or rather, the men) told her what they were doing, introduced their families if they were present or mentioned their marital and parental status otherwise, asked after this or that teacher, and whether 'school was still the same'. More than half the time, there was another question that would crop up at some point – 'Achcha, Ma'am, are you still *Miss* Bose?' – to which she would always answer with the same, slight nod. On occasion, some of them would seem determined to visit her at home, and would even insist on taking down her phone number, but few ever called afterwards, and not one ex-student had yet made it to her doorstep. In this regard, it didn't hurt her too much to admit another truth to herself: not all teachers were equally memorable.

Yet the first meeting with Viju was entirely different. To begin with, she recognised him as soon as he drew close under the streetlights, from the newspaper photos of a few years before. He'd lost weight, but this she only inferred from the odd outfit he was wearing. It was a double-breasted cream suit (conspicuously formal in that marketplace-roadside setting, surrounded as they were by buses and cars, taxis, rickshaws, autos, cycles and thelas) which, understandably for an early February evening, was buttoned all the way up, but this couldn't conceal the fact that it looked perhaps two sizes too big for him. Then, for someone she had never actually taught, or interacted with in any meaningful way (apart from being in silent attendance at his traumatic disciplinary hearing), he seemed disproportionately pleased to see her, and took her by surprise by kneeling to touch her feet, while Haran, her regular rickshaw-wallah, waited and watched, still holding on to her bags of shopping. (Later, while being pulled home on the rickshaw, it occurred to her that Viju might have thought of her as an ally all those years ago, simply because, amid that chorus of condemnation, she was the only one who hadn't spoken).

Because not only had Viju been one of those extra-keen students who'd taken down her phone number and insisted he would come by to visit, he'd even asked for her address right there and then, handed his briefcase to a bemused Haran, and noted it in his phone. She had been so surprised at this request – indeed at the overall pleasure this hulking, square-shouldered, slab-faced man (whose suit nevertheless was too big for him, which meant he must have been even larger once) had exhibited upon running into her, based on one previous meeting in the most unfortunate of circumstances – that she hadn't had time to stall or refuse. And what could she have said, now that she played back the meeting in her head as the rickshaw trundled homewards, that wouldn't have hurt his feelings, that wouldn't have led him to believe that he was being rebuffed either because of that silly incident with those mean-spirited chief guests over two decades ago, or worse, because of the other thing in the papers (also now some years past), about some desktop and a laptop, where no one had even had a chance to hear his version of the story?

Of course, she told herself – remembering to grip her shopping bags more tightly as the rickshaw picked up pace once it had turned off the main road into her street – she knew the bribery incident had been much more serious than that, but how could she have allowed it to determine her manner towards him? Should she have sidestepped him instantly upon recognition, ignoring his warm, enthusiastic greetings; or should she have timed her rudeness even more effectively, and moved her feet away just as he knelt to offer his pranam, then climbed onto the rickshaw and asked Haran to set off? *Or*, she addressed the faceless prosecutor in her head (which part – had Miss Bose ever thought about it – probably would always have been taken by her younger sister Malu), should she have played along for the duration of the encounter, acted innocent and unknowing (as in fact, she had), and then, as people did on American TV serials when dealing with various forms of unwanted attention, left him with either a fake address or a fake phone number, or both?

In either case, Haran would have been a witness to her behaviour. He, who had known her for twenty years, would have understood most of the exchange with Viju (since it had been in Bengali: Viju, although North Indian by origin, was of course a lifelong Calcuttan), and realised she was giving him a false address. Then, leave aside her opinion of Viju, how far would she have fallen in Haran's eyes? He didn't know any of the background; all he'd have seen would have been some barefaced lying.

In fact, Viju had made an impression on Haran, because he indirectly remarked on his appearance as he followed her with her shopping bags down the side-passage of the building to her door. 'That Dada must have a very big job, na?'

He had clearly liked the cream suit. Miss Bose told him that Viju worked for a medicine company. What Viju had said was

that he was a 'medical representative', so she was probably not too far wrong.

Then Haran proved he had been paying attention to the meeting, because he first said, while setting down her bags in the drawing room, 'Didi, your students respect you so much,' and then, when she'd waved his remark aside and was looking for the bundle of ten rupee notes in her handbag, added, 'He said you were like a mother to him.'

So he'd heard it too, baffling and baseless though the comment was, coming from someone she literally had never spoken to, and been in a room with just once before. Viju *had* said, as Haran lifted up the bars of the rickshaw and they were about to turn and depart, that he'd always thought of her just like a mother! What a strange sort of exaggeration to employ. She'd briefly pondered and dismissed the statement while riding home: she must have heard him wrong, or misunderstood what he meant. But here Haran had unwittingly confirmed the exact words (and implied spirit) of the comment; and just for that, without any pause to think about it, any word of acknowledgement or particular expression on her face, in one smooth motion she counted out Haran's money and placed into his hand his usual fare, and an extra ten rupee note.

5

Ordinarily, Viju's next appearance in Miss Bose's life would hardly have registered on her mind, unsettled as she was at the time by extremely threatening developments. Her landlord wanted her out, fast, of a flat that she had rented for twenty-four years (almost the entire duration of her teaching career, pretty much ever since she could afford to live alone). A couple of years ago, on a rare personal visit downstairs to collect the rent (he lived with his wife on the first floor: they had a son

who worked as a chartered accountant in London), he'd vaguely mentioned the temptation he faced on a regular basis from promoters who wanted to demolish the two-storey house and put up a block of flats. This had made Miss Bose nervous for a long time, but then he hadn't said anything further about the matter, or called on her again, and she'd finally let herself breathe more freely about three months later, deciding it had been just a passing fancy. But suddenly in the last couple of months, he'd visited her thrice and sounded much more definite and adamant, saying he was certain now that his son would never leave his job in London and return to live in Calcutta, and so he and his wife might as well sell up while they still had enough years left to be able to use the extra money. He was sorry to have to do this to her, he'd said on his second visit, because over the years she had been as much a friend as a tenant, but after much thinking they had concluded as a family that this was the only practical option.

For some reason, and even though she was aware of the tendency herself, and aware that it was ultimately futile, Miss Bose reacted to these increasingly unambiguous signals by becoming something of an ostrich. Although they preyed on her mind constantly whether at work or at home, she discussed her worries with no one the next couple of months (not even Malu and Animesh, who had no idea what was going on, even though she saw them at least once each week, and spoke to Malu daily on the phone), nor did she begin to take any definite steps on her own.

It was at this point that Mr Chatterjee, her landlord, had started to lose his patience. He visited her once more, asking politely but forcefully for a definite date, telling her that they themselves had arranged a place near Ruby Hospital on the Bypass that they would move to before the Pujas, to live in during the demolition and construction. If she started looking

quickly, especially through a broker, there was no shortage of flats to rent. Perhaps through a good dalal who knew this para well, she might even land somewhere not too far away.

But when he received no clear answer from her even after this third and final courtesy call, he began mentioning the matter pointedly, and with less grace each time, whenever they ran into each other on the street or outside the house, or even when he was standing on the balcony upstairs and saw her returning from school. Sometimes, when Sheela was with him, her reasonably good friend of twenty-odd years would remain silent and try to avoid her direct gaze, while her husband would ominously say, with no preamble or greeting, 'Before the Pujas, Nandita, don't forget, before the Pujas, just another four months,' and they would continue on their way. Most recently, as she alighted from the rickshaw after her last weekly visit to the market, even though Haran had been present beside her, he'd quite deliberately raised his voice from the balcony, asking about her plans to vacate the flat, as if he wanted the entire street to know how unreasonable she was being, and coerce her into promising him a definite date in front of multiple witnesses.

This incident took place two days before Viju's visit, and had (finally) forced her mind into deciding to take some sort of action. First she would talk to Animesh and Malu, perhaps this weekend itself, and with their help, initiate the process of finding a broker, as Mr Chatterjee seemed to insist was necessary. Enough was enough: God knows what had been paralysing her until this moment, but today she had been deservedly humiliated for her tardiness. The man had thrown any last pretence of politeness to the wind. If she had any remaining sense, *and dignity*, she would be in a new house before the monsoon was over.

It was strange then, considering she had made up her mind on what steps she would take before Viju unexpectedly showed up again (four months after he'd almost pleaded with her for her address), how he persuaded her to change direction, this near-complete stranger whom, if anything, she had ample reason to mistrust. And perhaps she wouldn't have been so easily swayed by his advice had he not promised to take care of everything himself: no matter what turned out to be the most feasible possibility, he would hereafter be with her every step of the way. Those were his exact sentiments, and his support was so unexpected, and his expression of it so vehement (within ten minutes of arriving, he'd managed to get her to begin telling him of her troubles, and when he'd heard everything, his offer of help had been almost recklessly instantaneous), that she had no choice but to agree to his suggestion. Not only did his idea hold out some hope that she might be legally entitled to challenge her eviction, but, perhaps more importantly, Viju's immediate and utter absorption in her worries suddenly made her feel she wasn't alone. Yes, it was slightly baffling coming from someone who hardly knew her at all and had taken four months to keep his promise to visit, but nevertheless this tall, strong, busy, worldly man was now her ally, who went out into the city each day with confidence and conducted business with dozens of people, who would have a surer grasp on how things worked and whom to approach for help or information than either she, or Malu and Animesh, or indeed that increasingly wolf-like Mr Chatterjee, ever could. This young man of the world, who thought of her 'as a mother'.

All Viju needed from her was her voter ID card for a few days, in case the solicitor friend he had in mind, the one who specialised in property disputes, wanted to draw up an initial letter, or required her full name and address for any other official registration purposes. He promised to be back with it within a week. It was while fetching the card that Miss Bose had realised she hadn't offered him anything even though he'd probably come in straight from work (judging from his briefcase and his clothes), and had sat there listening to her worries for forty-five minutes. Goodness, why was she letting this depressing matter weigh upon her so? This big young man, too polite to even ask for water, must have been starving. She rushed back into the drawing room, placed the ID card on the coffee table, and then told Viju to wait while she brought out some coffee and snacks for him. He protested, but only briefly, and followed her to the kitchen door, where he stood and chatted while she boiled water, and looked for the chanachur and some biscuits.

To change the subject from her boring house-moving woes, she'd thought about asking him about his family, and specifically his mother, while she got the tea-tray ready, and also whether he still wrote. But then she rejected that idea, in case any reference to their first meeting, no matter how indirect, might embarrass him. If he wished to speak about any of those subjects, surely he would in his own time. So Miss Bose quickly apologised for serving Viju the same sweets he'd brought, and asked about his work instead. And he talked quite readily about it, so that even though she could only be half-attentive, she learnt about a new profession that she had previously never heard of or imagined. Viju was a medical representative who spent much of his time in rural areas, on behalf of a major private hospital near Salt Lake Stadium that maintained a database of organ donors, people it could turn to in cases of patients requiring emergency transplants. His work took him all over Bengal, all the way up to Darjeeling, as well as parts of Bihar, Jharkhand, Orissa, and even a few times a year to Assam and the North East. He usually teamed up with a local doctor in each region, who performed check-ups on prospective donors, and was often away from Calcutta for weeks at a time. On occasion, his duties included bringing the donors from their village to the hospital here (whenever an operation was necessary), and then taking them home again. He even helped several of them open bank accounts in their villages, so that their payments could be safely deposited.

It sounded like exhausting, harrowing work, and as Viju spoke, as well as later on that evening and frequently over the next few days, Miss Bose mulled over various aspects of the many new things she had learnt. First, it explained why he hadn't been able to visit for several months. Second, what a strange yet brave change of career, midway through his thirties, for someone who had once been an English teacher. This led her to think again what a sheltered and narrow existence she led between her school and home and her few weekly outings, the fact that she wouldn't ever have conceived of such a job until she'd heard about it, although in a way, difficult as it must be, it made a lot of sense, matching donors to needy patients. It also proved that her earlier hunch about trusting Viju had been sound: he was exactly as experienced at dealing with the world, and as well-acquainted with all sorts of useful people, as she had imagined.

And finally, one more thought she had – in fact this she'd felt while he was speaking, and agreed with herself afterwards – was that he still described whatever he was doing with as much energy, detail and gusto as that desperate boy once had, fighting not to be expelled from school twenty-two years earlier.

6

It did occur to Miss Bose three days after Viju's visit that she'd forgotten to take down his mobile number, but she didn't worry about it too much, aside from making a mental note to ask for it next time, which would of course be within the next few days. Besides, he'd promised her he would call as soon as he'd met the solicitor to pass on his advice, so, in any case, she would have his number presently on her phone.

The first time she told Malu anything of what had been happening over the last few months was seven weeks later, a full two months after Viju had disappeared without a word. Once she began, with Mr Chatterjee's now-impossible behaviour towards her (he appeared to be set on forcing her out through a conscious day-by-day strategy of intolerable rudeness), slowly, hesitantly, the rest came out, culminating in the utter irresponsibility and callousness of Viju, who had not only done nothing for her, he hadn't even had the decency to return her voter card.

'Didi, why didn't you tell us any of this?' Malu repeated over and over, unable to believe what she was hearing, about her sister's imminent eviction from the house she'd lived in for almost a quarter-century. It was early August; the Pujas, apparently her outermost deadline, were just two months away, and she'd kept silent on this matter since the start of the year.

'You trusted an outsider, a student you hadn't seen in twenty years, rather than your only family. You saw us every week, you spoke to me every day, and still you said nothing?' At this point, the baffled, indignant Malu didn't even know about this particular ex-student's chequered back-story. Miss Bose said nothing, glad to be sitting down, glad this first disclosure was happening over the phone.

'We would have called in a lawyer: Animesh's office has an entire legal department. What were you thinking when you trusted him? Why on earth would he need your voter card?'

Right then, briefly, a new worry landed like a thunderbolt on Miss Bose's head. Oh my God, what if he registers me as an organ donor without my knowledge? One day, one of his colleagues would just arrive and cart me off to the hospital to donate God-knows-what on the spot, and I would be legally obliged because my name would be there on the computer screen, and my voter card in their files. This is exactly the kind of scam that shaitan would pull, and earn himself a nice commission.

Thankfully she was seated, and despite her momentary terror, managed to remain silent. In any case, Malu was too involved in her own tirade to notice how long her Didi hadn't spoken. When Miss Bose had calmed down slightly, and decided it was unlikely even Viju would attempt a thing like that, and that in any event she probably couldn't be taken to hospital and operated upon against her will, she reflected through her sister's yelling that she would have to face all this again in person the next time they met, and from Animesh as well, who would be every bit as incensed. And also that the help she had believed, against all the signs, was well underway this past couple of months (how could it have been, she wondered now, what *had* she been thinking: wouldn't Mr Chatterjee have said something if he'd been contacted on her behalf by a lawyer?), had probably never existed. Not only had she never moved from square one, two more months had slipped away waiting. Viju had most likely contacted no one, or else he'd found there was nothing a lawyer could do and had been too ashamed, after all his big talk, to come back and admit his failure.

A little later, Malu realised during a pause after posing her sister another infuriatingly obvious question, that she had begun to cry.

7

It was Haran who pointed Viju out on the footpath the last time she saw him, close to the main entrance of Gariahat market, as they were about to go in, not far from where he'd hailed her eight months before. 'Didi, isn't that your student over there?'

Her first instinct was to pretend to be in a hurry, and she ushered Haran into the main market ahead of her. But only a few steps later, she realised a voice from within her, not entirely under her control, was telling Haran to go and wait outside the shobjiwallah's stall, and she would join him there shortly. It was probably better that he didn't learn how this supposedly 'son-like' ex-student had discharged his filial duty towards her.

He was picking out oranges or mosambi or something like that from one of the fruit stalls on the pavement. It was a pity they were going to be surrounded by people, but that would have to do. Besides, after sending Haran away, as she approached Viju, she had momentarily reflected that it might be no bad thing to be in a crowded place when confronting a scoundrel such as this.

When Viju turned around in response to her tap, he behaved as if he'd expected to find her standing at his elbow. Before she could launch into her long-rehearsed (and hastily-refreshed) list of charges against him, he begged her for just one minute's respite with a gesture, ordered the phalwallah to pick out eight oranges for him and set them aside in a paper bag, reminded him sternly not to try and slip him any duds because he would come back and check, and then, turning to Miss Bose, asked if they could talk just a little distance away, past those scooters parked over there, behind the fruit stalls, back on the road. Then he led the way, walking away from Miss Bose so that she had to follow.

'You're a very bad man. You're not at all to be trusted. I made a big mistake believing in you,' she made sure to say as soon as they were on the roadside, away from anyone's hearing. She wasn't going to let him snatch her chance to speak again. But he seemed to have no further wish to run, and stood before her, head lowered in apparent shame, hands clasped in front of him.

'You've always been full of mischief. Whatever you touch turns into trouble.'

Still he wouldn't look up or speak. She briefly imagined what an odd pair they made to passersby in buses and cars, standing on the road like that, a short middle-aged lady berating a shamefaced hulk. People would think a grown-up son was getting an earful and wonder why.

'Where's my ID card?' And then, 'You've done enough, I want no further help from you. Just give me back my card.'

He finally mumbled something, which she couldn't hear over all the horns and other sounds of the street. He was still looking down at the spot of ground between them. She asked him to repeat himself.

'Ma'am, I'm your culprit,' he seemed to be saying.

'I don't want to hear any of that rubbish. Just hand over my voter card, and we'll be done with each other.'

She had been demanding it all right, but she hadn't really been expecting Viju to be carrying her card on him. Why would he be? Besides, in some obscure way, she'd envisioned him to have used it for his own gain, or even sold it on to criminals of some sort, although she wasn't sure what that could have achieved. Perhaps her photo would have been replaced by someone else's, to perpetrate some kind of fraud.

So she was in fact quite taken aback when, without any delay or protest, he took out his wallet and handed over her card. She peered briefly to be sure it was hers, and then clutched it along with her phone, wondering if she should place it without delay into her handbag. This minor surprise had done nothing to redeem Viju in her eyes: if anything, it only proved he had probably put the card away in his wallet and forgotten all about her problem and his fervent promise to help.

Should she tell him about that, she wondered? Should she tell him what his irresponsibility had led to, that she was going to have to move to her sister's place next month until they found an affordable place to rent? Animesh had looked everywhere, in all the newspapers and on the Net, while she had asked several colleagues at school to let her know if they heard of any available flats, but there was nothing suitable just now in South Calcutta within her budget, even though in the last few weeks they had expanded their search to include out-of-the-way places like Kasba, Santoshpur and CIT Road, just in case something cropped up. And it was all because of Viju that she had lost two months of searching time, not to mention the false hopes and the anticipation (while enduring Mr Chatterjee's jibes on an almost-daily basis), as well as the worry over her missing ID card and what trouble that would cause in the future (aside from any devious plots Viju himself was cooking up: what if he framed her in some crime, Malu had repeatedly asked, how could you be sure with such a track record, of school suspension, bribery, exam-paper fraud, and what the two of them insisted on calling Viju's current involvement in the 'organ racket'?); and finally, the shame of first being scolded by Malu and Animesh for being so naïve and unworldly, and now having to move into Raja's old room (her nephew, who was studying civil engineering at IIT Kharagpur) while most of her things would gather dust in a spare attic room lent to her by one of Mr Kapoor's friends. He was her fellow Maths teacher, in Classes VI, VII and VIII, a young well-meaning soul who had originally proposed the room (in Bhowanipore) as a place she could stay in, probably without seeing it for himself; but when Animesh accompanied her for a viewing, he rejected the idea as soon as they were back in the car and driving home. There was no way she was moving into a single third-floor room, with her bed, dressing-table, almirah and sofa all in the same space, and a tiny attached kitchen and bathroom. She would be much better off in Raja's room, and he'd refused to hear any more on the subject. Miss Bose had been secretly relieved, her heart too had sunk the moment the room had been unlocked. It was only afterwards that she had managed to persuade Animesh that they could at least rent it as a storage space, and this way Mr Kapoor would also save face with his friend. After all, he had honestly been trying to help.

Sometimes, as the day to move to Malu's drew closer, Miss Bose saw herself in their eyes, as one child moving in to replace another, and their parental responsibilities beginning all over again. 'Didi,' Malu had said on the phone more than once (she frequently forgot her own rebukes, or else she really believed in the ultimate effectiveness of constant reiteration), 'do you know how much teachers with your seniority, and especially in your subject area, make with their tuitions in this city? Several of them have not one but multiple properties with all their undeclared income, and here you are, still refusing to teach a single child privately. The world has changed; you don't need me to tell you, that is the norm these days. Raja says teachers deliberately don't teach anything in class so that students are compelled to join their tuitions. And maths is probably the most popular and important tuition subject. You just need to accept a couple of students, Didi, and the rest will come by word of mouth. No one minds, no one thinks anything of it. In fact, *not* doing tuitions these days is abnormal. Would you be in this position today, looking at lousy, far-flung flats all over the city, if you'd built up your savings over the years? But even now you can start, you have such a great reputation. And the best thing is, you can do it at home, and you can continue to do it even after retirement. You'll be doing students *a favour*. Parents are always crying out for good maths teachers. Raja still says, even after three years in IIT, that you were the best teacher he ever had, that he understands every concept from scratch only because of you.'

Raja, her nephew: the only child who'd ever been coached at her dining table, trying his best to evangelise on her behalf.

And now she was calling in the favour by moving into his room, and his parents had taken it upon themselves to show yet another child what was what in the 'real world'.

All these random things ran rapidly through her mind as Viju grew quiet again, and although she was filled anew with anger and hurt at the thought of what she had undergone over the past few months, she decided silence would be the best rebuke for this incorrigible character, especially in this public setting. Everything she had prepared to say to him had been premised on his visiting her house one day, skulking in some evening with bowed head, but it would be undignified to stand there inhaling exhaust fumes and trying to shout over all the noise. (What would he have done if she had already moved, she'd also wondered – he wouldn't have known where to find her, in fact Mr Chatterjee's house mightn't even have remained standing.) Besides, she suddenly realised that she didn't want this swine to know how much he had managed to upset her, how anxious she had felt when she hadn't heard a word from him and meanwhile the Pujas were drawing closer, and there was increasingly no option but to confide everything to her sister and brother-in-law.

It had probably been less than a minute since Viju had handed over her card, but it was an awfully long time for two people to face each other silently standing on the road just outside Gariahat market. Miss Bose became mindful of this, and also remembered that Haran was waiting for her outside the shobjiwallah's, so without another word, she turned around to walk away. Dignity had won out over righteous indignation.

Except of course dignity could be allowed to play no part in any episode that Viju was involved in – the very concept was probably alien to him. Miss Bose had not even walked two steps when she heard a plaintive voice saying 'Ma'am, won't you even ask about my side of the story?'

Later that evening, on the rickshaw-ride home, she analysed why she had turned around – after a moment's hesitation – in response to his outrageous question. Yes, ridiculous as it sounded, part of her did want to hear his story – what could have caused him to so callously forget his confident guarantees of help – although, paradoxically, she knew she wouldn't believe for a second a single thing he said. How smoothly and deviously he had explained his involvement in the organ-trafficking industry, she remembered, almost as if it was a social service he performed on behalf of the relatives of desperate patients, slogging through dusty villages in unimaginable temperatures, thinking only of expanding an innocuous 'database' of willing donors. And she would have continued to believe in this version of his job, if she hadn't by chance mentioned it one day to Malu and Animesh.

But today, after she'd let him spout his usual pathetic tale (how typical that he should beg *her* to hear *his* story, without having asked once what had happened in all these months with her flat), in which he was always the victim of accidents far outside his control, she *would* – on second thoughts – allow herself the satisfaction of letting him know, in no more than a couple of clear sentences, the destructive consequences of his lies, without once raising her voice.

These were her intentions, but in view of what happened soon after, it's important to remember that when she turned around, she did have full knowledge not only of Viju's deceitfulness, but also of a proven history of borderline criminality.

And when you decide, against all your better judgement, to talk to a person like that, without Haran or any other able-bodied help nearby, the least you can do is put your phone away in your bag – this being the most expensive visible thing you're carrying (you who doesn't wear any rings or necklaces, or else he would have snatched those too, in the name of pawning them for much-needed cash) – and then keep that firmly under your arm.

Because unbelievable as it may sound, the conversation that followed culminated in Viju stealing Miss Bose's phone. No, this should be rephrased, it isn't quite fair to Viju, and doesn't fully reflect the truth of what happened. Because Viju actually asked her for the phone, and ok, while she was still searching for the appropriate words with which to refuse him (keeping in mind what she had just learnt, and the ten-percent chance that some of it might be true), he did sort of prise it out of her incredulous fingers, but it's not like he dashed off immediately after, and she had no chance to ask for it back. In fact, even as she turned and headed towards Haran after Viju had touched her feet, reiterated his image of her as a divine mother who always appeared in his life exactly when he needed her most, she was already aware of what she could do by way of effective retaliation. She could cut him off at the fruit stall, where he would have headed to pick up his oranges. Then, in front of witnesses, she could denounce him for the thief that he was, or else simply demand her phone back and be done with Viju once and forever.

8

Of course Miss Bose had anticipated when and how Malu would find out. All she hoped for, strangely enough, was that Malu would have heard something of the story from Viju himself. Then perhaps she'd have an idea – although it would have been over the phone and she wouldn't see his six-foot frame pleading and shaking before her – how persuasive and difficult-to-refuse he could be.

Malu, who had insisted on gifting her the phone three Pujas ago (there were nine numbers stored in it: Malu, Animesh,

Raja, three colleagues including Mr Kapoor, the once-friendly Sheela Chatterjee whose name she was determined to delete the day after she moved, Bina the maid who would call to announce with barely an hour's notice whenever she was 'too ill' to come, and Haran, who had made her note down his name and number with great pride while he'd watched), called every afternoon at 3.30 to chat a little and make sure she was safely home. If for some reason she didn't answer, Malu immediately tried her landline. Miss Bose had been tense and absentminded all day at school, dreading what would happen during this afternoon's call. She'd even thought of calling Malu first, just to say she'd had an absolutely normal day, but this would have been so unusual that Malu would have suspected something and probably called again (on her mobile) later that evening. Besides, what would she do tomorrow, and the day after that? One day soon, if not today, Viju would most certainly answer Malu's call.

At least on that count Miss Bose was put out of her misery that afternoon itself. She'd even been granted another of her unlikely wishes – Viju had said something to Malu about how desperately ill his wife was, which was why his 'mother-like Ma'am' had lent him the phone for just a few days, until his wife was out of the nursing home, so that she, and the nurses, could get in touch with him whenever necessary. His own phone, he had explained the night before to Miss Bose, and she now relayed to a most sceptical and displeased Malu, had been demanded back by his company when they had sacked him, owing to his inability to travel while his wife was so ill. He hadn't been able to afford a replacement yet, not while coping with the ever-mounting medical bills.

But Malu, who after all had only the poorest possible opinion of Viju to begin with and hadn't had the benefit of receiving this latest story from him in person, had not been swayed by anything she had heard. In fact, Miss Bose could hear in her voice what she had probably started to believe, that this satanic young man had some sort of hold over a foolish (and lonely) older woman.

'After all you know, after all our warnings and everything we told you, you just let him take the phone?' It was at least the fourth time she'd said that.

'Why did you even talk to him?' Malu demanded of the silence.

'Why didn't you keep Haran with you?

'Why didn't you go over to the fruit-seller and tell everyone there what he'd just done and what kind of man he was?

'I couldn't believe my own ears when he told me his name. Can you imagine my shock, Didi, when I call you and this criminal answers? Can you imagine the things that ran through my mind? He was babbling some nonsense when all I wanted to do was to hang up and call you at home, to be sure you were all right.'

How could anyone think up such absurd scenarios? How useless and weak did they think she was? Miss Bose suddenly felt so annoyed by the implications of Malu's 'worries' that she wanted to say something cruel in return: get over yourself, Malu, only a phone has been taken. He didn't lock me in a dungeon, and make me sign a new will. Whatever else I have will still go to you and Raja. Or perhaps you think he is my new lover, who will make me start a private tuition class, and use me to amass a huge fortune.

But she only said, 'No one calls me on that phone except you and Bina, and Haran sometimes. All of you have my home number, and you can tell Raja what happened, because he occasionally texts me jokes.'

She was going to add that this was why she'd felt the phone would be of more use to Viju, just in case it was true that his wife was down with hepatitis, but Malu cut her off by asking if she'd lost her mind, and what on earth any of that had to do with anything. She had *handed over* her phone to a renowned crook in the middle of a crowded market who might now use it to conduct a whole range of shady business that couldn't be traced back to him. That is what they were discussing.

'Just for a few days, Malu. He said he'd lost his job because of his wife's illness. Didn't he tell you that? He said he was running around each day just trying to cope with the bills. And he was buying oranges for her. I saw that with my own eyes.'

'Since when did oranges mean hepatitis, Didi? And what job was he talking about – the one where he persuades poor villagers to part with their kidneys and god-knows-what-else for less than the price of a bicycle? Wasn't it you who told us you've known him to make up these stories since he was seventeen?'

Yes Malu, I have, and you know what, the truth is that each time they made my life more interesting. At least I remember the occasions I see him. What am I meant to be so level-headed for anyway? What are these great rewards for being sensible?

But what Miss Bose said, in full recognition of her only sister's good intentions, as well as the validity of her objections regarding Viju, was: 'The phone will be back in a few days, ré. And anyway, by this time next month I'll be living with you, so you won't need to call me every afternoon.'

It was after a further fifteen minutes of repeating several of the statements she'd already made, in just as aggrieved and disbelieving a tone, that Malu finally hung up. She promised her older sister one thing – she was going to call Viju every single day until he returned that phone. If he didn't answer her calls, or return it within ten days, she would report it as theft to the police. Somebody had to call his bluff sometime. He should have been behind bars ages ago. This guy had got away with bullshit his entire life, and had become more and more dangerous as a consequence.

9

It's been two weeks since the phone was taken. Malu, as promised, does call it every afternoon, and each time, although it rings, she receives no answer. She keeps Miss Bose updated on the matter too, and for the last four days, has been insisting she accompany her to the local thana to file a formal complaint. Since it's her phone (even though it was Malu's gift) and she was present at the actual theft, she will have to make the charge, otherwise it would have been done already. She cannot understand *what* is causing her Didi to hesitate. Has she forgotten that the SIM card Viju is using is registered in her name? Has he called *once* on the landline to tell her about his wife's condition?

Miss Bose by now resorts to her two stock responses: one, she knows from the experiences of several students that hepatitis can be a very drawn-out illness, depending on the strain; and two, what do they need the mobile for anyway? Aren't they talking each day as usual?

Besides, it's only another two weeks, and then she will be their house-guest. In fact, she tells Malu, trying subtly to change the subject, she's already started setting aside a few things Haran and Bina would find use for, and Haran is coming in on Saturday to climb up and fetch the two old suitcases from the loft, and whatever else is up there, long-forgotten, including the boxes they put away after Ma died. Would Malu like to come over to be present at the grand dust-off when those were opened?

But it still seems very unreal, Miss Bose adds – after Malu has relented and laughed to say yes – that in a few days everything around her will go into that attic room in Bhowanipore, the furniture she has gathered over twenty-four years, and she has no idea when she would be able to bring it all out again.

Part II: Jaya

1

It was after his fourth assignment as courier that Viju decided to disappear with the money. This wasn't the quite-easily-accommodated, almost-cosy-after-all extra bit of business within his regular travelling routine that the first two deliveries had led him to expect. On the contrary, after their behaviour during his third hand-over, fleeing might even have been his most sensible option, because these assholes were clearly as unpredictable as they were (infuriatingly) deaf to reason.

Briefly, this is what had happened until then. A month-and-a-half before his last (chance) meeting with that sweet former teacher of his (or, rather, ten days *after* he'd promised to put her in touch with a first-class lawyer who would definitely help her keep her flat: Viju forgot about this commitment in the wake of what happened soon after – perhaps an understandable lapse, although it cost Miss Bose so dear), during a routine visit to D. district to pick up a twenty-year-old woman due in Calcutta two days later for a kidney-removal operation, Viju had been kidnapped and roughed up by some Maoists. Or at least four men who claimed to be Maoists, and seemed deeply displeased by Viju's activities in the region. They let him know they'd had an eye on him for several months, and, during the initial rain of slaps, after he'd been stripped, blindfolded and gagged, and his arms and legs were also bound, even asked him for one good reason why they shouldn't cut him open and sell him for parts just like he had been doing to their people, with little conscience and for even less cash.

Of course Viju wasn't expected to answer this charge, just as he needn't have feared being actually dissected. The beating and the blatant misrepresentation of facts (every donor-to-be was customarily informed *at length* about all the potential health-effects of any kind of organ-removal during Viju's first home visit itself, and each fully-informed villager who then went ahead with any of the procedures received exactly the generous five-figure amount that had been promised him or her at that initial meeting – no later cuts or commissions, no sneaky deduction of travel or recovery expenses, unlike so many other hospitals and agents he could name) were solely intended to soften him up for their yet-unstated ulterior purpose, so that he would agree to anything in return for staying alive.

And truly, after two further hours of being kicked and punched (all administered carefully in zones that would usually be covered by clothing, Viju later realised, although he was specifically forbidden to go to any doctor, even in Calcutta), it did seem almost like a let-off to be ordered to stand by as an occasional courier, to have to regularly submit to them a list of his forthcoming rural trips at least a week in advance (through a drop-off at a particular fruit stall outside Gariahat Market, not far from his house near Golpark, so that it wouldn't appear suspicious), and be ready to pick up money from the same shopkeeper whenever he received a late-evening call with a specific opening line: *Have you arrived home yet?*

In the days after the abduction, after he began thinking clearly through his persistent mid-section discomfort, Viju realised pretty quickly that for the moment he had no option but to obey, despite the obvious dangers of being involved in any way with anti-national, train-bombing, policemen-killing subversives. First, the dangers of disobeying them were even more immediately apparent. If that beating was their way of asking for a favour, imagine how they dealt with someone who'd turned them down. Also, equally importantly, he needed free and constant access to every single district in the neighbouring states: in fact, some of the areas with the worst Maoist reputations were the most lucrative hunting grounds for potential donors. There was nothing for it but to play along until he had a better idea, or a different job, or at least until he was clearer as to the risks and demands involved in the actual couriering.

And once he'd managed to convince himself with this reasoning, and get over the immediate anger that followed the beating, Viju got used to his new routine with quite-surprising ease, and even began to buy fruit regularly from his contact-person in Gariahat (who remained as unsmiling towards him as ever). There were no delivery assignments for him during the first six weeks. Perhaps they wanted to confirm that he was methodical and reliable, or else they were waiting for a suitable destination to appear on his itinerary.

Then one evening, while Viju was picking out some oranges (he'd now resorted to handing over his weekly list in one handful with his payment for the fruit, no attempt to make conversation), the phalwallah told him tersely, without any change in his expression, to get a new phone under a different name and pass on the number to him. Viju asked once, to make sure he'd heard him right, if his present phone wouldn't suffice, but the man didn't deign to dignify this query with a reply, and went back to polishing some Australian apples.

Viju was working out the implications of this new twist, and how exactly he was going to arrange for the false ID and proof of address that would be required for a new SIM card untraceable to him, while still sorting through the piles of oranges and mosambi absentmindedly and putting a few in a paper bag (it would certainly be better to use a grocery store in a small town during one of his trips than one in Calcutta to buy a new prepaid card, especially if he was going to try and put one over the shopkeeper using borrowed, fake or inadequate documents; or perhaps he could get one of his clients to buy the card for him), when he felt a tap on his shoulder, and turned to see Miss Bose facing him. To his credit, despite having so much on his mind, it took him only an instant to remember the promise to her he'd forgotten – to put her in touch with Subhashish, who would have been able to offer useful legal advice regarding her options with the flat. The run-in with the Naxalites had entirely erased it from his mind.

From her grim expression, he guessed he was in for a yelling, and he knew he deserved it. So, once they were out on the road, where the fruit-seller wouldn't learn what an untrustworthy idiot he'd been, he bowed his head and prepared to take his punishment. But as at that awful expulsion meeting all those years ago, when she alone had remained silent amid that bloodthirsty pack of so-called teachers, Miss Bose seemed to have no wish to judge, scold or condemn him, although she looked disappointed and tired. All she asked for after the most minimal of rebukes was her voter ID card, a request that stumped Viju momentarily until he remembered what she was referring to, and thankfully was able to find it in his wallet (it hadn't moved from there in eight weeks). Although she'd kept a tight grip on her feelings, he was genuinely saddened by her evident distress, and wondered for a moment if he could share the truth of what had happened directly after their last meeting to make him forget his well-intentioned promise. Somewhere in his mind another voice even suggested – and this proposal was accepted – that he at least dedicate himself to hunting out a suitable flat for her over the next few weeks, and that this time, instead of falsely building up her hopes, he should just show up at her sister's house with a perfect new home ready for her to move into.

In other words, the impulse to make a play for the phone in Miss Bose's hand was wholly spontaneous: Viju was thinking about very different things in the run-up to his next extraordinary action (such as how to make reparations to Miss Bose, rather than another impossible demand upon her trust and patience). His eye might have fallen on it as she reached out to take her ID card, or even as she was turning away immediately after, and from somewhere within him, before he could consider or curtail the idea, a voice had spoken up to call her back, imploring her to hear 'his side of the story'. And then, from that same place whence it had spoken on so many earlier occasions, the place obviously within him that was nevertheless a mystery to Viju – in its wellsprings, its motives, its precise whereabouts, and how, from a standing start, working apparently from nothing, it obtained the raw material for its elaborately-spun stories – emerged first a wife and then her life-threatening illness, followed closely by the loss of his own job and the desperate need for a phone!

And as always, it was the half-dazed momentum of the same impulse that carried him through his next action right on the back of drawing out all these surprising words and details, when he grabbed the phone from her hand, promising to bring it back as soon as his brand-new wife was better, and thinking to himself as he walked away, heart triumphant and thudding at the same time, that everything would be put right when he could show up at Miss Bose's sister's doorstep within the next month or so, with her phone in hand, a huge box of sweets, and a set of keys for her new flat by way of a thank-you card.

Miss Bose's phone number was good enough for the phalwallah and his Maoist overlords, and the first couple of times during the train journeys Viju carried the bundles of cash as instructed in his usual travel bag, spread out and concealed among his clothes. On either occasion, once in Bengal and once in Bihar, someone showed up at his hotel within an hour of his arrival, exactly as promised. This was the cosy, convenient phase of the operation, Viju's honeymoon period so to speak, after which he'd even found himself musing that if this was the level of danger in the specific anti-national activity being demanded of him, sure, his pulse-rate could handle that.

But the third assignment changed his thinking completely. For a start, he was called shortly after his arrival in the district town, and told to head with the money to a village seven miles away. This in itself was a waste of time, as Viju had planned for several home visits in exactly the opposite direction that morning and afternoon, which would now spill over into the following day; but he knew the area well, including the actual village of the rendezvous, and initially didn't mind the imposition too much. After all, he couldn't have expected someone to meet him at his hotel room on every occasion (these guys were in constant danger from the police: sometimes, when the pressure was on, they probably couldn't emerge too far out of the forest), and even taking into account the dreadful stretch of unsealed road that began barely two miles out of town in that direction, he reckoned on being back in the hotel within at most an hour and a half.

Or perhaps not, he then had second thoughts, maybe he could stretch this unscheduled trip to take in a few home visits in that neck of the woods. After all, there was no way he was going to be able to visit both his originally scheduled villages today, so he could do them tomorrow instead of making two trips in that direction. Besides, this village where the handover would take place had precisely forty-two huts, and yet had yielded him three kidney donors in the past.

Later on Viju would recall with bitter irony, that on the way to the village in the back of the auto-rickshaw (he would normally have taken the bus: he tried to save as much out of his travel budget as possible, and only used auto-rickshaws when journeying back or forth to a station with a donor, another of the little humane touches on which he prided himself), he had conceded to himself the cleverness of these bloody rebels in picking him as a courier. His job was the perfect alibi for these trips. He'd even suddenly wondered how many of his other colleagues had been recruited for such purposes, each anxiously keeping it a secret from everyone else.

Well, as long as there was no police trouble, and he himself wasn't asked to cough up for the cause, thought Viju with an inward grin and shrug, he could handle this minor inconvenience for the further year at most that he expected to remain at this job (while constantly looking for something better in Calcutta). What was that Bengali proverb from his childhood: if you want to fish in the water, you have to deal with the crocodile, or words to that effect? Perhaps Viju had been a bit unlucky to be spotted by the crocodile, but for now, he certainly needed the fish in these parts.

Except on this third visit, the crocodile that had been basking in the sun these past few weeks, seemingly content to let him swim around and do his thing as long as he nodded occasionally in its direction, proved to have much more malign intentions. It had lured him close and then suddenly lunged, nearly taking Viju's arm off in one mouthful.

There was someone waiting for him at the turn into the path that led alongside rice fields from the main 'road' to the village. Viju had expected some such arrangement, and had planned to make the hand-over some way down the path (where they would be briefly unobserved) and continue to the village for a couple of visits. Then he could return to the roadside to catch the two o' clock bus (he wouldn't be carrying any money, so there wasn't any need for a rickshaw), and be back in town in time for a late and well-earned lunch.

But this man, a young, surly fellow, refused to take charge of the money, and, despite being barely half Viju's size, instead insisted that Viju follow him to the village. Viju, although put off by the hostility of this scrawny runt, reminded himself he'd been planning to go there anyway, and decided not to argue the point. Maybe he was in training: they deemed him too young to handle such a substantial amount.

Unfortunately it turned out that the Maoists had a whole other drama waiting for Viju in the village. The tight-lipped youth led him to his apparent senior (in a hut) who did ask him right away for the money. A woman sat on the floor to one side, looking away from everyone towards the floor and wall. Viju sensed some tension in the room, but didn't want to waste any time with some domestic quarrel that was really none of his business (already this whole out-of-the-way trip had cost him a morning, even though he was trying to squeeze some use out of it). He didn't make any motion to sit down after handing over the cash; in any case, the other man had the only chair. But the man quickly counted the bundles, and ordered him to sit on the floor. Viju noticed the boy had blocked the doorway.

At this point, the man in the chair asked the woman a baffling question, 'Is this the guy?', to which she nodded, still without facing Viju directly. Instead, with her gaze fixed downwards on her lap, she started to cry.

Shortly after that, the slapping began, but by then Viju had at least learnt the crime of which he was supposed to be guilty. The woman's husband had been one of his patients, *allegedly*, who'd donated a kidney a year ago. Last week, after a month of complaining of internal pain, and constantly passing blood, he had died. The woman, who couldn't have been more than twenty-two, had apparently been left with two children.

Of course Viju had never seen her before, although she had so readily identified him. The womenfolk often didn't come out while he was talking to their husbands, unless it was a wife or daughter who was being proposed as a donor. So, with the husband having been cremated the previous week (supposedly), there was no immediate way of confirming whether or not Viju had been the agent who'd arranged for his operation.

Fuck that, was Viju's first reaction when he realised what he was being accused of, and what was probably being angled for; there was no way of confirming anything. First, you can bring in any local woman here and claim without a scrap of evidence that she is the widow of a deceased donor. At least have her point her hut out to me so that I can confirm whether I ever visited them at all. Because, secondly, even if this isn't an out-and-out broad-daylight stitch-up, even if I briefly believe – without any supporting evidence – that this drama-queen here has lost a husband, and not to alcohol or tobacco or even dengue (had he remembered and followed all the precautions we warned him to take while living with one kidney – how were we to be sure?), but to complications resulting from an organ-removal, doesn't she think I know how many other agents constantly visit these villages? Who's to say, until she shows me her hut, that her husband was operated on at our hospital? If he agreed to be cut open at some fly-by-night joint in Asansol or Bardhaman, they've got nobody but themselves to blame.

And finally, finally, my dear Maoist fuckheads, always on the lookout for something for nothing, even if I entertain, just for the heck of it, the notion that this isn't a scam cooked up by you guys, who might be planning to use the 'compensation' money to buy some more mines and bombs, and it isn't a shakedown by Little Miss Titty over there, whom you've probably come all over while this other idiot was walking me here (Viju could clearly tell, as expected, that there was no blouse under that sari, and yes, even in this most inopportune moment, the presence and fullness of those babies just beneath that thin blue fabric had registered their due impact), and that I did in fact sign up her supposedly late husband as a donor, and who then did subsequently die not of any other illness or vice, but of complications resulting from the surgery, she should have asked her Pati Parmeshwar before he ascended to heaven (come to think of it, she wasn't even in white, though Viju admitted to himself he had no idea if that was also a tribal custom) if he remembered any of the clauses that had been carefully read out to him before the operation, from the contract he'd most likely thumb-printed rather than signed. Remembered how the one-off payment, once duly made, was to be considered full and final settlement of dues: no further claims *on any grounds whatsoever* would be admitted. Not in the event of complications, or illness, or death – and how could one be sure of causes anyway in these malnourished, mosquito-infested hellholes where there were a hundred-and-one things to catch and die of? This particular clause Viju religiously spelt out for every client, slowly and loudly, before they signed or finger-stamped anything, with the same truthfulness and solemnity that he counted out every single note in front of them after they were discharged from the hospital, in anticipation of exactly a situation such as this, so that there could be no later claim of misunderstanding or incomplete information. And because he was certain he'd followed all the right steps in the enlisting and payment procedures, now, in no event – even if this had been one of his clients who had suffered some surgery-related aches and pains – did he have any further obligations. End of story.

Indeed, there were so many distinct objections to the charges being brought against Viju and the hospital, that he would have been forgiven for losing his cool while spelling them out. Here's another one for you, chutiya, he thought but didn't say, have you ever heard of a limited guarantee period? If her husband died more than twelve months after an operation, but was fine in the meantime, how can you be so sure it's the hospital's fault? Except, being absolutely professional and above-board in all his dealings with his clients, being as confident of having fulfilled his earlier responsibilities to this woman's husband with transparency and integrity, if indeed he'd been one of his donors, as he was of the legal flimsiness of her claim, and finally, being aware that he was after all on their territory, and these were volatile, trigger-happy dickheads, and therefore politeness, a calm voice and a show of concern wouldn't do anyone any harm, Viju began his response with admirable restraint and reasonableness. If the young woman would only come outside, point out her hut, and tell him her husband's name, he could immediately confirm whether or not he was the agent who had signed him on.

That was when he was cut short by a shove from behind that sent him sprawling almost to the feet of the weeping woman, who shrank back in her surprise. The skinny kid, probably less than half his age, had pushed him while he was speaking. In his shock, Viju couldn't be sure if he'd noticed any signal from the man in the chair.

'What's the meaning of this?' he made to scramble to his feet as he demanded, but it was the wrong thing to ask, because it resulted in a stinging slap from the older man, who had now got up, followed by another punch between the shoulder-blades from the kid. Viju was so enraged by this second sneaky blow that he turned around determined to choke the life out of the madarchod boy, who however was ready for him and gave him a backhanded slap, which opened up a cut on his right cheek from a ring the kid was wearing.

Suffice it to say, without dwelling further on the ugly details, that Viju never got a chance that day to present any of his excellent objections. Moreover, while he was being slapped around, two other awful realisations landed on his already sore head. The kangaroos who had decided to try him in their blind-and-deaf court-of-two decreed by way of a verdict that his hospital had to come up with one lakh as compensation for this alleged widow (who might very well have been one of their whores, and would be thrown three or five thousand as payment for her valiant sobbing efforts). When Viju tried his best to remain reasonable in the face of such extreme provocation, and to explain slowly that there was no way he could persuade anyone in the hospital administration to even listen to such a possibility ((a) because it had already been nullified in their initial agreement with any donor, and (b) because it could open the floodgates for any number of similar claims, both from impostors as well as genuine relatives), all he received for his efforts were two further slaps from the older man (who was still at least five to seven years younger than him), followed by the most ludicrous suggestion of all – that he himself might have to make good on the compensation then, out of his own pocket, because her husband had been his client and therefore it had been Viju's responsibility to ensure the best possible medical attention for him.

Viju might have started laughing at this point, he wasn't sure afterwards, so extraordinary was this idea that salesmen personally fork out compensation on behalf of their companies. No wonder these jokers had never made it out of the jungle, they were completely out of touch with even the most basic realities of the modern world.

If indeed a smirk had burst forth from him, it certainly didn't help his position. The morons stuck to their guns and became even more hostile towards him (just to show they weren't entirely indelicate brutes, the woman had been asked to wait outside after the first few slaps), and that was when the second, still more terrible aspect of this incident dawned on Viju. At a stretch, in the worst possible scenario, if these fuckers persisted in their idiocy, he could imagine fobbing them off with a couple of bank statements from his two most inactive accounts, in which he and Ma kept a few thousand rupees apiece, to prove to them there was no way he could personally pay such a sum, along with a letter from the hospital (typed by him, of course) making clear their own policy in such cases. That should take care of that. If they wanted anything more out of him, they could roll up their own sleeves, open him up, and collect a kidney for a kidney. How about that for a fair counter-offer?

But no, the most simultaneously hair-raising as well as revolting aspect of this whole incident that struck Viju while he was lying on the floor, too tired to try and make his points anymore, was that this sort of thing could easily happen again, over and over, with or without a big-titted weeping widow by way of prop or scenery. Any time these bastards liked, or others just like them, they could pull him in on a delivery and rough him up, make him personally answerable for all their complaints and frustrations about society, either toy with him and slap him around as if they were playground bullies, or dump more and more of these cooked-up compensation cases on him, and demand that he obtain restitution from the hospital. Speaking of which, where would he stand with the guys in Administration if he ever started seriously submitting these claims? Ghoshal would find it funny the first couple of times, and thereafter decide that keeping Viju might not be worth the trouble, since he, alone out of all the field-agents, repeatedly seemed to be bringing in the wrong kind of person, a string of bumpkins too dumb to respect their agreement conditions or to remember the post-operation rules.

On the bus-ride back to the district town (despite his smarting face, he had got on board the bus when it came along, instead of waiting uncertainly by the roadside for an auto), squeezed in among local passengers, it was the thought of being violated at will by other clowns such as these and being absolutely helpless about it, having to write it off as another of the hazards of this piece-of-shit job (along with riding these buses, regular bouts of amoebic dysentery from the food and water he often had to shut his eyes and swallow, and lately, enforced collusion in treasonable couriering activities), that made Viju's skin crawl, much more than the pain from the beating. For a while now, even before this nightmare came along, there had been very sound reasons in favour of getting out and looking for something in Calcutta itself, but this afternoon had decided him. He would rather go hungry, quit Calcutta, and move with Ma to his uncle's home in suburban Mumbai than tolerate such abuse a second time. And what if they – and it was clear from today's behaviour neither their stupidity nor their greed should ever again be underestimated – stuck to their threat of squeezing the money out of him, or passed the word on to their 'comrades' in other districts that hey, there's a sucker doing the rounds who's ripe for the taking? Make sure you shake him down for your fair share.

2

It is clear in retrospect that Viju's response to this incident developed in stages. First, there was a somewhat firm decision to quit his job in the very near future (he also thought on the bus-ride itself that he could put out a classified ad offering his services as a private English tutor who would willingly travel to his students' homes anywhere within the city limits: this would tide him over while he looked around for something more solid) and thereby get away from these thugs for good. If they ever got on his back to find out why, it occurred to him he could even turn his resignation to his advantage, and tell them he'd left out of disgust at the hospital's refusal to pay that poor widow any compensation. Yet this was all he had for the next week or so, when probably every day he told himself he'd draft a succinct resignation letter as well as a snappy advertisement that very night and send them off to their respective addressees first thing tomorrow. But come morning, he'd show up at the hospital as usual, except the days when he brought in two donors from Narendrapur and Barasat, and didn't say a word about his resignation plans to anyone, not even his mother. In his uncertainty and inability to follow through on his decisions, Viju even dropped off his weekly list of upcoming trips to the fruit-seller, telling himself it was best to do so in order not to arouse suspicion.

Unfortunately, his period of procrastination lasted so long that the summons for the fourth pick-up presently came along. At first he was dismayed, and after taking the call on Miss Bose's phone, finished his dinner absentmindedly while wondering if he could sneak in his resignation the following morning, and then call at the fruit-seller's to beg off this next assignment. But he remained at his office desk the entire morning and afternoon without even opening a new Word document. That evening, as if nothing was on his mind, he visited the fruit-stall and picked up the money, and bought some surprisingly good-looking late-season lychees from the sullen phalwallah without quibbling once over his named price.

It was after dinner, and a dessert of lychees, as he was absentmindedly concealing the bundles of cash beneath his underwear, socks and hankies in the bottom drawer (he was leaving early the day after tomorrow), that, out of nowhere, he decided to take it all and run. Although on previous occasions, out of some unnamed anxiety, he hadn't been able to bring himself to count the money he was delivering (all he'd noticed was that there were never any 1000-rupee notes), he had subconsciously registered that this time there were more bundles than usual. The paper bag in which the fruit-seller had handed over the money had been heavier, and there had definitely been more piles to hide away in his drawer. Perhaps it was a sign that they were starting to trust him.

Well, big mistake, motherfuckers, thought Viju, and after counting out the two lakh twenty thousand twice to be absolutely sure, he actually did a little jump of glee in the middle of his bedroom. Suddenly this seemed like a solution to so many problems at once. First, it would be the perfect retort to those junglee assholes, a most satisfying act of revenge, to make off with all this loot they probably gathered from harassing rickshaw-pullers and vegetable-sellers and jamadars and people like that, grubby piles of ten and twenty-rupee notes that the bastard fruit-seller changed into fifties, hundreds and paanch-sous. Then the logic of the action itself, the certainty there would be repercussions if he stayed, would force him to do what he'd been half-dreaming of for so many years now – finally quit Calcutta. In fact, and this is why he first jumped, and then had to sit down on the bed from dizziness brought on by over-excitement, not only would the money be a perfect springboard for a fresh start somewhere else, Ma and he would both, by sheer force of circumstances, *have to be* out of this bloody house (which so often he'd thought he would only leave on the shoulders of a funeral procession, like his brother and father before him) latest by day after tomorrow. By doing this, by deciding to take off with the money, the die would have been cast, there could be no second thoughts or nostalgia: for better or for worse, out of the fear of awful reprisals, Viju was going to jump-start the future, and force it to take a new direction, far away from the city he was long convinced would never again give him a decent break, not after the public blackening of his name by the stupid tuition affair.

Besides, speaking of sudden windfalls, once safe in Bombay, he could carry out the sale of this house through a broker and earn another, much plumper financial cushion to buy themselves some time before choosing the next step in his career.

It was amazing to see how much he achieved that night and the following day, having embarked on such a dangerous, irrevocable and uncertain path, especially compared to his inability to act on a far less momentous impulse (that of handing in his resignation at the hospital) the previous week. First, after a brief consideration, Viju decided to save himself a lot of time by telling his mother the truth about why they needed to lock up the house and leave Calcutta as soon as possible. Well, *some part* of the truth anyway; at least the word 'Maoists' was in the story, which, along with some skilful emphasis on key details and facts, proved more than enough to terrify the old lady. He first reminded her of the bruises on his face from the week before that he'd claimed were caused by walking into a door, during a midnight power-cut in the town where he'd been staying. Now he solemnly revealed the truth about his injuries, much to her horror and disbelief – they had been part of a brutal extortion attempt by a group of Maoists who'd been hounding him on his village trips for the past month or so. As Ma gaped and the tears began inadvertently flowing down her cheeks, Viju remorselessly pressed on to informing her of how they had graduated to death threats within the last week, because now they wanted him to hand directly over to them the fees paid by the hospital to its donors, although he had repeatedly made it clear he would never stand for that kind of daylight robbery of the poor. Finally however, in a last-minute veer from his original intention, he decided leaving town 'for a while' sounded better than 'perhaps forever', when you're asking a sixty-four-year-old woman breaking down before your eyes to leave within twenty-four hours the city, and neighbourhood, she'd come to as a bride forty-three years before, and the house in which she'd lived out her entire married life and raised her two boys, and where both her husband and older son remained constant, vivid presences to her years after their passing.

He also decided it was best for the same reasons not to mention any idea he had about getting rid of the place long-distance from Bombay, not just now, at any rate. Instead, he put his arms around her and drew closer to speak into her ear.

'We're going away just as a precaution, Ma. Once they realise I've left this job, and there's no further point in threatening me, they'll probably leave me alone and move on to the guy who replaces me at the hospital.'

A few minutes into her tears, Viju did feel some guilt about the fate he was inflicting on the poor woman. Ma was used to periodic upheavals in *his* life, even overnight changes of career, such as the move from being a high-school English teacher to a rural hospital agent, away from home in search of organ donors for days at a time. At the height of that scandal a few years before – in which a student's father had not kept his promise to gift him at least a working computer, if not a new one, and then had managed to turn Viju into the villain of the piece when his stupid son failed his annual exams (with absolutely no interference by Viju) – he had done his best to shield her from the long-running coverage of the story in both the Bengali and English presses, by the simple expedient of cancelling their newspaper subscriptions for a month ('Since they have no interest in the truth, Ma, the least we can do is keep their poison out of the house. You saw that junk computer Mr Das gave us, hanging on average three times a week. That was supposed to be in lieu of the whole year's fees, because he told me he was having a cash-flow problem. Why shouldn't I complain about teaching his son for free when the bloody thing won't even work?'). On that occasion, although there had been no way of keeping from his mother that he'd been detained for four nights at the police station, he had later

– successfully for the most part, he believed – been able to persuade her of his entrapment by a malicious plot, in which a devious parent employed some spectacularly underhand tactics to shift the blame for his son's utter ineptitude onto his hapless teacher, and St S's School used the opportunity presented to them on a platter to get rid of a popular and efficient non-Christian member of staff and replace him with one of their own. Viju had confided afterwards to his mother that they'd initially offered him the option of converting, in which case not just his job but also a promotion and a pay-rise would have been immediately secured. But he had turned them down on the spot: he could not imagine the pain such an action would have caused his dear and devout mother.

Even though she had taken ages to recover from the various shocks of that affair, it hadn't been too difficult to convince her of the perfidious nature of present-day school administrators, perhaps especially the Christian ones, not after her first-hand experience of the total lack of compassion that had so brutally terminated Viju's own high-school career, and had irrevocably twisted out of shape his entire future. But this was a shock of a different order, in which overnight they were going to have to leave the house where she had first arrived as a bride, the house in which Raja had lived and died, and become refugees at her brother's home in Bombay.

And yet, after all the pleading and persuasion, when Ma had finally agreed to try and sleep for at least a couple of hours at four-thirty that morning, Viju nearly had a change of heart once again when he returned to his room. Suddenly a much easier solution presented itself to him, in which (for once) everything he'd said to his mother could actually be turned into the truth. All he had to do was to return the money the following morning to the phal-wallah, and tell him he was quitting his job. In a note along with the money, he could even throw in the bit about resigning in indignation when the hospital wouldn't admit the poor widow's claim. Then no one would have to run to Bombay, and there would be no (real or fabricated) sense of danger.

Lying in his room with his earlier exhilaration fading, and the enormity of what he was about to unleash within just a couple of hours (but could still back-track and reel in even now if he wished) beginning to press down upon him, there was a period after dawn when Viju had travelled a full one-eighty degrees and changed his mind. When Ma woke up, he would explain to her that while he was certainly going to resign from this job, perhaps he had been overstating the threats by the Maoists, who after all had no actual reason to kill him. If he quit, they might merely move on to harassing his replacement. Of course, she would still be worried about his safety, and probably have her heart in her mouth every single time he left the house for the next three years, but that would be nothing compared to her relief at being able to stay in the only home (and neighbourhood, and world) she'd ever known as an adult, despite all her reiterated vows to return one day to Patna if only Viju would settle down with a wife.

By six a.m., the craziness of last night's plans had been starkly exposed in the daylight. By seven, Viju had printed out his letter of resignation, in which he'd mentioned the Maoist menace that was making him take this extreme step with immediate effect. Ma would normally have been up by then for at least an hour, but he assumed she was tired after having wept and worried until just a couple of hours before, and decided to awaken her both with bed-tea as well as the good news that they were staying.

As he threw the tea-leaves into the boiling water in the saucepan, trying not to make noise and spoil the double-surprise he had in mind for Ma, Viju could see only a few minor disadvantages to not going through with the original, audacious plan. First, he would be relinquishing the satisfaction of handing those sons-of-bitches one in the collective eye by making off with their money. This vision had been one of the most pleasurable aspects of that idea, even though Viju realised it was immature, and that the (after-all) paltry sum of money was grossly outweighed by the risks. Besides, he would again indefinitely be putting on hold the long-held dream of 'the fresh start' – there'd be no fleeing to Bombay, no immediate financial cushion, and no delicious prospect of selling this house shortly afterwards. One way or another, he was going to hand in his resignation that morning, but now he would have to look for something new in Calcutta itself. Once more would follow the uncertainty of being unemployed as the savings leaked away, and the leaden assurance that the next job would be another arduous ill-paid slog of some description. This city would *never* have anything better to offer him, yet nothing short of a death threat would convince his Ma to leave.

Thus it was that Viju was almost depressed again by the time he appeared at his mother's bedside by her tea. She was flustered about over-sleeping as soon as she heard the door open and looked over and noticed the time, but one look at Viju's face reminded her that none of last night's conversation had been a lurid, impossible dream.

It was the perfect moment for him to tell her about the revised plan. And he was about to, after laying down the tray and handing her a cup, except, to his own astonishment, he found himself describing his hectic schedule over the next few hours. He would have to call Mamaji in Bombay just after eight, before he set off to catch his train. Then a quick stop at work to hand in his resignation, from where he would head directly to a travel agency to book tomorrow's flights. Meanwhile all Ma needed to do was to pack one suitcase for herself, take whatever she normally would for a month-long holiday. He'd return home right after buying the tickets, to pack as well as take care of everything else around the house before leaving.

Viju and his mother flew out to Bombay the following morning. Every part of his plan had worked out perfectly. His uncle, although initially as perturbed as Ma by the news of his run-in with the Maoists, welcomed them with great warmth, and after hearing all the horrifying details several times over from both his nephew and his younger sister, promised to ask an ex-colleague from the legal department of his former company (he'd retired three years ago) if Viju was eligible to seek compensation from the hospital for distress and injury caused in the course of official duty. (Another unexpected bonus if it works out, Viju thought to himself, to add to what he had already mentally titled the 'Mumbai seed fund', as well as further evidence that he'd jumped off that bus at exactly the most profitable time).

In the meantime his resignation – which he had handed in at the hospital front desk the day before and asked to be forwarded upstairs, because he had to be at the travel agency as soon as possible – had sparked off a couple of phone calls that very afternoon, in which Ghoshal (his manager) was offered the same version of the truth that Viju had put together for his mother and uncle, emphasising the regular harassment and extortion demands that he'd stoically endured for nearly two months, until they had stooped to death threats, personal blackmail and beatings. 'No more, Ghoshal, I'm sorry, I love my job, but no more. Please remember that I have a sixty-four-year-old widowed mother who has already lost one son, and who relies on me for much more than material support.'

Despite having only twenty-four hours, Viju had made himself a to-do list and attended to everything crucial around the house and at the bank before they left for Bombay early the following morning. It was only at the airport while clearing his pockets at security-check that he realised he'd forgotten to drop by Miss Bose's place to return her phone. From here on, he wouldn't be fielding any further calls from Maoists. Ah well, he'd definitely return it during his next visit, probably in a month or so, when he would have to come back to initiate arrangements for selling the house.

Yet, meticulous as he'd been, there was another woman (coincidentally around Miss Bose's age) that Viju had forgotten about in the all-consuming haste of that penultimate day. Probably because their paths never crossed most days of the week, he'd omitted to say anything specific to his mother about Jaya, who'd done all their housecleaning and washing and plant-watering for over twenty years. Or perhaps it was because Viju hadn't really ever imagined their house was being watched, or even that the Maoists would know exactly where he lived. He'd mentioned living near Golpark in a general way, which was why they'd picked the fruit-seller in Gariahat as the contact-person, but had certainly never passed on his full address.

In any event, while his mother had told their neighbours on either side and upstairs what Viju had coached her to say about their brief disappearance (her sister-in-law in Bombay had suddenly been taken ill), she acted in other ways exactly as she would have on the eve of her annual Puja trip to Patna, and repeatedly reminded Jaya to come in each day to thoroughly dust and wipe the house, and equally importantly, water the plants in the front verandah and the back garden. Jaya followed the path of least resistance as she always did, by nodding and assenting vigorously, while being fully aware that a daily drop-in to water certain plants and a quick floor-wipe every other day would suffice perfectly during this absence, as it had the last many years.

So it was her bad luck that Viju's antagonists chose to pay him a call to find out why the latest consignment of money hadn't been delivered, on one of the alternate days when she was inside the house, sweeping the floors. Perhaps they wouldn't have dared harm her at eleven in the morning if she'd been in the front verandah watering the plants. In any case, it took another day and a half for Viju in Bombay to hear the news from Mr Mani, who had spare keys to their house, and was calling with a police inspector standing beside him. Jaya's son had contacted the local thana two evenings ago when his mother had failed to return home after her usual round of work, and after a night of waiting as advised by the OC, they had finally made their way over around noon the following day to the front door of the Sinhas, which appeared to be padlocked with no one home. They'd gone next door to the Manis; it was a Saturday and Mr Mani had been home, and had immediately produced a latchkey for the Sinhas' back door. Jaya had been found tied up with some plastic clothesline just inside the kitchen. She'd been dead for about a day. Beside her lay her broom and an old floorwiping rag that looked like it had been used as a gag. The rest of the house had clearly been ransacked. Obviously, neither the police nor Mr Mani could confirm what exactly had been taken.

Later that evening, Mr Mani was able to call Viju back with a probable cause of death. Although of course there would be a post-mortem, the examining doctor had said Jaya didn't have any obvious injuries. It was clear the burglars had tied her up and gagged her while they raided the house, but then the doctor's opinion was that she had died of a heart attack, most likely brought on by fear.

3

Perhaps it was some sort of lifetime first, but on this occasion everybody bought Viju's story – the police, his family, Jaya's family, the hospital. They believed that he'd been terrorised for money by the Maoists for over two months until he'd had no option but to quit his job and hide out temporarily in Bombay while figuring out how best to get them off his back. They believed that he hadn't imagined the Maoists – who always waylaid him during his rural trips – were watching his home in Calcutta, otherwise he would have never allowed Jaya to be exposed to such danger. They even believed (although his mother had been virulently against the idea) that he was something of a hero for returning immediately to Calcutta (the very next day, in fact) after hearing of Jaya's terrible death.

And the most amazing thing of all – *even the Maoists appeared to believe him*, because they didn't take any further steps to harass Viju after their money was returned to them. It was the first thing he did upon arrival in Calcutta, head to the fruit-seller's straight from the airport and hand him a brown paper parcel wrapped in thin rope, in which he'd also enclosed a letter fully explaining the reason for his absence, as well as informing them of his resignation from his job. Viju had intended to return to his taxi without a word, but since there was no one else at the stall when he arrived, he couldn't resist admonishing the phal-wallah at least slightly with the following words:

'All the money is in the package. Count it carefully: you'll find exactly the notes you gave me. There's also a letter in there. My aunt suddenly fell ill in Bombay, so I had to rush with my mother to see her. That is why I couldn't deliver the money. How could you think I would run off with it? What you people did in my house was not right. Because of you, an absolutely innocent poor person, who worked all day in people's homes even though she was a grandmother, lost her life. Enough is enough. I'm leaving my job, and I'm saying goodbye to you. Everything is explained in my letter.'

The fruit-seller had turned to face Viju halfway through this loudly whispered speech, but as usual he didn't reply. It was only after a month had passed without any further word from them that Viju decided at last the Maoists too had swallowed his story and forgotten about him. Thus, in a way, everything had turned out ok – except the falling-through of the plan to resettle in Bombay, and of course Jaya's tragic death. The local police were perfectly satisfied with the amount of detail Viju gave them about the beating he endured in the village (of course he omitted the encounter with the weeping widow and presented it solely as an extortion threat, for him to hand over the monies he was transporting to needy donors), as well as of their intimidatory visits to his hotel rooms in various district towns (he understandably included no word of his delivery assignments for them, nor of the Gariahat fruit-vendor's intermediary role). Not only did the story sound specific and genuine (and it was corroborated by all his other actions), Viju reckoned it had an added benefit for them: this way, they could keep the case-file open without needing to take any further action – after all, the actual culprits might have melted away into some village or forest across the state border, and that was clearly outside their jurisdiction. The contented Gariahat-thana inspector even respected Viju's fervent plea to keep the full story out of the press, because of his concern about further reprisals: it was eventually carried in two Bengali papers as a single paragraph name-suppressed news-item, about an ordinary burglary during which a housemaid had suffered a fatal heart-attack. But Jaya's two sons were touched by the fact of Viju's immediate return from Bombay, and his offer to take over the full costs of her funeral ceremony, and they seemed to believe the inspector's personally delivered account of a routine break-in gone wrong. And as for his seniors in the hospital and his mother and uncle in Bombay, who (thought they) knew the full story of the dangers he had faced, and Mr Mani and the other neighbours, who had witnessed first-hand his concern for his poor housemaid's family, Viju was suddenly revealed to be an unassuming hero living in their midst. In fact, as if to prove the maxim that one good turn begets another, once he'd had a chance to fully debrief Viju on the events of the past two months, his immediate boss Ghoshal called him three days later with two astonishing offers – a desk job at the hospital that would involve no rural trips (which Viju graciously refused), and an offer of a cash settlement – in return for a promise of no further claims or lawsuits – of three hundred thousand rupees, because of all the distress Viju had suffered in the course of trying to protect his clients' interests with remarkable integrity, which of course he immediately accepted with unaffected pleasure and surprise. After receiving the news, he thought briefly of calling Jaya's older son to share some of the money with their family, but then decided not to act in the heat of the moment, because perhaps the payment of the funeral expenses had been generous enough.

The compensation settlement from the hospital did have one other ironic implication for Viju, and it struck him in the back seat of the cab while riding home from his meeting with Ghoshal. Three lakhs was a good deal more than two lakh twenty; this time he was being *gifted* more money than he'd tried to steal with extreme recklessness just a few days before; and moreover, if he announced within the next fortnight or month that he had decided to move with his mother to Bombay to make a fresh start far away from the scene of his harassment, everyone would nod understandingly and sympathise. Jaya's awful and accidental death had provided him with both the means and the perfect alibi to pursue his earlier plan, and best of all, he'd be entirely in the clear, with no need ever again to look over his shoulder in fear. The truth, and the ridiculousness, of this thought forced Viju to shake his head and smile.

And of course, in so many ways, Bombay would also be the best option for Ma. For starters, she was already there, because he'd asked her to remain at her brother's to spare her some of the distress of Jaya's death, all the neighbours' talk, and the regular police visits. But even when they spoke each evening over the phone, it was evident that Ma had taken the loss of Jaya very badly. Jaya had been a twice-daily presence in her life for twenty-two years: their sons were the same age and had grown up in parallel. Would Ma really want to return to this house, to which another ghost had just been added?

Within the next few minutes, Viju had made another couple of significant decisions. He wasn't going to mention his sudden windfall to Jaya's sons, but besides paying for the funeral, he would open a fixed deposit account in the bank on behalf of Jaya's family for a decent five-figure amount (perhaps something like eighty thousand rupees).

And the money from the hospital also meant he didn't have to rush through the sale of their house just yet. They could take their time over it: after all, they wouldn't be paying rent to his uncle in Bombay. And in the meantime, they could rent out the place for some extra income, although only if the tenant was familiar and a decent sort, just to be sure he or she would vacate the flat whenever required.

Thankfully for Viju, there was someone he knew who exactly matched that description, and needed a place just then for herself. She would only have to move to the other end of Gariahat: she would hardly notice the difference. He would also help her out by asking for a very reasonable rent.

Some good was going to come (for someone) out of all this, and when he dropped by to see her, he could finally also return her damned phone, which to him in any case was now only a reminder of a most unpleasant time. In fact, he must make it a point to ask Miss Bose to change her number.

They were already at the Deshapriya Park crossing, so Viju leaned forward to tell the driver they wouldn't be going to Golpark after all. He'd just remembered another call he had to pay at the other end of Gariahat, so the driver should carry on straight ahead instead of turning right at Triangular Park.

City Lights

When I cut my left forefinger one night last week, while slicing a capsicum for my chilli paneer, my landlord – who lives on the ground floor and religiously takes the air in his front garden after dinner – noticed me on the balcony wrapping one of my dish-towels around my hand, and insisted I go straightaway for an anti-tetanus injection, even though I pointed out more than once that the knife hadn't been rusty. But it was no use. In fact, he was so startled when I replied after a moment's thought to one of his questions that my last booster injection might easily have been over fifteen years ago, because since college I hadn't had any cuts or scrapes that merited such an overwrought response, that even I grew slightly nervous and promised to get my injection the very next day, although I'd have to go after work. And when he learnt upon further cross-examining (shouted up across two floors) that I didn't really have a regular GP even after all these years in Bangalore, he managed to extract a promise from me that I would go over to a particular bus stop on Residency Road and wait for some mobile clinic that would come along, which apparently specialized in immunisation drives for children.

The following evening the van (actually more of a converted mini-bus) showed up two minutes ahead of time, and a cheerful man asked me to step inside and sit down. Its back had been turned into a screened-off doctor's chamber, while the compounder, who'd greeted me and then resumed his work, had his corner, and a basin, on the right-hand side. There was room for maybe six patients to sit along the left, three on either side of the door. For now, there was only me.

In these dark, cramped surroundings however, there was an incredible surprise in store for me, because shortly after, the doctor emerged from behind his curtain – and it turned out to be my childhood physician, whom I hadn't seen in over twenty years. Of course, he would have never recognized me, but was able to place me as soon as I named my parents and mentioned where we'd lived. But all that had been in Calcutta, over a thousand miles away: what was he doing here, in a mobile clinic that toured the outlying slums and suburbs of this faraway city?

'I too have signed up for this scheme,' he told me. 'Go to the children if the children cannot come to you. I get to feel useful, and also to see different places around the country a few times each year. What could be better?'

'But this is remarkable,' I said inadvertently, meaning both such an undertaking at his age, as well as the coincidence of our meeting. He must have been at least seventy.

The doctor beamed, delighted at the impression he had made.

'My mother would have been so pleased. She always said you were the best diagnostician she had ever known. Sometimes, all it took was one look as we were coming through the door from the waiting room into your chamber, and you would guess what was wrong with me even before we'd sat down, from my cough or the way that I was walking. You know what I've always believed, that Ma secretly wished she too could have consulted you.'

All this was true, the details were coming back clearly to me, the layout of his waiting room (near Deshapriya Park) and the brightness and high ceilings of his chamber. I also saw no harm in mentioning these things to a man who was just about to administer me an injection.

The thought of an injection suddenly reminded me – he'd pulled off the same trick today. His first words, as soon as he'd parted his curtains, and before I'd exclaimed in recognition, had been 'Injection lena hai?' upon seeing my bandaged finger.

'Arré Doctor, you did it again!' I burst out. He was grinning widely now, as if to say he'd been waiting for me to notice.

The compounder turned around from his counter to smile at us: he'd cottoned on that we knew one another, even though we'd mostly been speaking in Bengali. He also seemed very friendly, and when he returned to his work, I realized he was preparing a large quantity of something milky in a big steel jug.

'Doctor, how long will you be in town? Would it be possible for you to come to my house sometime, or we can meet at a restaurant for dinner? Whatever suits your schedule. I'm free after work pretty much every evening.'

The doctor was preparing my injection, and said, 'I better give you this quickly because we're expecting a big group of kids at the next stop. The van will get pretty full.' Then, in response to my remark, he added, 'I will come, I'll definitely come.'

The injection was painless, and as the doctor pulled it out, he asked after my parents.

'Ma went away three years ago, and Baba two years before that,' was all I said.

'Oh, I'm so sorry.'

'Not at all, Daktarbabu. It's fine.'

'Do you still go to Calcutta often?'

'Once every year or so, mostly to see a couple of elderly aunts. But otherwise no, this is now home for me.'

'And marriage?' he asked with a smile.

'Not yet,' I smiled back. 'Still interviewing candidates.'

We both laughed as he discarded my syringe and turned to wash his hands in the basin, next to where the compounder was working. The driver of the van was separated from us by a steel mesh. I hadn't thus far seen his face.

'Well, listen,' said the doctor next, 'Vinayak here has made a big jug of chocolate milk for the kids who're about to get on for their injections, and you've just had yours, so I feel you deserve a glass as well. Want one?'

'Yes please, Doctor,' I said immediately.

'And also, if you don't have to go home or be elsewhere this evening, just stay on the van if you like. We go through a few different places, Abdul in front knows the exact route, but we can definitely drop you off around ten o' clock at the stop where we picked you up. What do you say? In between patients we can chat.'

'Won't I be in your way?'

'No, there will only be a few people on board while we're moving, the ones who need a bit more time. So there'll be plenty of room. It's entirely up to you.'

'In that case, I'll stay. I'd like to see what route the van takes. Thank you so much.'

In reality, the way the night turned out, with sizeable queues at every stop and always some children who needed further attention, the doctor didn't have much spare time to chat with me. For instance, there were about twenty kids at the next stop he had to vaccinate, and four of them, with three accompanying parents, remained with us after we drove off. But it didn't matter that the doctor was so busy: the children were amused to see that I, a grown-up, was sipping the same milk-shake they'd downed in one go, and I smiled and talked to them (to those among them who responded to English or Hindi) while they waited their turn on the bench. Afterwards, I was content to see what little I could of the areas we stopped in or passed through. Aside from the pleasure of running into the doctor and all the particular, long-unvisited memories it had brought back (especially of my parents), the other interesting aspect of the evening was the fact that I didn't recognize many of the large crossings or main roads we drove through, before we passed into more outlying districts of half-lit villages, uneven, narrower streets and dark fields. I had been living in this city for six years, I wondered, as I stretched my legs on the back streets of a still-bustling market area where we had stopped, and yet there were so many parts of town I'd never had a chance to visit. I finally could place where we were again only at about ten-fifteen, as we suddenly took a left-turn onto a major road and ascended a familiar flyover.

The doctor recorded my mobile number in his phone, and promised he would call me before he returned to Calcutta.

'Hope it wasn't too long a night for you. Will you still be able to find something to eat?'

'Yes, of course, don't worry, Doctor. There are plenty of leftovers in the fridge. I cook enough at a time to keep me going for a few days.'

'Well, one day I'll definitely come and sample your cooking.'

I thanked him again and left, wondering if he'd have the time to call me during this visit itself. They had dropped me about a thirty-five minute walk away from my house, but although I needed a bathroom at some point soon, I decided not to hail an auto-rickshaw after my four-hour-long van-ride all over town. Halfway through my stroll, the sight of an open supermarket reminded me that I needed eggs and bread for tomorrow's breakfast, or else I'd have to set aside a helping of last night's chilli paneer to go with my morning coffee.

I was fourth in a surprisingly long line at the checkout for ten-forty in the evening (of course, the store only had the one till open), when a voice came over the public address system reminding shoppers in both Kannada and English that the big deadline for some 'Max' competition (I might have missed the full name) was coming up in twenty minutes time, and that there were still forms available at the back of the store for anyone wishing to enter. The first prize was a year's supply of rice and pulses. Although I did wonder what particular pulses they were offering and whether the rice would be Basmati, and even more, on the basis of whose reasonable rations they'd calculated 'a year's supply', I wasn't at all moved by the urgency of the appeal. And even less so when the three people ahead of me miraculously vanished – squeezing past me with their baskets on their way to the back as if they could not believe their good fortune, of being in the supermarket at such an opportune time – and I was suddenly promoted to the top of the queue.

It was probably because I was distracted, first by the checkout guy's insistence that I too grab my chance and enter the contest as he bagged my goods and counted out my change (I tried to counter him by pointing out that mine was a one-person household in a one-bedroom flat – there was no one to eat and nowhere to store a year's supply of dal-chawal: he replied with a triumphant smile that they would deliver it in monthly consignments, which point I checkmated before walking away with the incontestable fact of my shift timings; I would never be home at a reasonable hour to meet the delivery-men), and then, as I was leaving the store, by the sight of five or six men approaching the entrance with what looked like their competition forms in hand, that I failed to spot Ashok outside, standing in front of his motorbike, waiting for me to notice him. It was only when I had nearly bumped into him, my eyes still following the local men heading for the back of the supermarket with their forms, that he reached out to steady, and greet, me.

'Oh, Ashok,' I said, as if it was the most everyday thing for us to run into each other there. 'What time is it? Is it eleven already?'

'No, it's still ten to. What's the matter, yaar?'

'Nothing. I was just wondering if all of them will make the deadline.'

'What deadline?'

'Some competition. It doesn't matter. What are you up to? Sorry I didn't notice you before.'

Ashok asked me if I would wait outside for him for just a couple of minutes. He had to buy a big bottle of Coke.

When he returned, he said he was going to a party, and that he needed the Coke to go with some rum he had in the side-box of his motorcycle. I said, Wow, Thursday-night party, are you planning to come into work tomorrow?

Ashok raised his eyebrows and shook his head as if I had asked a Dad-like question. 'No worries, yaar, tomorrow I have the evening shift, na.'

Then he added 'Want to come? I'll drop you home afterwards. It's only four kilometres away.'

'No, man. This week my shift starts at 9 a.m.'

'Chal na. Lots of people from the US shift will be there. You might know some of them. Babes too.'

I demurred again, and told him a bit about the long evening I'd already had. Ashok looked bemused at my idea of nighttime entertainment, and said so as well. When he reacted to it like that, hanging out in a mobile medical unit full of sick people with God-knows-what infections, bumping along on unpaved roads, did sound like an odd form of recreation. But the doctor had known me as a child, and had remembered Ma and Baba, and the evening had been nowhere near as dusty and depressing as (I suspect) Ashok imagined. The breeze had been so pleasant, and I had exchanged smiles with virtually all the children, and several of the adults.

'Ashok, listen, I have to go home, eat, and most of all, I really need a toilet,' I said in my final attempt to wriggle away.

'There will be plenty of food at the party. And no. 1 jana hai na? If you can't hold on till we get there, we'll just ride for a while, and then, when there's a dark stretch, you go by the road.'

'And my groceries? I've got eggs here.'

'You carry them for now, and when we go inside, we'll leave those in the side-box. I also keep an extra jacket in there, in case you're worried about getting cold sitting behind me.'

The slightly strange truth is that I agreed to go to the party precisely because I didn't know Ashok all that well in the office. He used to be in the UK team with us during his first six months, and of course we'd all gone out together several times, but he and I hadn't been especially close. Yet that was what touched me now, that someone I didn't even consider a good friend really wanted me to come along to a party. That, and the idea that I already had had a special evening solely because I'd agreed to the doctor's spontaneous suggestion to remain in the van – so perhaps this was a day of being open to the unexpected.

In the end, nothing noteworthy happened at the party, although it was nice to feel the breeze again on my face sitting behind Ashok on his bike (I did take up both his offers – to borrow his extra wind-cheater and also to stop off for a necessary pee by the road ahead). I suppose I expected too much: how many new friends could one hope to make in a night? Ashok did his best to introduce me to the new faces in his US team, including the women, and even pointed out my bandaged finger at the start, which led to a brief discussion about anti-tetanus boosters, but they naturally returned to talking amongst themselves whenever he headed off to some other corner to greet a new arrival (he seemed to know everyone at this do, whether they were from our office or not; it made me even more reluctant to try and monopolize his attention).

I did eat my fill of the snacks on offer and also downed a couple of beers (I was careful not to drink too much, since I was conscious of not having contributed anything to the party), before I decided to leave at around one. Ashok was on a sofa talking to two women from his team, and I realized I'd have to make my own way home. I didn't want to drag him away from the fun. On my way out, I noticed a room in which three or four guys who looked like they were from the North-East had taken off their shirts for some reason. One of them was bare-chested while the others were in their vests. They were in good spirits, and I wondered if they were playing some kind of strip poker. I also thought to myself that I was leaving just as this party was warming up: perhaps I should go over to these guys instead and ask to join their game. But tiredness won out, and I waved goodbye to one of them who had noticed me at the door and was beckoning me to enter, and stepped outside the house.

The night was cold, and it was the thought of Ashok's wind-cheater which I'd returned earlier to the side-box of his motorcycle that reminded me of my bread and eggs. I picked those up, and tried to remember the right way out of the neighbourhood back onto the main road. I hadn't really been paying attention while Ashok had brought us here, and the first turn I took only led me deeper into the suburb, until I reached a small playing field with a pond at one end. On the other side were a couple of narrow lanes amid a row of older cottage-like houses that didn't seem to lead to the main road: in any case, I had no memory of going past this field or pond on our way to the party.

And yet, as I turned around to retrace my steps and try following the lane in the other direction, and as part of me was also wondering whether it would be a good idea to re-enter the house and ask someone, not necessarily Ashok, the right way back to the main road, something made me pause, and reconsider the open space I was leaving behind – the field, the pond fringed by palm trees to the left, the light mist passing over the scene from right to left, and on the other side, visible because of the streetlamps, the row of whitewashed single-storey bungalows from an earlier era. I was certain I had never been to this corner of Bangalore before, and yet I felt equally sure that I knew it. How was this possible?

I was on the auto-rickshaw home twenty-five minutes later, after having agreed to pay twice the meter fare, when I answered my own riddle (reaching the main road again once I headed back up the lane, past the party house and in the other direction, hadn't been a problem). Over twenty-five years ago, back in Calcutta, we were just starting Class Five when my close friend and desk-partner, Aftab, had suddenly announced his father was being transferred to Bangalore, and that they would leave within a month. I still remembered how long it had taken me to understand, and then fully accept, that this really meant he was going permanently, and would never again rejoin our school.

Anyway, Aftab and I wrote to each other fairly often after he left (for at least a year if I recall correctly before the letters grew more infrequent and eventually tailed off), and from his occasional descriptions – although he never sent any photographs – I had put together a mental picture of the neighbourhood in which he lived, and the scene outside his window. What had stopped me in my tracks half-an-hour before was the astounding similarity of the place I'd stumbled upon to the image I'd once constructed (entirely) in my head, complete with field, pond, palm trees, and low bungalows on the opposite side with open verandahs.

I shook my head in disbelief the rest of the way home, and nearly forgot my bag of eggs and bread on the back seat of the auto (the driver was good enough to notice and call after me). I'd of course looked Aftab up online when I first arrived in the city – even though we'd not been in touch for nearly twenty years – only to find he was now a lawyer based in Singapore: since then I had not thought much about him. But now at least three distinct memories had returned on the back of the first one. I recalled his eyebrows – how thick they were, and how they nearly met in the middle above his nose. Then I remembered his singular running style: Aftab ran like no one else I had ever seen. He never moved his arms, and always carried his elbows bent at perfect right angles before him. At that age, and although we were close, I didn't ask him whether he had any theory behind running in such a unique fashion, or whether it was the only style that came naturally to him, but he never ran in any other way, not at break-time, not while playing football, catching the school bus or in a race. In any case, he was in the house relay team, and one of the three fastest runners in our class, along with Abhay K and Anand I, so his strange style clearly worked for him.

And after Aftab left, sometimes when I wanted to remember him, I would run like that for a few paces, during a game without saying anything to anybody, or just along a footpath by myself, with unmoving, perpendicular arms. This odd memory also came back to me during my auto-ride home.

If that doesn't sound foolish enough, here's a final thing I recalled last Thursday night, although this is not so much about Aftab directly as it is about me. About a month after his departure, I was about to cross Rashbehari Avenue (opposite Triangular Park) and head home one afternoon around four-thirty, when to my right I saw a boy, out of uniform, who from the back looked just like Aftab. He was walking up the pavement towards Priya cinema and Lansdowne Road, whereas I had meant to cross over and go home, but the degree of resemblance was so stunning I decided I had to follow him.

I had read more than enough mystery books (Hardy Boys, Five Find-Outers, Famous Five) to be aware of the kind of distance I should keep in order for the boy never to suspect he was being tailed. And he didn't, although I figured out well before we'd even reached Deshapriya Park that it wasn't Aftab (how could it have been: why would he return from Bangalore within just four weeks; and in any case, he would have called me). There was no reason for me to keep following him after that, but still I continued, giving up only after we were somewhere past Lake Market several minutes later. I had diverted myself a good fifteen minutes away from home, following someone I knew to be a stranger, all in pursuit of a fleeting quality in his walk that reminded me in some way of my friend.

And that recollection was the last of the somewhat strange run of events that evening. There's been a weekend between now and then, but I didn't go back to that neighbourhood to see the pond and the field again in the light of day. I guess the doctor wasn't able to call me on this visit, but I did run into Ashok on Monday as I was leaving the office, and told him I'd had a good time the other night. He said there was another party he'd been invited to this coming Friday, and I was more than welcome to join him if I wanted.

Down to Experience

(A Novella)

Introductory Note

It is the late 1940s, and although most of Europe is yet to recover from the recently concluded war, tensions are fast developing between the world's two remaining great powers. Virtually every country on the continent must choose a side, but for many nations that find themselves on the front-line between West and East, the 'choice' is often forced upon them through instigated violence and external manipulation, leading to years of internal conflict that tear these societies apart, setting against each other different classes, regions, towns, ethnic groups, and sometimes even neighbours, friends and family members who believe strongly enough in opposed visions of the future to be willing to fight and die for them.

This story takes place during that dark time in two neighbouring nations of South-Eastern Europe, each of which has suffered years of civil war. In one country, there has recently been a victor: the prize has finally fallen to the West. But in Ivan's homeland, even after three years the fighting continues, apparently with no end in sight…

Ivan

1

It was a clear sign of how nervous I was the way I snapped at the child. Poor gypsy, probably a loner, barrelling along cheerfully peering at everything through his treasured eyeglass, neither loud nor inquisitive, and when he removes it there's a large sheet by the river laden with food not ten feet away. Four rows of food gleaming silver in the midst of three people, none of whom is eating. They've all got their eyes, it seems, on the full moon playing on the water, lighting up the field beyond. So he steps closer to examine the feast, and the kind woman notices him and asks him to help himself, to select whatever he likes. She even passes him a napkin to carry things away. He stands there disbelievingly until she repeats herself and I, turning around for the first time, reassure him: 'Go on, don't worry, we've eaten already. Put that telescope behind a tree and come back for it tomorrow so you can use both your hands.'

So, while he was trying to recognise what everything was so he could pick the things he liked, he didn't notice that his feet had stepped onto the edge of the sheet and that his toes were touching the sandwiches. Suddenly this thickly-bearded hulk – well over twice as tall as him, and with a rifle slung across his front – yanks him right off the ground by grabbing his pants and hisses into his face whilst he is still in mid-air, that he has to take the sandwiches he'd touched with his feet because who else was going to eat those? But the kid was barely six or seven and got so frightened he ran straight off the second I put him down, forgetting even his eyeglass. By bringing it to a climax, his leap actually broke the suspense for a moment and, although I immediately felt ashamed of my behaviour and wanted to run after him to apologise, we all laughed gratefully for the relief.

Things began to happen not long after that. Eugene emerged noiselessly from the river ten feet away from us, and I had just rushed up with a towel and open arms to embrace him when he shoved me aside so unexpectedly I slipped and sank in the mud at the water's edge. But though he managed to turn around, he couldn't dive back into the water before the bullets dispatched him there, face down with an echoing smack. I was screaming, both from the understanding that Eugene had saved my life, and from the certainty I was next. My rifle remained uselessly over my shoulder, because we hadn't been expecting any fighting. But everything that followed defied my expectations. A sniper emerged from the woods behind us; yet he wasn't accompanied by any soldiers. He had no more bullets to fire and nothing to say: instead, he put away his machine gun in a case before disappearing, still without a word, towards the road. Most of all, I then realised, Elena and Marc were unmoved. They were quietly packing the food and shaking the sheets clean as if a normal picnic had just concluded. Then Elena arrived to help me up saying we had to be in town again before daybreak, and that Marc would follow us once he'd 'tidied up Eugene's body'.

On the long journey to the city, it occurred to me repeatedly that none of us (except Marc who would be 'tidying up') had even cared to turn Eugene over and look at his face one final time. What would he do, I wondered – weigh the corpse down with rocks, or bestow the minimum dignity of placing it in a coffin before pouring concrete all over it and sealing the lid? That is the most Marc might do for Eugene, the same best friends who once sat at the back of the tram roaring with laughter and egging Elena on to consider me for the key.

It had been my first visit ever to our capital, nearly four years ago, days after that other great war had just ended, and the Americans (briefly) were being honoured as our liberating heroes. Like thousands of other young men and women from our provinces, I too had lost no time in heading for the big city to be part of the festivities and the crowds. It was only my second afternoon there, and with wide-open eyes and ears I was riding the tram as it trundled through the centre, first across the river and then through the old town, before it would drop me again at the riverside further west, right opposite the National Museum. It was three o' clock, and there were five people left in the tramcar – Elena was with two male friends and her neighbour Teresa. As soon as we were alone, I had become aware of their teasing: their actual words to one another were drowned out by the noise of the wheels on the tracks, but not their shameless hoots of mockery. In my rage, I didn't even notice that first time those streets and houses I would grow to love, or the plane trees that lined the river; all my enthusiasm had turned to bitterness, and I was thinking only that everything I'd heard about the arrogance and superficiality of folk in the capital was totally justified.

At the terminus I rushed out through the front exit desperate not to catch their gaze, and was already on the first steps of the over-bridge leading to the museum opposite when I heard Elena calling out to me. I turned at the second call, but remained on the stair, surly and unwelcoming. Such were the last seconds of my life before I fell in love once and forever.

Elena skipped towards me, took the stairs and announced she had something to give me. She handed me a key saying it would open the door to her flat. It was up to me to find the door. As she returned to her friends grinning at how dumbstruck I appeared (so she told me later), not knowing how best to communicate either my fierceness or my haunting suspicion of being scored upon, it was the now dead Eugene who'd shouted out to rescue me: 'She's been carrying that key for two years, looking for the right stranger to give it to. No one else has ever had it. Good luck, my friend-from-out-of-town. We voted unanimously for you.'

And there it was, as they boarded a tram heading back into the old city and Elena didn't even turn around to confirm for me what I could not believe I had witnessed – how the most beautiful thing ever to have happened in my life had already just taken place.

It was at this point I barely managed to get my head outside the van in time to vomit, as the sight of the first two bullets ripping open Eugene's face flashed before me.

2

It was four hours to the capital by way of back roads and forest trails, and all that time I wept uncontrollably for Eugene. After all, I had had the most recent and intimate contact with him when we hid out in my mother's cellar for a month until just a fortnight before, and her kitchen was still stashed with our leavings. Irrepressible even as he hid from a capture that would certainly have been appalling and prolonged before it was fatal, Eugene came up with the idea for an 'exhibition' that he then insisted we prepare, if we were not to lose our sanity spending day after day in the windowless cellar. And though it was evidence for which we could have been executed on the spot, I had left our invaluable 'artworks' rolled up behind the oven out of an unreasonable affection for those dark yet incongruously blithe days we'd endured together. However, our instructions to my mother were clear: any hint of a police or military search-party approaching our village, and she was to toss the entire heap into the fire.

What we had done was meant to be comic, and now the very memory of our light-heartedness was unbearable. We collaborated on a large collection of sketches – pencil drawings, and a few with more detail in charcoal – that were caricatures of leading lights from all walks of life: artists, tyrants, thinkers, film-stars, saints and world leaders, in which they either slept, shat, urinated, were captured masturbating or blowing their nose, or else were sneezing or eating. We drew everyone we could think of: Rita Hayworth, Gandhi, Stalin and Napoleon, Einstein, Aristotle, Himmler, Dietrich and Bogart. Our own leaders, generals and 'philosophers' of the present time occupied pride of position. The point of it, if there was any, was not just that they too inevitably succumbed to these urges along with the rest of us – we wanted to say that all humans are essentially harmless and identical when involved in one of these numerous pursuits, which taken together consume an unexpectedly enormous portion of our lives. It is only what each one pursues during the rest of their waking hours that defines whether they are killers or geniuses, clerks, Mozarts, or madmen. The idea evolved out of the unstoppable momentum of a schnapps-soaked night, and the sketches were stored away in the hope of a better time, when both our friends and our foes might have the humour necessary to allow us our silly point.

But already in those first hours I was grieving in a vacuum, because even Elena yielded me nothing by way of sympathy or support. For a period of time that I didn't notice, she was silent; then, halfway through the journey, she quietly moved over, gripped my left arm, and expected me to believe she'd always mistrusted Eugene because he was born fortunate, and hadn't made an effort for anything in his life. Even his part in the struggle had been dilettantism, she insisted, a hobby, and it was such deep-seated frivolity that made him lethal, because it could turn either way, or perhaps he would one day have outgrown it.

'Life has been hard for every one of us,' she pronounced into my left ear, 'and from long before this war. We have all lost friends and parents or seen them transported, never to return. That is why our commitment is beyond question. But what class did Eugene belong to? What had they to gain from change? His parents have supported the government all their lives, haven't they? That is what led many of us to begin worrying about him, and then as we observed more closely there were more and more signs that didn't add up, that began to confirm our suspicions. Initially we dismissed it as a mere lack of seriousness that a straightforward talking-to would correct, but gradually the evidence started to point towards a more sinister possibility. He was a double-agent, and the moment we understood this, we had to act, before he was aware that we knew.'

'What evidence?' I barely managed to whisper. I couldn't look directly at her face.

'It'll be presented to all of us shortly, I promise, and then you can judge for yourself. He was a saboteur, Ivan. We're certain about that. But he was also a master at covering his traces, which is why he went undetected for years.'

Such was the bilge I was served up and ordered to believe. Further, I was rebuked curtly when I wailed out that mine was the last face Eugene had seen, which meant he would have died believing that I spearheaded his betrayal, after all we had been through together. No one else had the courage to either contradict or attempt to comfort me on this point, except Elena, who sneered at what she deemed my unbelievable degree of willed naïveté.

'Are you just sentimental, or are you completely deaf and blind? Do you even understand the scale of what just occurred?

Did you think you were in a film, or a play, and there was an audience watching in the shadows that will go away believing that you are a heartless villain? Or do you imagine that it's all being counted on your score and you will pay your account on Judgement Day, when Eugene will accuse you in the afterlife? Don't you ever have any wish, Ivan, to outgrow your adolescence, even after everything you have witnessed in the last three years? When will you begin to understand the significance of what you're involved in, and that it's not about you or me or Marc, or any other individual who may come or go?'

3

We have murdered Eugene and re-entered the capital. I have been bundled into the front of the van by the others, unable to walk or say anything from shock. We are passing through outskirts in which already-immense crowds are celebrating with cheering, dance, festoons and crackers. Up ahead and on either side, I can see how balloon and paper-flag sellers are conducting a brisk trade, as are the vendors of candied fruits, sausages, ice-lollies, and cakes. Photographers have set up booths all over the parks and squares to take advantage of this historic occasion, which families and lovers, friends and patriots will want to recall and commemorate in their own ways. There are some that recognise us in our van and jump onto the running boards, pushing their faces in through the windows so as to be able to kiss us. A woman smelling of garlic and sweat has planted herself next to me, and it appears to be her unshaven son that wants to embrace Marc.

Suddenly, in the midst of being pulled forward in an arm-lock by the well-intentioned woman, I spot Robert in the crowd behind her, except he is dressed as a policeman. Amid the raucous distractions, he is involved in deep conversation with a colleague as if they were alone on a stage. In one move synchronising scream and action, I open the door so suddenly that the good middle-aged woman is thrown to the wayside behind us, while I leap onto the board and land on the street running. I push through layers of the crowd and arrive behind Robert. I'm about to ask him what this means, this awful altering of allegiance, when I understand there's no time for talking. His colleague has noticed me and realised I recognise him as Eugene's assassin. But it is all he can do to turn around and make his escape because I have already got my arm around Robert's throat, and am soon dragging him back to the van, oblivious to any resistance. The killer might flee for now, but Robert was our friend. His treachery is a body blow even on this sunless morning when anything seems possible.

Robert makes no effort at excuses. The van continues, the silence inside forming an extraordinarily resilient drop within the tumult around. But very soon I again am the one to break it, because I have recognised another comrade – someone not close to me personally, but who regularly speaks at our meetings – now in uniform, forming part of the human cordon that is keeping some sections of the crowd at bay. This is the only time Robert talks; he has noticed him too, and sullenly affirms as I sit him up beside me that this runs far deeper than anything I can gauge, and my efforts are futile, since everyone I know is implicated, and there'll never be room in a hundred vans to round up all those who are not as they seem, all those in different guises, all those I know who are in the crowd this nightmarish and miraculous dawn.

4

Even in my near-faint condition, I could tell we were being escorted as honoured guests to the very front of the auditorium, that we were expected and were being led to seats actually reserved for us. There was, as if clairvoyantly, even one for me, into which I was placed gently by the two huge arms propping me up. The gigantic flags and banners all around made clear that this was organised on the scale of a national gala, a landmark celebration to mark the end of hostilities, even though until last night, the war as I knew it had been grinding on just as it had for the past three years. Every second banner that, brightly lit from below, had been unfurled from the ceiling or the balconies, and ringed the sides of the enormous theatre and the back of the stage, was scarlet and had at its centre our great symbol; but always next to these were others of equal size displaying the old national flag of the loyalist government, with the eagle and the royal coat-of-arms at its heart.

By now I suspected that everything I'd been fed since the shooting was drugged. I had also extrapolated the obvious – that there were inconceivable alliances at work organising and co-ordinating, who were completely at home with the events of the previous night, and had scripted in the very seats we would occupy on our return from Eugene's murder. But perhaps even these omniscient nexuses had their limits, or they occasionally miscalculated, or they simply couldn't choreograph every level of a nation's history down to the littlest details. They had provided the choir that opened proceedings with a new national anthem, one that none of us knew, but which was obviously intended to signal a fresh start. But from the beginning, despite being led by our most famous conductor, a unanimously cherished treasure, the choir's different parts sounded ill at ease, mutually uncoordinated, and lacking both fervour and practice. Bass interrupted tenor lines, twice the lead soprano missed her cue, and the orchestra in the pit below was possibly going too fast for the singers to find their stride. By the second verse Sir Edgar, with as much briskness as his ramrod stance would allow, had actually walked onto the stage and was conducting the singers directly, but it was no use, and far from rousing the crowd and swelling their hearts, the bad music and the unfamiliar words had the effect instead of setting off the first mutterings of doubt.

It was thus amidst a growing restiveness that I heard my own name being called from the stage, as the host, one of our leading classical actors, and perfect for the purpose, invited 'a devoted foot-soldier of the nation – rather than one of its leaders – to break with tradition and proclaim the renaissance of our beloved motherland. Ivan, who until last evening, was hiding and fighting for his life on behalf of some present in this hall and *against* others among you; Ivan who could not have imagined peace anywhere on the horizon when the sun rose even this morning, let alone a great Day Zero, a new beginning, a glorious reconciliation made possible by the visionary statesmanship of our leaders who had been secretly working towards this day for months; yes, Ivan the ordinary soldier is perhaps the most appropriate candidate to express his awe, surprise and overwhelming gratitude at this unprecedented turn of events, this miracle whereby our collective destiny has been altered overnight, because in doing so, he'll voice the as-yet unformed sentiments ready to pour forth from each and every one of you!'

Although the same sturdy pair of arms once more lifted me as far as the steps to one side of the stage, although there were others to assist me onto the podium where they, along with the great thespian, remained behind me reassuringly throughout, and most of all, though I did not have to find the actual words of gratitude and awe myself because they had been thoughtfully laid out before me (exactly the same ones uttered before, with the leading pronoun altered to 'I'), from the beginning I fluffed my speech. It was as though I couldn't read – I committed each of the cardinal sins of oratory. I was slow, I slurred my words, I interrupted myself, paused to find my line, read paragraphs out of turn, and frequently spoke away from the microphones. After what seemed like a very long time because my throat was as dry as crumpled paper, one of the helpers stepped up behind me and instructed me in a steely voice to faint – to do or say nothing more, simply collapse and stay on the ground. And that was when I realised how loud and disrespectful the crowd had grown, how their shuffling and combined whispers were drowning out even the actor's trained declaiming as he tried to excuse my performance in terms of overawed exhaustion, because even as late as last night, I, like many hundreds in this hall, had been hiding out cold and fearful in the woods, and had been brought in without any sleep or refreshment to be present at this extraordinary birth anniversary.

I was being carried away on a stretcher as the next speaker's name was announced: it was our leader, the man in whose name I had killed and lived underground for the past three years, who I'd imagined was safely in hiding in Moscow. But there was no chance for me to sit up and ask to remain in the auditorium. I was being speeded down the aisle and already we had arrived outside, where we continued through the crowd right until I felt myself being lifted and placed to rest inside a vehicle that turned out to be an ambulance when I opened my eyes. Yet now, for those next few seconds, there was no concern that I had missed such an immense occasion, missed the speech that might finally explain this unremitting nightmare, the speech during which Elena would possibly have been present on stage beside me if only I could have maintained my composure and played my little part, because as I opened my eyes and realised I was inside an ambulance, in that same instant I saw Eugene lying on the opposite side, turned away from me, so that part of his head looked eerily intact. And the last thing I remember is the immeasurable pain that terminated my screaming and banging of my forehead against the cold steel bench.

Paul

1

'OUR DRAWING OF OUR HISTORY teacher offering the royalist salute to the new Communist flag has been discovered, and there will be hell to pay. After all, our region fell to the partisans just weeks ago, and they're still searching for loyalists everywhere. He could get into serious trouble if anyone ever reported some of the things he regularly ranted about in class. He is raging all over the classroom, kicking down chairs, lifting and pushing desks over. As we stare helplessly, he demands the names of those who began passing it around, 'the royalist snakes born of royalist scum,' he calls us, 'who will shamelessly defile the reputations of others,' and our own names are the last words we hear. By sheer force of terrified reflex, Martina and I have simultaneously headed for the back door, and thankfully no one is alert enough to heed the teacher's order to stop us. Anyhow, all his pets, who would have thought nothing of grabbing hold of us or tripping us, sit in the front rows.

'We ascend a dizzying, ever narrowing spiral staircase and my only worry is that Martina might fall through one of the large spaces between the iron steps. Floor after floor goes past: our knees nearly knock our chests as we climb. We have never been to these parts of the building before, always assuming that the older boys and girls would eat us alive for such audacity. As it happens the staircase runs out abruptly and we find ourselves in the middle of an ongoing trial, a summing-up speech against a senior student standing in a corner, probably indicted for a crime similar to ours. The jury of parents and teachers is looking on, but suddenly the fury of the prosecuting master turns on us, who have emerged into the classroom between himself and the Head of school. We realise this is no place to rest and before we can be surrounded, I have grabbed hold of Martina's arm and raced out through the nearest door onto the adjoining passage. Judging from the sound of footfalls, by now our teacher and probably half our class is pursuing us up the spiral stairway. We'd also heard shouts and cries of abuse growing louder as the feet of people slipped and landed on heads below them, but drowning them all out had been the bellow of our history master's voice cursing at our names.

'We have run, it seems, for several minutes, turned many corners and even climbed a few more small stairways, and thinking fast, because I'm aware of the risk that we'll soon come full circle and head straight into the backs of our pursuers, I push open a door and rush into what we later discover is a large bathroom for the cleaning staff of our school.

'And that is where we remained for four days. Every door and wall was made of dark, solid wood, the stalls were in a big circle around us, and we slept on the benches and often found ourselves staring at the black and white squares of the floor. We would never have survived if it wasn't for one of the teachers on the jury in the classroom trial we interrupted, who entered late the first evening long after the hunt had been called off. We'd hidden behind heaps of dirty towels in a cupboard while the bathroom was searched, and remained there afterwards until the teacher convinced us he was a friend who had only brought us some bread.

'Over the next few days a massive search was conducted; a dragnet was cast over the entire school and even the lanes around it. Guards were posted at our homes, and our parents forbidden from contacting us. Our history master took up residence within the building, and searched those wings of the school himself that would be well known to us. But all this we learnt by note, since that first evening was the only occasion our ally showed up in person, although he continued to find ways of getting us food each night, that was left in one of the toilet stalls.

'We remained in one or other of the linen cupboards most of the day for safety though this was only a bathroom used by the cleaners to change and wash before and after work. One of them must have been bringing our food; another would just as likely have betrayed us. We slept on the benches on beds of dirty laundry, but would wake up and wash as soon as it was light. We made sure to dry the sinks we'd used.

'The only positive to arise out of it is that I realised I was even more in love with Martina than before, and that no period seemed boring or too long in the darkness of the cupboards as long as her fingers were in my hand. There was obviously no opportunity to bring it up given our situation, but I knew already by the second day that I was afraid but not unhappy. I only wished I could have dared to hold more than her hand, and that she would agree to sit a little closer.

'The escape took place on the fifth day, when the young, friendly teacher returned to alert us that the guard around the school was being relaxed. They were now certain we were no longer in any of the buildings. We were smuggled out buried deep (and separately) within huge baskets of laundry, bumpily pushed down a long staircase, and just as I realised we were being loaded onto a van, I suddenly heard cries demanding for the van to stop. Then my basket was shoved in on its side, and though I escaped injury because of all the padding, I had to fight my way out to breathe. While struggling myself, I could hear the sounds of a scuffle, and as my head emerged into some air, I felt our van moving. There must have been a leak somewhere, a snitch amongst the cleaners, and we'd certainly be pursued. But just then all I could think of was Martina, and whether her basket had also made it onto the van. I shouted out her name in order to be heard above the noise and the muffling, because whatever new phase was beginning, it only mattered to me that we stayed together. There was no point to my being rescued alone. I would have much preferred to remain indefinitely in our cupboard.'

2

And that was the remarkable, take-it-or-leave-it, straight-faced story with which Paul entered my life, unfolded over many interruptions during our unrelenting plate rounds, as we brought in stacks of used dishes to the main tent from the endless carousing at the long tables near the other end of the field. Finally we had to sit down, both from our aching arms and because I wanted to hear him to the end, although just for a few minutes before the other waiters insisted that we return. There we were, a remarkable duo (or perhaps it was *not* coincidental at all, rather what would soon emerge as a typical phenomenon of this extraordinary day, once things became clearer and other people like us compared their recent experiences), both far from home, uncertain as to how we were brought there unconscious in the backs of vans, quickly handed a few razors and sent to shave and wash from a large pail whilst still drowsy, then handed waiter's suits and aprons and assigned to work at what seemed like a round of organised festivity deep in the southern countryside. Neither of us knew how we would be instructed once this party broke up, whether we were to be rounded up and driven home, or set free to disperse as we pleased. Did all the other 'waiters' have such stories of sudden exile and itinerancy? Should we feel afraid or secure; should we plan an escape or accept things as they happened? Most of all, we each wondered without being able to discuss it with anyone else, should we risk trusting one another?

In fact, the oddest and yet most reassuring thing was that the only faces we all recognised instantly, when we had a chance to break through the crowds for a quick (shared) cigarette – once the dining was over and everyone thronged around the stage at the centre of the field – were those of three of the country's most celebrated performers, obviously transported from the capital just like ourselves, although they had probably not been dumped unconscious into the back of a van: our leading clown, folk singer, and the wench whom everyone in the cities was curious to see because she had raced naked through a forest in her debut film. Of course, this didn't feel like a crowd that often visited a cinema, and she played her part suitably as the demure maiden in local costume, standing to one side of the stage, while the clown and the singer worked away at a double act, in which the clown in his eager nervousness kept trying to brush down his hair and smooth his suit in order to meet his sweetheart, whereas his mother the singer wanted him to ditch her and come out to celebrate the most unexpected and important day in the long history of his people. This he tried to dodge in the most ingenious ways, while she threw everything she had at him from her armoury of songs, from the humblest country tune to the most soul-swelling of patriotic hymns, in a vain attempt to rouse his non-existent sense of historic occasion.

Like everyone around us trying to stir themselves to spontaneous merriment on this enforced festival day, outside of any expectation or calendar, on a borrowed field that misty afternoon, ordered to forget their dead of the last three years as if it had all been a bad dream, we too were lost in their antics, and momentarily freed from the unaddressed misgivings just below the sounds of our laughs. I imagine many locals in the crowd had questions too, even though villages like this one (and my own), despite our best efforts to convince them of their inherent closeness to *our* cause (that of the peasants and the workers, a great Revolution just like the one that had transformed our mighty ally to the east), had always tried to keep an equal distance from both parties in the war. I, who had initially been dispatched to my own district for just this purpose, had never understood this deep-rooted reluctance to be involved. In fact, it was my consistent failure to recruit friends and fighters for our side – even amongst people who had known me as a boy, who otherwise trusted me, listened to me, and would never dream of betraying me – that led to my transfer from the propaganda wing into the fighting arm within three months. An expedient decision was taken up above: there would be all the time in the world to convince villagers to support us once we'd secured some actual territory.

But now, in the fragile tranquillity of standing there among them, it was clear to me that perhaps they thought of today as simply another incomprehensible imposition, unleashed upon their heads by unknown agencies in the capital, to be seen through while the going was good. Until yesterday we'd tried to convince them about a war, and either faction had killed them in turn when they wanted no part of it; today we had joined forces and invited them to an equally ludicrous feast.

And yet, as I rose to full consciousness in the space of that cigarette after the numb, drowsy activity of the last many hours, such questions could not remain distant ones for me – my involvement in events from the previous night onwards made every new twist seem especially sinister and personally threatening. Of course, what I could not have known at the time was that such drowsiness had in fact been merciful, a craft of sorts that would soon crumble but for now was keeping me from drowning, from disappearing under the combined pull of so many irresistible currents: my grief for Eugene and the yet-to-explode panic of losing Elena, the sensation of sliding down a long darkness without beginning or end along with the rest of my ordinary countrymen, and finally, most submerged for now, most buried of all – my nameless, shapeless, tasteless fear about my own immediate survival.

3

But the next phase of my story is all about Paul. Paul, who leaped onto the truck that was headed for the border with a smile and without a hint of doubt, as if only mulish folly or unforgivable dithering could induce anyone in our position to even consider taking the trucks returning to the capital. If we were finally being offered a free choice, Paul knew exactly what he wanted. His clarity, even in a muffled voice spoken to the side of my face, was exemplary: there are certain opportunities we have to seize – the window of time is very brief. In the last few days something throughout the country had steadily gone insane, and he for one could hold his questions. If they were actually letting him go, he was going to jump ship with a smile.

For those few hours Paul was wonderful, because he slept without a break right through our journey to the border, against all the odds, against the worries and the jolts of the much-damaged road, eventually settling into comfort upon a mattress made up of folded sacking and with my lap for a pillow. I frequently gazed upon him, stealing glances while he slept, full of an affection that had no place in an acquaintance of seven hours. Strongly made though he wasn't tall, lean and muscled with brown all-weather hair, and I kept recalling the smile he turned on like a tavern lamp, when everything around him was in shadow.

As it transpired, his bold leap had led the way not only for me but for nine of the other 'waiters', and although most of us were not too forthcoming with talk, or trust, as the truck braved through the late afternoon into dusk, their earlier speech had made evident that they hailed from different regions of the country. It wasn't as though we all fell asleep: most of us simply sat around looking up or ahead or to the sides, at the endless, darkening woods or at the sky with its brief, distant, sunset glow, or the road behind that we soon couldn't see any more. Perhaps in our silence we were all contemplating the vehicle in which we travelled, as it conveyed us between mystery and mystery. Whose orders were we unknowingly following, and why should we believe what we had been told? Even if there was only one soldier escorting us, who rode with the driver in the cab, it wouldn't take any more than him to stop by a wood somewhere and gun all eleven of us into oblivion. Were we all inconvenient troublemakers who'd been too stunned to step in line immediately, and too full of memories to discount the last three years? Did that make us natural allies as we moved through the bowels of the reconstituted state towards a smooth excretion of the undesirables? But then why had our neighbour, a Western ally, agreed to accept us – perhaps they were doing our 'revolution' a favour, but of what sort? Was *Elena* doing me a favour, but of what sort? Did I owe my life to her intercession, or else why wasn't I at the bottom of the river like the man I spent a month with in a cellar, with whom I'd surely and amply plotted the downfall of Elena's new masters? And most of all, was it credible, no matter what Elena's new powers, that they would allow us to freely vanish without any price to pay, any form of imprisonment or surveillance?

That was the point at which my longing for responses repeatedly short-circuited, because I looked around and felt unable to identify the near-certain informers among us. Thankfully I could also intermittently return to longing for Elena, recalling (curiously) memories from our early months, rather than raiding desperately, as one would expect, the last two weeks for any signs of her involvement in all this. I suppose I needed the respite. So I remembered the months when I was put to work printing leaflets in our 'head office' (the little two-room rooftop apartment in Elena's neighbourhood, where the afternoon sun shone upon my table), during the post-war period in late '45 when we were considered to be harmless agitators and were therefore still allowed to operate legally, and I was directly under her command, which at first drove her to discontinue spending the nights with me, since, as she never tired of repeating, we were now involved in a much more serious endeavour, part of a higher undertaking. By choosing this path, surely I could see how I must make that sacrifice with her. But – when I still refused to stop coming up from behind and kissing her neck, or slipping my fingers down her shirt – if she had to state it baldly since I didn't appear to understand any other way, she was my boss, and that drew the line, she insisted, before looking furious when I sheepishly confessed that thinking of her as my boss only aroused me more.

But so often she would weaken when we were alone, and we ended up covering each other's faces with kisses, the softest, fiercest, warmest, hardest, most tender and most searching kisses. Despite resting against the back of the truck, I found myself flailing momentarily amid my memories, of taking hold of her lower lip or kissing her eyelids, the caress of her downy cheek, the distinct fragrances around her neck and in her hair, the breasts just visible below the check shirts she usually wore. I remember then being afraid of waking Paul and of being spotted by the others, because of the heaves I couldn't control, of dry retching and lack of breath, and the tears I tried to squeeze back. Eventually Elena had yielded to my relentless pressure, and we had stayed together at her place, and after the first night we slept together regularly once more, Elena's sorry (but accurate) justification to herself being that we clearly got much more good work done during the day if she just let me have my way each night, and therefore overall it could be seen as a strategy that was *beneficial* to our cause (I always nodded earnestly at that point). One of those mornings when we'd spread out sheets on the office floor after working late, we were awakened by 'Cagney' himself, our leader who looked so much like the firebrand actor (and had no idea of his secret nickname). He appeared disappointed in Elena and gave us a brief talking-to about the sanctity of our workplace: I tried to look suitably ashamed and even whispered to her to explain about the effectiveness of our new strategy, entirely devised to hasten the coming of the Revolution, but she only pinched my stomach hard under the sheets and refused to speak to me all morning.

Elena's even now breathtaking body and the many angles I seized it from, the diverse ways to clamber over, slither beneath, entangle with, grasp and savour her various perfect parts, all the incomparable alternations of soft and firm. I tried to hold on to the few glimpses I could manage for as long as possible, but they were soon mixed up with recollections of another early and happy episode. She'd warned me about a big pro-monarchy procession that would take over her area that afternoon, in which most of her neighbours would be out with large flags, the cowards and the bastards all, and of course you could imagine the numbers of police, secret as well as visible, out in force to compile their lists so that they could persecute each person afterwards that had been absent from the march. But I thought all this would only add to the amusement of me strolling through the crowds and up her stairs to visit her, and disregarded her half-hearted caution.

By the time I arrived, the crowd was greater than I'd have guessed, and altogether more drunk, more raucously affable than usual (a sign already of the government's weakening grip; the capital would fall to us before the year was out) – all of which made it steadily more impossible for the police to impose any sort of rank or timing upon their progress. It almost seemed a conscious ruse, not so alcoholic and unruly after all, the way the swirl kept swallowing and digesting the few hapless blue-shirts within it. And it was an experience and an entertainment to push through this gregarious disintegration, shaking dozens of hands, raising my voice to join in a new song or the chant of a slogan that might have nothing to do with the government or the monarchy, swigging from a few beer-bottles passed to me in affectionate approval, and occasionally waving at Elena, who stood smiling at us from her balcony with a bottle in her hand marked out against the grey sky, beside her scowling mother, certainly furious at me for drawing attention to them by waving.

I suppose I thought of that scene because of its contrast with the crowds I'd encountered earlier that day: neither in the capital that morning nor in the field while we all watched the clown together, was there anything of that bluffness, that reckless, warm-hearted disorder, from three years before. Or perhaps it was the memory of Elena hovering above me then, and the great distance I seemed to have been hurled in so short a time – so far now from such a moment when she had felt so close, so familiar, so living and attainable and real, only a few floors above me, a mere staircase away.

4

It was my turn to be waking-dead for the next leg of the journey. There was no trouble at the border despite our universal lack of papers. Normally the border was open because relations had always been relaxed, and inextricable, with our western neighbour: most local people went to market as well as to graze and marry on the other side, and there had never been any fencing beyond the checkpoints. But we, who had held this corner of the country for nearly six months now, had had to initiate a programme of tight and armed supervision, complete with fences and regular checkpoints, because of the open support shown by their new pro-Western regime for our royalists. The worst – infamous to us but little known outside the country – incident that had finally forced our hand, was their barring of three hundred desperate villagers a year before, who had fled an oncoming army purge (a hunt for partisan sympathisers that had predictably turned into one of the regular massacres of 'deterrence'), yet were simply held at gunpoint at the border until enough forces arrived to round them up. *And then they evaporated the evidence.* At great risk to themselves, on territory far from our strongholds and where the border was no longer a neutral refuge to be taken for granted in an emergency, some of our boys had searched for a week, but never found the ditches in the steep woods all around in which those villagers must still lie. Of course this, and countless instances of such behaviour, the Americans and the slavish Western press never reported, although full details complete with eye-witness accounts were openly available for reference in several of our local newspapers.

Yet this evening we were friendly again with our neighbours, open house, no questions asked. But while Paul was delighted and most of the others noticeably relieved (we had all been inwardly incredulous about being allowed past this point), to me it made everything more sinister, more beyond limit or encompassing, even more vertiginous. *What was going on?* Had everyone gone crazy, as Paul so simply diagnosed? When did I go to sleep and where had I awoken? In an askew world where everything was familiar but nothing unfolded as I foresaw it? Had I been fighting a war in a forest like those legendary lost souls scattered on islands all over the Pacific, who were still being found each month hiding from 'the enemy'? How far and deep could this possibly run; exactly how many layers and knots did this alliance involve; and how pre-planned could it be? This was more than a war: how could an entire country, and its neighbour, be forced to overlook the most awful, conflicted and immediate past and run overnight to this new clockwork?

It was Paul's excitement that roused me hours later as we approached Market Square in the heart of E.. It had been just the two of us since we crossed the border, as no one else wanted to exchange one capital for another, and perhaps wisely had decided to disperse elsewhere around the country. After fifteen hours of working and journeying together, we had parted with odd, mistrustful handshakes without even learning which of us had been on the same side during the war and who amongst us was informer or recent enemy?

Then, with our wages from the banquet, we'd hired ourselves a horse-drawn cart for the three-hour ride to E.. Dawn found us plodding along a muddy riverbank, winter branches marking out the dull sky above, the pleasant crunching of iced leaves our constant accompaniment (the land was flat, and the river almost silent). Another daybreak, another riverbank; but there was too much ache and lethargy in my back and limbs just then to make anything of the coincidence (besides, who was there to share it with but an impetuous sixteen-year-old excited by everything?).

After two hours of this shortcut, as our old-fashioned driver insisted it was, we finally met the steeply uphill new highway on the outskirts of the city, and Paul and I realized suddenly why its completion had been so loudly celebrated. The astonishing

American-built bridge-road on pillars fifty feet high taking in woods and rivers in its effortless stride, with gigantic slides that opened on either side into huge clearings in the forest meant for new factories and settlements; all this we knew about at home from legend and rumour, and from the unrelenting military propaganda that had promoted it all of this past year as if it was one of their own achievements, as being merely one of the many fruits of 'peace' our country would immediately earn, 'peace' on their terms of course, but peace that would win us powerful friends with deep pockets, large armies, and goodwill in their hearts. Friends that our neighbours had wisely adopted, and look at the society they now fostered, and along with it we had been repeatedly shown photographs of their recent elections, and of this miraculous suspended highway that was completed in record time and would allow for the expansion of their capital E. to almost twice its ancient size.

'You know we have to hurry,' we heard our driver admonish his horse, before he turned around to explain, 'people like us are not allowed on the bridge from seven in the morning until midnight. They complain we get in the way of the cars and lorries and slow everyone down. If they catch us they'll fine me my day's wages, but the policeman will go further and search the cart and steal everything valuable you have.'

But that pace was just fine for Paul, who moved to the front to ask him about each new construction he saw: the villas and the smaller houses, the towers of apartments supposedly 'for workers' whose tops even I could see though I was lying slouched against the side of the cart, the half-completed factories and warehouses in the distance, the newly cleared lands to both sides of the river. I dropped even lower, curled up and kept trying to shut out Paul's excited cries, but it was useless. All I could do was picture everything he was describing, imagine brand-new homes and towers and parks under this sky with the lid firmly screwed on, another morning with all the light throttled out of it.

'Yes, yes, all this is new. While you people continued to fight this is what happened here. You don't know about it because those Communists closed the border. Why they did that I don't understand. Drivers like me made half our earnings bringing your folks to market in the morning and taking them home at dusk. Now of course the markets are gone because the fields are over there, but today is a special day. It's the first time since last year that anyone arrived from over the border. You are my first passengers from there in months. In fact, it's the first chance I've had to speak the language since last spring, so I'm sure there are many mistakes.

But the driver too had questions for Paul, about recent developments on our side of the border. 'What's happened? All sorts of stories are doing the rounds. The guards said there are celebrations in every village, with food and drink and dancing. Is the war really over? Did you know that would happen? Why did you come over now after surviving the worst, when there is finally peace and celebration?'

Paul handled the moment masterfully. 'Well, the first thing you do when there is peace is go on a holiday, and that's what we both decided. Ivan wanted to come to E. and so did I. We met on the way and here we are together. We wanted to be the first to step over that open border. I'd heard about all the changes, and more than anything I wanted to witness them for myself.'

The driver was mildly surprised to learn we weren't brothers. But the last phase of the journey was quiet as he sped up, anxious to be in the centre of E. by early morning. Paul grew tired of pointing out things that I refused to sit up and notice, and returned to the back of the cart, placed his head on my chest as though I was indeed his brother, and dozed off. I think that was the first time I realised we were in this together, whatever it was and wherever it would lead us, and that Paul took this implication for granted. I adjusted myself so that his head could rest easily, and when I was sure he was asleep, stroked his curly hair. In that way we finally approached the old E. that I recognised, after a steep and rapid descent, into the narrow, uneven lanes of its heart.

Just over an hour later we had jobs, at the Hotel Bristol in Market Square, in the kitchen and the lobby respectively. The cobbled streets had awakened Paul, and the first thing he noticed was his mother's cousin Marlene, bidding a guest farewell into a shiny black Daimler outside the great front-porch of the hotel. He had enough discretion to let her finish her job, but the moment she turned around, he began shouting her name without any warning (our driver dropped his reins temporarily from being startled). Yet his enthusiasm was matched by the warmth of her acknowledgement, for giant though she was even from this distance across the square, she couldn't check herself but began running towards us at an impressive pace, all of which together with Paul's earlier screams, quite upset our horse which now wanted to flee in the direction of the river away from the source of the confusion. Paul apologised repeatedly to the driver, shouted out further calming words to the horse, turned around to me and explained that this aunt was one of the best, which made it the second lucky thing to have happened to us today, after being allowed across the border without difficulty. 'The tide is turning, I can feel it,' he yelled. 'Just look at her, she's a darling. The best thing about her is that you always know it's her even from such a long way away.'

So that is how exactly twenty-nine hours after Eugene's murder, I came to be the new 'runner' at the concierge service of the Hotel Bristol in E., our pro-Western neighbouring capital.

The Hotel Bristol

1

'I've recently lost a right-hand man, who's gone to work for an insurance firm, because he insisted his new wife wouldn't tolerate the hours here. And he even met her on the job!' Franz explained, speaking with what I later understood to be characteristic slowness (not just because he thought he was talking to a foreigner), and taking further care to disdainfully enunciate the word 'wife'. 'Meanwhile there are no suitable assistants available in E. just now, which proves underneath all the improvements this is still a one-horse town. So the management requests me to commence the perilous process of training another one up from scratch, which is asking a lot at my age, but what are the options? This isn't Paris, or Vienna, or London. There all we had to do was call a friend in the business, and within an hour, we'd have a list of fully qualified young fellows to choose from.

'Now, I can't tell straightaway whether you'll make it that far: I don't even know if you want to, but I need to fill the gap with at least a reliable runner. In a certain sense the work is simple – in the first stage it only calls for agility and perseverance: you have to be prepared to turn swiftly on your toes, sleep on your feet, and never take 'no' for an answer. Later on, a couple of additional attributes are essential, but if these aren't qualities you recognise in yourself, I know they're looking for help in a few of the kitchens, so you can just walk out and present yourself once more to Marlene. But don't pretend to be what you are not, or I'll find you out within the first evening, and we'll have wasted each other's time.'

After she'd introduced me and left us alone together (knowing there were vacancies in Franz's department), I had answered his question about my previous working experience with a list of my varied occupations since leaving school: post-boy, waiter, dark-room assistant, chauffeur, bus conductor, and finally a dogsbody at a detective agency, dispatched to cover, and submit detailed reports of, numerous day-to-day shadowing assignments. That last one had actually been my first job upon arriving in our capital four years ago (my boss was my mother's uncle), and I was invariably assured that each and every case involved assuaging or justifying inflamed marital suspicions. Yet only a fraction of the suspects I had watched ever seemed to pursue any dalliances. Most of them, usually men, met other (male) acquaintances in pubs and cafés, spoke in low voices, or retired straightaway together into a private chamber. Frequently my subjects whiled away entire days alone. Sometimes they visited apartments, but when I returned at the end of a session to check up on their hosts in order to complete my report, few seemed likely candidates for affairs of the heart, unless I conclude a very large proportion of our targets were men who practised love in the unusual way.

Thus, even before I met Elena, although I was a greenhorn in the capital and didn't recognise many of its prominent personalities – a number of whom I was soon to consider crucial allies and leaders – I guessed that I was in fact hunting political prey. My great-uncle made no secret of his royalist sympathies, and it wouldn't have surprised me if he'd willingly undertaken surveillance duties on behalf of the regime. Even someone as apathetic, provincial and ignorant as I used to be, who only kept his mouth shut and his eyes on the girls, could scarcely ignore the almost-daily street clashes all around us, the rallies and processions, the constant exchange of arrest anecdotes in any pub you entered. None of this however I shared with Franz in answer to his question, just as I remained silent about my fugitive life during the war. For his benefit, I stuck to the script about tracking extramarital ins and outs. It was sufficient, since this diversity of experience seemed to be exactly what he required.

'Have you heard of Gandhi and his three monkeys?' he asked.

I shook my head. 'I know who Gandhi is.'

'Well, the old man could have been spelling out the job requirements for a concierge. Each of the monkeys is supposed to have its eyes, its ears or its mouth tightly shut. See no evil, hear no evil, and speak none either, is Gandhi's lesson. In fact, you'll soon realise there's not much difference from what you encountered as a detective's assistant, except no one asks you to, no one *wants* you to, file any report. Just list all charges and expenses, and a brief note explaining them. Nothing more.

'But here I am filling your head with much more than you need to know. For now I seek a strong pair of legs, a thick skin and a smooth voice on the telephone. Just say you're calling from The Bristol on my behalf, and it should be sufficient to open most doors.'

A few weeks later, Paul and I would move into a room the size of a generous broom closet, deep in the bowels of the hotel, with a vent near the ceiling that opened just above street-level at the building's rear. By then it seemed as though Franz had overstated the character traits vital for this post, at least to handle the uncomplicated tasks he assigned me: picking up theatre and opera tickets, usually last-minute, forcing through restaurant reservations, hand-delivering important packages, making telephone appointments, conveying unorthodox or sudden requests for withdrawals and deposits to banks, and the occasional warding-off of irate creditors determined to cause a row unless they were allowed to meet certain guests in their rooms to demand their dues. This was clearly unacceptable, no matter how righteous their grounds, but placed no real strain upon me, since we held Malik and Anthony, two extraordinarily proportioned African gentlemen, in reserve for precisely these difficulties. Along with Franz, they had acquired a reputation in E. for smoothing over such creases, and especially for a hothead such as myself, it was something of a wonder to watch these gentle giants leave their daylong games of cards to perform their assignments without breaking sweat. The word 'violence' never entered into it. It was closer to a dance, albeit with one set of extremely unwilling partners, who mostly swirled with their feet well up in the air. They were disturbed only when absolutely necessary, and this was all they'd been retained for. The price the establishment charged for such a service was to discreetly inform the concerned client about the incident, since the hotel could step in on his behalf just once more, ever. This policy was adhered to without exception, I was told, and somehow it goaded people to settle their affairs outside our walls, since I never witnessed any guest being expelled during my employment.

As Franz promised, a mention of The Bristol eased almost every situation I had to manage, and anything more delicate or demanding, he was personally on the case. I will not spell out what I imply by that, although for my fellow countrymen struggling under years of dictatorship and strife, much of it might be difficult to imagine, especially upon our doorstep. Ever since the Western takeover of our neighbour thirteen months before, our people had been receiving swarms of rumours across the border of all conceivable forms of decadence and indulgence thriving in the city of E.. Some of the more far-fetched stories were admittedly propaganda, and I can confirm that, since we partisans ourselves cooked them up. Yet I can confirm now that those canards about rampant debauchery were nowhere near as interesting or sinister as some of the other encounters that took place regularly at 'the Dowager' (as I soon learned to call The Bristol), between men (usually) who certainly never took their clothes off. In fact, gossip about the more mundane human vices was common even among other departments in the hotel – Paul, who worked in the kitchen, told me often that everyone there speculated endlessly about how the concierge desk helped procure companions for several guests, facilitated infidelities for others, and above all how much and exactly what the inscrutable Franz knew about the surprising weaknesses or fatal-if-revealed character twists of the many eminent personages who were his long-term clients. What was possibly far more scandalous, and going on right in the open, was everything no one ever gossiped about.

Because, although virtually every guest at The Bristol took care to adhere to its unspoken golden rule – that no unseemly scenes must ever take place in any of her public areas, since the Dowager had a reputation to uphold – and even though Franz dealt with the most sensitive matters of all strictly behind closed doors, and Malik and Anthony warded off any curious queries from other staff members with the most winning and irresistible of grins, after a while it was impossible for me not to sense that a great hive of questionable activity flourished all around me, and that Franz was probably aware of every vital meeting that took place here. Every now and then he would himself drop a hint with a smile ('You know that man who just walked out, Ivan, half of the police forces in Europe would be interested to learn he is in E. tonight.'), but never elaborate on the story behind such a remark. Normally, I awaited orders in a little room behind his office, but when he was attending to someone in private, or receiving an important phone call, he would send me out to man the front desk for a few minutes. On such occasions, I would put into practice the training I'd received as a detective, and take a closer look at several innocuous-seeming meetings in progress all around, in the bar and the restaurant, at the lobby and outside the lifts, or when certain parties left the hotel one after another at precise intervals, clearly to regroup elsewhere. Within just a few days of joining, I gradually understood (without anyone having to spell it out for me) that this vast, pillared, gilt-edged honeycomb was used by many as a rendezvous, or further still, as an actual market-place, where Westerners from all over Europe met frequently with each other to conduct transactions, as well as with visitors from the Americas and the Near East. As I stood by and watched men of different nationalities, dressed in suits of varying cuts, greet one another in the lobby and go on to the bar or upstairs to one of their rooms, or sometimes move to a sofa directly in front of me to confer closely, I would try to imagine the subjects of their discussions, as well as make guesses as to which of them were well-known tycoons in their own countries, which ones were diplomats and official representatives, and which notorious criminals? So this is what the West is like, I thought, recalling everything we had been told during the war. This is what it means 'to do business'. Then I wondered if perhaps it was here, in a suite somewhere in the Dowager, that the present fate of my country had been planned. After all, the venue was ideal for our leaders to meet and arrange such a plot, screened from the gaze of our people (and the men that were dying in their names), yet less than an hour away on the new miracle-road from the border.

In fact, Franz would occasionally tell me with a wink that a particular task I had fulfilled had been requested by a countryman of mine. Although with the reopened border they were once more fairly common to notice or hear in the streets and markets of E., the prices at The Bristol, the general poverty of our people, and the few notes of our war-ravaged currency that they probably had in their bags and wallets, kept all but a tiny number away from our door. Which is why, whenever I passed through the lobby or took a brief turn at the concierge's desk, I looked all the more keenly at the faces of those compatriots who did come in, who had a meeting in the bar or the lobby, or stayed a couple of nights, or those who approached me to see Franz about a personal favour. Part of me was always expecting to spot a renowned enemy, someone from the military, the royal family, or the former government, a man whom until recently we had vowed to kill, but now I must serve with a smile. Or, much worse, I dreaded the moment when I would look up one day into the face of a recent friend. In either case, I doubt I would have been able to react with restraint and composure.

But I was fortunate at least in this: no one from my earlier life ever crossed my path without warning during those months at The Bristol. And if I found myself on occasion next to a fellow countryman at a pub during my free afternoons, I claimed to be just an ordinary arrival, who had been lucky to get here straight after the ceasefire and find a job.

I wasn't alone in trying to interpret the ever-altering patterns within the walls of the Dowager, or to tell apart the ordinary from the suspicious: there was a bunch of designated policemen who liaised every other day with Franz, in private of course, mostly over the phone. And although he always sent me out of the room once I had passed him the receiver, I realised within the first month that he in fact was like a great ringmaster, a tamer of wild creatures who would otherwise tear each other apart with their teeth, the one who fed all parties with a subsistence diet of information, just enough to keep everyone in equilibrium. Enough arrests, enough warnings, enough assistance in mutually antagonistic clandestine purposes. If I'd been a neutral, it would have been a demonstration to admire, in how Franz maintained his composure and held himself above everything, untainted, unruffled, never ceasing to shine in his lustrous black suits, distributing favours and (probably) receiving rewards ceaselessly like the many-armed gods of the East, all three of Gandhi's monkeys fused into one virtuoso that thrived – with nature's own indifference and zest – upon the number of battle-lines drawn across the world.

But I was a warrior, who until recently had taken sides, bled much and lost even more. I would have had to be insane to be indifferent. Our confrontation was only a matter of time; only I never suspected which corner of the sky it would fall from.

2

After ten weeks at my job, I browsed through my new diary one night; I'd never kept one before, and it was still something of a mystery that I felt such a need at all. Because it was nothing like a chronology of daily occurrences that I maintained, rather the opposite – everything but the day-to-day, everything odd, incongruous, sudden, far-fetched, and out of keeping with the tranquil routine that enveloped my waking life and often seemed more suffocatingly surreal than any of my recent surprises. No wonder its pages were full of unlikely connections, and constant leaps of time and logic.

For example, after one especially long evening of sitting with my work-mates watching their card-games, occasionally holding up my glass for more brandy, and half-listening to the harmless gossip and dirty jokes, I returned to our room, and instead of collapsing into bed with my clothes on, I switched on the desk-lamp and began a new page in my diary. It had occurred to me that these Monday nights were the first time in over three years that I'd actually spent time with people who hadn't belonged to our side during the war.

'We wanted new inheritors of the earth; they were our single constant point of reference, but when did we last speak to one of them? Who was I fighting for? When did I ever discover them? How many times during the war, or even before it began, had I concentrated and imagined something simple outside my immediate experience – an old schoolmaster in the mountain district putting on his coat each morning and walking down the path to work; a woman in the valley resting momentarily from labour amid the peach orchards?'

In the course of writing, further distinctions forced themselves upon me – *'The elite versus the people, the unseen against the seen. Reality or the great game; Elena's path or mine – was truth to be sought in immersing myself within the sheer plenitude of everyday life, or in those rarefied realms that she had chosen? There were numberless actual people on the one hand to belong and dissolve among; a few corridors and vaulted rooms on the other, in which entire nations were mere counters on a global chessboard and the players always remained in the shadows.*

'Live in the all, and then you will be happy,' I recalled Elena once quoting to me an expansive promise by Goethe. *'But then she had succumbed to everything wrong – her prideful delusions and games – so far from 'the all' they were. And so far from the all seemed our war: why had we been instructed to hate and mistrust so many of our fellow countrymen as reactionaries and likely betrayers, when all they wanted was to work by day and gather harmlessly to drink in the evenings?*

'Such distinctions seemed so facile, the way we'd once defined

them and I now saw I had merely memorised. How many irredeemably "un-revolutionary" souls, including the Eugenes from amongst our own ranks, would have had to die before our vision was ever realised?' But I never recalled these questions being raised once during those three years, let alone satisfactorily answered.

'And what then did events signify? What did they point towards: how to decipher their purpose? That anything could happen was clear, anything could happen and everything did. This was the only thing to say about life that you'd not immediately have to modify or retract. It was the sum of all that was. But what does that imply for me? Why did I feel so supple and able only recently, and yet now I'm so broken and lost?'

For a while I tried an experiment in 'balance', trying to keep in my head all the time as many simultaneous ideas as possible, believing that the more I could hold on to a full view of things, the more likely I would be in a state of peace. So I chose to focus on the cessation of war and slaughter, the soon-to-be-explained presence of my close friends at the highest levels of the new government, the gradual, if diluted, introduction of some of our most crucial policies, and, not least, my own precarious but ongoing survival. This particular phase, the attempt of which lasted a fortnight, culminated in the reflection that *'in fact, meaning is like a magic wand, and it is up to us to wield it. The world is what it is, cranking out the consequences, the entire range of possible outcomes, just like nature, indifferently and without respite. Yet we can decide which events to confer significance upon, and how much, and which to forget or deny. No one underwrites any value but us – just as money would be mere paper or gold a shiny metal in a land where no one prized it – and we can change our minds on the matter whenever we wish.*

'But this business is a black art,' I concluded the paragraph, *'of endowing and subtracting meaning. It takes great experience and*

a level head, and still the fumes of phenomena are very strong, and frequent error followed by injury is both costly and inevitable.'

Finally, I decided that *'perhaps the true distinction lies between those who wake up every morning to the luxury of spinning themselves a story and the freedom to believe in it, as I happen to enjoy at least for the moment, and those who awaken trapped in one they cannot recognise, a story imposed upon them, like our Jewish citizens during the German occupation, or my countrymen today across the border.'*

Exceptional incidents and dreams also made their way into that book of the non-real, the non-daily. For instance, the diary began out of a wish to remember an encounter with a guest, a Mr Goldman, who stayed only two days and was visiting from America. One evening he wandered into our office, with no clear purpose, and after a while Franz asked him why he seemed so morose. Goldman replied he was a native of E. and a survivor of one of the great death camps in Poland. After the war there was no one to return home to, so he'd made for New York, where he now had a family with children. Last year, he had felt a strong need to visit his birthplace at least once. Their house was exactly as they'd left it: the present resident willingly let him in. Inside too Goldman realised not much had changed; in fact, most of their furniture was still being used. Even the very chair he sat on had been his father's morning chair, in which he would routinely take his tea.

Yet Goldman was refuted when he pointed this out simply as an observation; the new owner claimed to have bought it himself. Goldman, not out of stubbornness, got up and turned the chair upside down, remembering one of his father's schemes on the eve of the transportation. 'Mark everything with the family name, to avoid confusion when we return.' He was right about the chair, and that was when the new owner could no longer contain himself.

'Come on, Baruch Goldman, why don't we stop the comedy and get to the real reason you're here? Nobody comes over from America to be nostalgic about a chair. You want me to spell out why you came? It's obvious as the nose on your face, if you don't mind my saying so. You want to pick up what you buried. It's a familiar story; I understand. You buried your valuables hoping you would return. And I'm a reasonable man. So whatever we uncover, we'll split it evenly. That is my promise, if *you* will now be honest.'

But he wasn't as reasonable as he claimed, because nothing Goldman could plead would convince him otherwise. Simply put, a Jew without a secret plan, without resources hidden away, was impossible for him to conceive. He cajoled, he argued, finally he abused, and Goldman realised it was pointless and left. That was twelve months ago, and the man had continued behind him down the street whispering threats and promises until he turned the corner.

For some reason he didn't mention, Goldman was back again in E. this year, and today, irresistibly, his feet had led him once more to the old street (in a quarter nearby that Franz knew well). But now the house was abandoned, in awful condition, beyond repair. It looked like it had been empty for years: most of the brickwork was exposed, damp had started to spread, and the upper windows were blind, empty holes. Nothing else was different about the street or the quarter.

He'd knocked at the neighbour's door, someone else he didn't recognise. But when he identified himself, she instantly had a lot to tell him. 'Oh, my God, so *you* caused all the problems. We all know who you are. The day after you visited, peace disappeared from this street. First the hammering started; then began the digging. He took apart the walls, he dug deep into the floor, then he thought of the roof. Six months later, when everything was broken, every plant uprooted in the garden, he realised he hadn't the money to fix things. So that is why the house remains as you see it. It's ugly and unfortunate, but at least there is silence.'

The next morning, Mr Goldman was gone. A few days later, at four in the morning, I went to my diary, and while Paul slept behind me, wrote down the dream I had just awakened from. I'd never done anything like it before.

'We were meeting in a disused railway compartment, the core of the old group – Elena, Marc, Eugene, and somehow Paul was with us as well – when suddenly we realised we would soon be surrounded. People in uniform with guns were racing towards us on the platform. We had been betrayed, yet as they drew close it became clear that everyone outside actually belonged with us. Those about to capture us were our friends.

'There was nothing to do but split up and run: Paul and I formed a natural pair. We jumped out onto the opposite platform and headed straight for our hotel lobby (yes, strangely enough it was The Bristol, but transported in the dream to its neighbouring capital), an entrance to which opened directly into the station. Instead of stairs though, what faced us was a long, twisting, red-carpeted slope going all the way up to the roof. We took our chances and ran up because our pursuers were now coming through the door, but at the very top we realised we'd trapped ourselves since there was no exit onto the roof from here. So Paul followed my instructions and we switched off the light and waited in the shadows.

'A. was the first to reach us, but he was expecting to follow us onto the roof, so it was easy to step out of the dark and push him hard over the banister. He fell with an echoing cry, and almost immediately after he landed shots were fired in our direction. Two of them missed me only because they bounced off the fire bucket in my left hand, with which I'd been about to attack A.. In a flash, I hurled it at Robert who was shooting at us from the floor

below. He had no resistance when it hit him on the head, and landed just beside A. at the bottom. Now we had them scared, and made the most of our momentary advantage, running down one floor in the hope of an exit. But here was a brightly lit reception hall where people usually purchased tickets for the cinema, with nothing offering us any shelter. We entered the first room we found, but the game was up. Soon three men – all comrades of mine but today their faces were unyielding – burst through the door, and Paul and I were taken prisoner.

'When we were outside again, we had to thread through a crowd entering the cinema. This time it was Paul who provided the cue; he shoved his captor in the stomach and pushed his way into the theatre. I kicked backwards sharply onto J's ankles and followed close behind him. The newsreels had started but people were still entering in columns along the aisles. Paul immediately climbed onto the banister rail in the middle of the upper circle stairway and slid all the way down, a silhouette against an immense image of aeroplanes raining parcels over Berlin. Even in the midst of our emergency, I could hear his long yell of glee.

'At the bottom of the upper circle we opened a trapdoor that thankfully led onto one of the lower roofs. From here escape was relatively easy, since no building was more than a few feet away from its neighbour in the old city. Leaping from roof to roof, we finally dropped through an open skylight and down the stairs of a house, the backdoor of which gave straight onto the railway tracks, a few hundred metres beyond the station. It took us less than a minute to climb on board the first open car of a slow-moving goods-train and shut the door behind us.

'When I had the courage to peer outside I realised we were in the mountains, which was territory I knew well from the recent months of hiding. I glanced up and down the great length of the train as it struggled uphill, and once I was sure no one was watching out for us, we jumped together into a soft-looking ditch overgrown

with heather. A brief hike through the woods and we were at one of our old camps, abandoned now, but near a village full of friendly locals. There I was instantly recognised; we were fed, and bathed in the lake, and spent the next few days in complete tranquillity, as I showed Paul around the routines of the old life, the trails and caves and streams, the lookout points, the places Elena and I disappeared to in order to be alone. This was how it went for close to a week, as the old security returned to envelop me, the rhythms of a life with which I had been most content, a time that I had secretly not wanted to end. We talked late into the warm nights, the stars so close above us, bright and ripe and ready to fall.

'Returning home from one such stroll, we found a crowd waiting for us outside the very first hut of the village. We pushed our way through, puzzled, but everything was cleared up when I realised my grandmother was standing at the heart of it, surrounded by relatives and well-wishers, so frail and yet expectant, waiting to greet her favourite grandchild. It was her hut; yet no one in the village had told me, and I'd unwittingly wasted the last few days walking past her door each morning. For a full hour we stood embracing, with barely a word spoken, and her somehow filling up my arms even though she was so ill. There was nowhere more to go and nothing needed saying: I could have remained like that forever. But after an hour she was gently prised from me and led away to rest. I was told I could visit later. She never stopped glancing backwards as she went inside, and I felt her embrace for minutes even after waking up, and only when it faded did I begin to write.'

It was an unbroken vision that departed from reality in only two details – the misplacement of Marc and Elena who shouldn't have been inside the carriage with us, but rather amongst our pursuers, and the encounter with my beloved grandmother, who had died during the second year of war, whilst I was in hiding. I didn't know for seven months: it was too dangerous for my mother to trust anyone with smuggling a message – it was a miracle she wasn't arrested just for being my mother. When I found out, I didn't cry, and though I felt guilty for this, Elena had been right in saying it was too far away now and pointless. The only involuntary reaction that overcame me was three days after receiving the news, when I was climbing down from the end of my watch, the birch woods in the valley around me, and suddenly the sky opened up ahead and my breathing stopped and my throat seized up for an instant, as I glimpsed the simple truth that my grandmother *was* dead and I really would *never* see her again. No matter how long I lived, no matter if we won this war one day, she would still be *non-existent,* nowhere to be found on earth. There was no journey I could ever take that could end in her arms again.

But I knew those two altered details in the dream weren't real: they were merely the representation of my wishes, as was the presence of Paul and the return to the idyllic mossy woods of our hideout.

Life wasn't entirely tranquil during those first weeks, though. One Monday night, we arrived home to our single rented room to find our few clothes bundled in the hallway, and the padlock reinforced with an extra lock and chain. Our landlord had obviously been listening out for us, and he emerged to give his reasons. He was bowing to extreme pressure, he claimed, pressure from everyone else in the building (it was a word he used repeatedly in his own defence), as well as from the rest of the neighbourhood and even from the policeman who patrolled our street. So many kinds of pressure too: some had informed him we were politically suspicious – we'd arrived the week after the ceasefire in our own country, so we must have been fleeing something. Others complained about our living together being *morally* suspicious. He couldn't bring himself to name the act within the hearing of decent people, but he forced us to admit we made it worse because Paul was clearly so young. And of course he didn't have to add that we were foreign, which in itself was nothing to be guilty of, except when you considered it on top of all the other reasonable doubts.

So we left that very night in search of new lodgings (and within a few hours ended up in the basement quarters of the hotel, with Marlene's help), quite cheerfully in the circumstances, although I had been taken aback by the hostility of our hitherto placid neighbours. Still, this was just a room; we'd left our country behind a month ago, believing we were running for our lives. Only Paul, who had been reluctantly kept awake many nights by my enthusiastic pronouncements on 'the profound decency of ordinary people', and my newfound resolve to immerse myself in 'the all' by cherishing their goodness and wisdom, couldn't resist urging me to embrace and shake hands with these just and open-hearted neighbours of ours, who'd come out unembarrassed to witness our departure while refusing even to wave us goodbye.

Exile in E.

1

It's much easier to remember the little things, the shared evenings and incidents that made bearable the burden of that pointless time. Paul and I saw each other in passing sometimes during the day without having any chance to speak, but we often dined together in the room behind Franz's office, and remained there over a bottle of cognac as long as no one called for me. Paul was the one with the most stories, owing both to his natural temperament and to his excitement about his new duties. They'd started him off as assistant to the man in charge of the hotel's silverware. Paul was entrusted with polishing and counting every last knife, teaspoon and fork from all the three restaurants at The Bristol, after taking delivery of them from the kitchens each night. (Apparently, since everything was actually made of silver, guest kleptomania was a severe drain on the hotel's cutlery expenses, a little-imagined fact about Western high society that Franz duly confirmed. There was no tactful way to address this, however, unless you actually interrupted someone in the act with the most winning of smiles).

During the month that he served there, I (and sometimes my card-playing comrades) were provided with regular updates on Paul's favourite kitchen colleague, Kapo, who was the man with the awesome duty of feeding the giant dishwashing machine, the miraculous contraption recently imported from America, in which the filthiest dishes and pots were carefully stacked in rows one above another, only to emerge spotless without needing to be moved! Kapo had been specially trained by the salesmen of the company, and he took his complex task very seriously. No one else dared approach this deity, I was informed in a hushed voice one night, when Paul sneaked me into the kitchen for a glimpse of it after Kapo had gone home. It rose three quarters of the way to the ceiling, with different-sized racks for every conceivable type of dish, plate and bowl, and I learnt how Kapo fed it painstakingly one object at a time using a specially provided step-ladder. But Paul couldn't answer for me how the dishes were cleaned without being scrubbed or moved.

We also learned of the irony that the official dish-washer Kapo himself never washed, and that he possessed two shirts, one of which he put through his machine along with the breakfast things each morning. Recently he'd complained of feeling unwell, but the kitchen couldn't spare him a couple of hours to go to the doctor since these weeks had been especially busy. Instead, Head-Chef Roland advised him to take the unprecedented measure of bathing. He even assisted him, by dispatching a man to reception to find out if any of the lower-priced rooms were currently vacant. Then Kapo was escorted to one of them by a bellhop, and thus became the first among us to experience another recently installed American marvel, hot and cold showers, in which you could (reportedly) adjust the water until it came out just right for you. He emerged after an hour in the bathroom, and spent another describing in detail his time inside, and also showed everyone the areas of his body where he'd been scalded without warning. But for a week after that, although his illness seemed to have vanished, Kapo complained of shivering constantly. Being clean had clearly proved too drastic a step for his system.

Still, he'd had a recent row with M Roland after going for three months without shaving with no explanation, especially when clean plates began to arrive on the chef's counter with long strands of hair lying across them. One day Roland summoned him; two sturdy commis-chefs positioned themselves behind Kapo in what was obviously a practised manoeuvre, and grabbed hold of his arms. Without any warning, Roland produced a cleaver, seized Kapo's beard and used it to pull his face close until he could lay the beard onto a chopping board, then lopped off its extra length with one well-timed strike. Kapo was mortally wounded (in his soul), and there seemed no hope for a speedy reconciliation. Franz, who of course had heard the story, observed sagely that the kitchen at present, like our continent, was functioning in a state of 'cold war'.

My own job demanded a high level of discretion, rigorously enforced by Franz, which made it a topic off-limits during the nights when I could join Paul and my other friends in the basement. According to Franz's 'system', there was a cooling-off period after the departure of certain guests during which gossip was strictly forbidden, no matter how tempting the anecdote. As for regular patrons, we were instructed to take our cue from the demeanour of the legendary English manservant, who, it was repeatedly impressed upon us, noticed everything, but with the impassive silence of God. Constricted by such stipulations, I was often just a quiet onlooker at these gatherings. This however changed abruptly one day (soon after we had moved into our room in the basement) when Paul came in and announced how excited several of the boys in his kitchen had been when he mentioned that I'd been a fighter in our civil war.

'What? Are you mad? What did you tell them?'

'That you were a brave partisan, and that I am proud to have you for a friend,' he said, his face disappearing and then beaming at me as he pulled his shirt over his head.

'Paul, I could be hanged if one of your friends reported this. And you too, for saying openly that I am your friend. This is a Western satellite now. They hate Communists here.'

'No, they don't,' he said, giving his hair a good brushing before hopping into bed, as if he was a girl. He was still entirely unaware of the danger he had created for me. 'These fellows all supported the partisans. They think you're a hero. Now they're dying to hear your stories.'

'What stories did you tell them?'

'I couldn't say anything,' he shrugged and seemed sincerely regretful about it, 'because you never tell me anything. But you can tell us all yourself on Monday. Believe me, to them you're a hero.'

Of course I didn't believe Paul. In fact, if he hadn't been quite so perennially cheerful, if it hadn't been quite so difficult to imagine reducing him to tears, and if he hadn't gone off to sleep almost immediately exhausted from his own high spirits, that night I came close to pulling out the belt from my trousers and thrashing him without remorse. With a few thoughtless words, he had jeopardised my safety here in E., and quite possibly, his own as well. It would just take *one* of his colleagues to pick up the phone and call a police station about a couple of Communists from over the border working at the Dowager under false pretences. No one would ever hear of us again.

I lay awake until very late, worrying over what to do, whether or not to make a clean breast to Franz and seek his advice and protection, or if that would be further folly. I couldn't come to a decision, not even over the next few days, so, on the outside, I went about my work as usual. Paul however seemed as cheerful and oblivious of danger as ever, and didn't bring up the subject again, until the following Monday when, true to form, he burst into our room – where I was spending my evening off with my diary at the desk – and insisted that I come over to their dining room immediately because '*everyone*' had gathered for my stories. It was a bigger crowd than he'd ever seen on a single night, and they were all there for one reason. They'd sent him down because I was late, and he couldn't go back without me.

'Paul, we discussed this. No one here should know…'

'But they want to know. They would never give you away. Just come with me once and see their faces. They all want to hear about the war from someone who lived through it.'

'They might want to hear about it, but what if Franz finds out? What if the hotel finds out? Think of your school, how you had to run away because of one simple drawing, and then compare that to a hotel like this finding out that I am a Communist. We would both be arrested immediately as agitators, yes, you too, because we arrived here together. They would assume you were the same as me. They wouldn't spare your aunt either. Marlene would be finished as well.'

When I eventually consented to be dragged to their dining room, despite Paul allaying not one of my fears, I was greeted by two minutes of sustained applause from a crowd comprising virtually everyone from the kitchen who had finished their shift for the night. Not one of them had gone home. Paul later described for me with added drama how I had remained rooted to the doorway in shock, but that a few moments later, although my face had broken into a smile, my eyes were brimming over with tears. I myself wasn't aware of any of this at the time.

Within minutes of sitting among them, I realised that absolute silence would only distance me from these new friends and create the wrong impression, so, after just a little more goading from them, and a request from me at the outset for their discretion, I told them one of the more harmless stories I could recall. That night, I had the pleasure of sharing with a spellbound audience the memory of one of my numerous near-arrests, this one in the northern town of D., where we were hiding out in the basement of Elena's ex-husband, Samuel.

'There was a workers' canteen at the corner, and every night after closing, the owner, a sympathetic friend, brought us our meals. Hermann would wait until the last employee had left, pretending to tidy up his accounts, but somehow we were still betrayed. His was a large kitchen, and it was impossible to be sure who the spy had been. I'm sure you can imagine the atmosphere of those days: two colleagues, working alongside one another for years, might support respectively the monarchy or us. Such bitterness was perfectly normal, and the brawls, betrayals and denunciations you must have known here as well. So a canteen full of workers and waiters would have had battle lines drawn all across it. Someone must have noticed food missing from their stocks one morning, and with typical cynicism would have waited outside and followed our friend Hermann setting off with a package that night.

'Anyhow, those divisions could work in your favour as well. Our host, Samuel, received a call from a contact at the police station moments after their vans had left, to warn him they were headed in our direction. We squeezed out through the bathroom window with a couple of minutes to spare. Add to that the time it took the police to quickly search the house, and weather Samuel's withering outcry against false denunciations and (literally) unwarranted harassment, and our head-start would have extended to about ten minutes. But we were running and they would have telephones and vehicles. Also, I had cut my foot, in leaping from the window and landing upon a shard of glass.

'As much as possible, we stayed within the poorly lit back-alleys in order to escape the attention on the streets. We were obvious fugitives: Marc was still in his bedclothes and I hadn't been able to locate my shoes amid the panic. We could have been surrounded almost immediately by one or other group of royalists at any of the bigger intersections: D. was still months away from falling to us. In fact, the local infighting had reached such levels that almost every wall in certain neighbourhoods had been raised recently by several feet, to prevent precisely such back-door partisan escapes as ours. The police, after all the desertions, were too depleted to search each household they suspected of harbouring our people, and this raising of the walls had been the army's alternative solution. The soldiers had worked night and day: they even transported extra workers from right here in E. as well as loyalist areas within our own country.

'Mostly we ran with just the moon for light, coming from up ahead, the huge walls and their shadows forming a looming open-air tunnel. We had to avoid alleys where work on the walls was still going on, because those crews would have armed soldiers among them. If they spotted two fleeing men, they wouldn't even attempt to take prisoners.

'Finally, after around twenty minutes of diversions through three or four different neighbourhoods, we arrived at a star-shaped intersection of streets and tramlines, with their overhead wires untidily knotted at the centre. There was a long roadside café and newspaper kiosk on a raised island around which the traffic moved. It formed an unusually large pool of light in that electricity-deprived town, and since I was at least in street clothes, despite wearing one soaking red sock, I volunteered to step out of the shadows and ask the way to the central bus station.

'Although I remained on the edge of the darkness, and kept my injured foot behind my other leg, I was aware of running a great risk, but there was no other way for us. We had to leave town immediately. Yet it is amusing to recall how coolly those men reacted. They must have sized me up immediately and figured out my story. So they simply started debating back and forth the shortest and most efficient route to the bus station, and presently, as if performing to a well-rehearsed script, every one of them responded on cue. They argued, called each other names, started drawing maps on napkins and newspapers. In fact, at one point, they appeared to have forgotten about my presence completely. Then one after the other they turned to me and pointed out how each of the six roads leading away from there could eventually take me to the bus station, and that there were arguments for and against every choice – of distance, safety, lighting, frequency of pubs along the way, and even the aesthetic qualities of the walk itself. It all depended on what was important to me.

'It was exhaustion rather than anything else that held me transfixed listening to this nonsense. They were playing for time, and I was simply catching my breath, wise to their game but unable to assess our other options. Another added reason for their malice, aside from politics, would certainly have been their contempt for my accent: as you probably know, many in the northern states at home look down on us southerners as illiterate peasants. I wasn't even carrying a knife so that I could make an instant reckoning with this bunch of clowns, who were probably unarmed as well since there would have been no need otherwise for this charade. Yet it was inexcusable that I stood there breathless and apparently entranced, until we could actually hear sirens approaching in the distance. At this point, Marc pre-empted everyone by rushing forward from the pavement and seizing my collar. By the unlikeliest stroke of fortune, he'd come across a taxi-driver about to enter a pub who had turned out to be from our region, and had agreed instantly to deliver us to safety. Of course this drove some of those cowards at the café to react as well, since they'd guessed by now we weren't carrying guns. A few of them rushed towards us as the taxi reversed to pick us up, and one of them even leapt onto the running board on my side, but by now I'd recovered my senses, not to mention my indignation, and punched him with great satisfaction flush in the face. Our newfound friend, whom we had after all taken a risk in trusting, proved to possess a peerless knowledge of the shortcuts and red herrings of old D., and the sirens never managed to draw close again, as we were deposited outside town in front of an inn where lorry drivers stopped for breakfast, and one of them would certainly shelter us among his goods until we reached the eastern border.'

Even though they had listened enraptured, even though they applauded long and hard when I had finished and then slapped me on the back and embraced me, I realised I didn't want to leave these fellows with an incorrect perception, that we were always like rats on the run, and had spent the last three years scurrying in the gutter. So the Monday after, I balanced my previous story with an example of how we swaggered in the towns that eventually fell to us, in an atmosphere of normality and unthreatened calm. In my home region the following year, we'd managed to bring about a state of stability within a few months to the extent of resuming the inter-club football tournament. The afternoon of the final, Marc, Eugene, a couple of others and I delegated our duties at the party office to a bunch of junior cadres and took off at the last minute for the stadium. We wouldn't have needed to be so irresponsible if the malicious scum of the royalist army hadn't destroyed most of the city's radio equipment during their retreat. Rest assured, heads did roll for that, but my point was, no live broadcast was possible from the stadium.

'We were about to enter an already overflowing and uproarious ground when the man inside the ticket booth stopped us. Within our regime, orders were very strict not to move around the city on regular business carrying any visible weapons, so he must have taken us for a group of visiting bumpkins. Well, we stuck to our part and asked him if there were any spare tickets. He immediately replied that depended on what we had to offer. Still, we resisted provocation from this royalist dog, and invited him to name an amount. Looking at his watch, and the expressions on our faces, he stretched and yawned as if to emphasise this would be the easiest bit of money he would make in his life, and quoted the impossible price of 250 Fo per numskull. I don't need to explain to you chaps how ridiculous that was, war or no war, final or no final. Perhaps that is what you would pay to spend a week being coached personally by Puskas. At such a moment, and only because of the situation, I pulled out my badge, and requested him with great sweetness in my voice to maybe reconsider. Let me round the story off with the little detail that we watched that game from seats just below the governor's box, which actually didn't work out so well for us. The boss was sitting right above, secure in the knowledge that we were looking after the office, and we were duly chewed out at half-time, especially since the club he supported was down three-nil.'

2

The door of our new cubbyhole opened onto a corridor that ran as a gigantic rectangle along the hotel's sides, and most of its five hundred staff were housed here in larger or smaller rooms depending on seniority. We had a bunk-bed, a desk and a set of drawers to share, and a skylight that opened onto the street to give us a view of countless moving feet. Since Paul and I usually worked alternate shifts, the room rarely felt overcrowded. In fact, I cherished the few occasions we were together, as he lit up the poor space with his irrepressible vitality. If one day he was full of delight about how M Roland had poured massive vessels of water over the vagrants who gathered behind the kitchen in search of scraps, another time he'd just pulled a prank himself during his afternoon off right outside the hotel.

Paul's Spanish friend and somewhat mentor, Ramon, who'd fled here as an orphan of another notorious civil war over ten years ago, had bet him he 'could expose the extent of human gullibility in a unique fashion' for the token consideration of 50 De. For this throwaway amount, and with the assistance of two aides, he would have fifty people clamouring for his autograph, all taken in by what he had grandly called 'the power of suggestion, and the operation of an unthinking herd-mentality innate in mankind.' Once his challenge was accepted, this sage of life, a mere sommelier, put on his best suit, slicked back his gleaming hair, and confidently strode off to assume a terrace seat outside one of Market Square's most exclusive cafés. He ordered a thé au citron and lit a cigarillo.

After a while Paul, playing himself, a passing nobody, happened to be strolling by when suddenly he notices this matinee idol, this living legend of an unspecified sphere – sport, the silver screen or the stage, you take your pick – relaxing incognito in our town square! Anxious not to miss this once-in-a-lifetime opportunity, yet equally concerned that he should not disturb his hero, he tiptoes over with great care, and in the most restrained of voices, requests the enormous favour of an autograph. The great man obliges, and also smiles, but in order to provide himself with some extra cover, summons the waiter after Paul's grateful departure (who is stepping away backwards, so as to steal a few last, longing glances at his god, and affix the incredible moment forever in his mind), and asks him to bring over the day's English newspaper, in which he then buries his head.

A reasonable interval later, another visitor to the café (played admirably by Miklos, one of our cloakroom boys), leaves his table inside and steps over equally circumspectly to Ramon's table, once more with a little diary and a pen, begging to disturb him just this once. He pleads in his own defence, in a voice that would barely make it to the adjoining tables, that it would delight his wife immeasurably, and that it happened to be their third wedding anniversary the following week. It would be a present out of her wildest dream, he added, and would buy him ample credit in all marital differences for months to come.

Once more, the legend shrugs his shoulders, obliges with his customary graciousness, and afterwards retires behind his paper. Paul and Miklos now take up their positions, sixty yards away seated on the edge of the fountain, to watch the crucial third act. This is the denouement of the challenge – the time has been precisely chosen, the wager will be won or lost in the next few minutes. There should be more than enough fools, both in the café and wandering about Market Square, to make up the numbers while they watched and counted.

It was remarkable. Paul was sharp enough to initially smell a rat. What if the real joke was on them, and they were being duped by appearances? But, as Miklos quickly pointed out, there wasn't enough money in it for Ramon to make a trick worthwhile. Why would he buy up fifty accomplices to win a bet of 50 De? Because soon after Miklos had played his part, it was as though a tap opened simultaneously within dozens of people and out poured a steady drip of folly. Age, sex, nationality, nothing seemed to insure or protect them. First, a pair of tourists at an adjacent table, followed by an elderly couple sitting behind Ramon, and then a bearded university student, each shuffling over in an equally ridiculous posture of supplication. What could they have been thinking? What was it they desired? Not to miss out on a moment they weren't even sure was special? The infection presently spread to the passersby on the square, who were drawn irresistibly to the queue that had formed at Ramon's table, each pausing only to pass and receive their slip of paper, so obedient, so inert, so afraid of appearing ignorant none of them asked him, or one another, what this supposed star actually did. Paul fell backwards into the fountain from laughing, but Miklos steadfastly counted until the number of certified fools reached sixty-three, in a period of only fifteen minutes. At this point, Ramon, quietly assured of his triumph, arose with supreme dignity, requested his bill, and began putting on his jacket.

The closing touch was to follow. The joke did require a couple more accomplices, certainly. The waiter made a great show of having been honoured by his presence, and set aside with a flourish any talk of piddling dues. All they asked was the pleasure of welcoming him regularly for as long as he chose to extend his stay here in E.. In an appropriate gesture of reciprocity, Ramon pulled out an obviously large note and stuck it under the saucer, raised his hat to everyone around, and strode off, fifty yards to the left, across the boulevard, and quite expectedly for a visitor of his ilk, up the carpeted steps of The Bristol.

He later revealed to his two delighted disciples that with a little cooperation from the staff across the street at Les Deux Anges, he'd been pulling this caper for newcomers at The Bristol for five years now. And success was assured every time, because the trick simply relied upon certain basic failings in human nature.

'But don't any of them ever spot you later working in the restaurant?' asked Paul.

'Of course not,' replied Ramon with unruffled serenity, 'although you're right, and I have faced several of my dupes in here soon afterwards. Some of them listen attentively while I'm discussing their wine with them, and still don't recognise my face, because it is not in their upbringing to glance too closely at their waiters. But others are more interesting. I look at them, and I can see the question in their eyes. Yet they are snobs of a different sort. How can they admit they have been such fools, and have queued up and bowed before a mere sommelier? It's best at a moment like that to disbelieve reality, and never to refer to such matters again.'

The other events that made Paul's eyes gleam as much as the recounting of such pranks, were receiving large tips from foolish Western guests (he was now being trained as a bellhop, and actually practiced his greetings and smiles in our room, in Italian, English and French), and the girls who agreed to return with him to his bunk for some fondling and kissing, though usually not more. Paul had exhausted the rounds of attractive girls within the hotel already, chambermaids, cigarette-girls, as well as those from laundry and household, and since he regarded our stay here as purely temporary, governed by different rules in a foreign land, and himself at sixteen as far beneath the threshold of serious obligation or loyalty, he permitted himself no lingering with anyone for more than a couple of evenings. Besides, he regularly professed that his ultimate destiny was to return to the girl Martina with whom he'd been holed up back in his school, and used this (much-compromised) vow of fidelity to ward off anyone else's demands or claims.

Out of comradeship perhaps, or pity, or simply plain cheek, he frequently offered to introduce me to several, more grown-up women who regularly crossed his path, especially when his old kitchen mates went pack-hunting on their off-nights. He genuinely worried about me, why I never took an interest in his exploits, or cared nothing about notching up my own. He said my war stories alone would draw them to me in swarms: a veteran, physically and mentally intact, holding down a job at The Bristol, could have anyone who pleased him from sixteen to sixty.

Perhaps that is where he misread me, although I used my long hours and fatigue as ready excuses, because I was far from mentally intact. Even though I missed his blaze of energy whenever I returned to an empty room early each morning, a part of me also welcomed this solitude, in which it could curl up, cringe, and shiver unseen. There was not a waking hour during those weeks when I didn't consider, or draw comfort from, my hypothetical freedom to commit suicide. At any time I chose, as soon as the balance tipped beyond the supportable, tomorrow, next month, any time within the year. This was what I'd been reduced to, the sum of what I could deem my freedom, but did I require anything beyond this guarantee of instant release? It was the only form of rebellion I had against the absurdities inflicted upon me by the mirages of politics and the betrayals of friends.

Because the arguments enforcing serenity, the logic leading to balance, that I periodically mapped in my diary, were actually useless and hollow, as was the applause and the back-slapping from the regular audiences for my Monday-night war-stories (although Paul proved to be right to trust them: not one of his friends from the kitchen, or from among the bellhops, ever betrayed me). Yet, unfortunately, far more vivid to me than their admiration were my nightmares, which I frequently noted down despite their incoherence and absurd connections, rising from bed and going straight to my desk, no matter the hour. As I read them over later, it was clear that these reflected more accurately the depths I plumbed each waking day – my hurt, incomprehension, and nausea. I swung between those appalling dreams and the empty, mocking work into which I'd been forced. Paul was too young to bother, but everything I was involved in – the procurements, the apathy, the deaf-and-blind ape-like indulgence of every manner of immoral exploit that Franz both recommended and praised – everything he and the hotel grew to symbolise, seemed a travesty of my previous life. How could I take out a woman and be sweet to her (as Paul suggested), pretend the world was innocent and we were starting anew, when earlier that evening I would have escorted a girl from my own province – a refugee forced into this 'work' in search of a better life during the war my comrades and I had fought in vain – to a taxi in which waited a visiting 'businessman'? This occurred not once, but several times, with girls from all over our country, many younger than me, lured here by the amazing fairy stories they had heard about the torrents of money flowing through E.. The first time it happened, I had been foolish and homesick enough to strike up a conversation, and even delighted when I found that we both knew many people in the village to the north of mine (it was her mother's birthplace), but the shame that had overcome me as I then watched her being taken away by a man old enough to be her grandfather, kept me from revealing my identity ever again. Instead, from then on I spoke as little as possible, in the accent I had learnt in our capital, and pretended not to hear any personal questions.

The distortion was too grotesque to ignore. I'd allowed myself to drift into the employ of precisely those forces we'd despised, and fought three years to protect our country from. And yet, what had been my options? To remain at home, skulking in Elena's shadow, irrespective of who she followed? Return to stand trial like a proud fool, certain of execution? Escape and organise a future resistance, but with whom, and on whose behalf?

All reports from next door, as represented in the slavish and triumphalist newspapers here, only confirmed that Elena and I were apart forever. They spoke of consolidating the recent reconciliation between forces that had murdered one another for years, now brought together wondrously in government by the unrelenting peace-efforts of our neighbour and her allies. There was never any mention of summary trials and mass executions, as if the happy spirit of pardon-and-advance could ever extend to the rank-and-file. The bitterness and hatred were much too entrenched for that, within me and our other comrades, as well as those we'd fought. Barring a targeted yet extensive cull, undertaken without sentiment or delay, no miracle in the capital could keep the disquiet in the provinces at bay. I knew this, and I considered myself to be on the good side. Yet none of the papers here, nor the ones from home that arrived in the hotel (each of which had speedily realigned itself in the wake of recent events), nor a single of the Western radio broadcasts ever mentioned any such retribution (no transmissions from Moscow,, that would certainly have contradicted this fairytale ending, were permitted anywhere in this country), although everyone in the pubs of E., as well as the staff dining-halls of our hotel, speculated endlessly about such actions. I was frequently asked to offer my opinion, especially by Paul's friends, but pleaded ignorance each time, and soon afterwards would leave the table. I found it an eventuality impossible to envision, since it implied imagining friends piled bloody and dead upon hundreds of innocent strangers in immense ditches throughout our forests and fields.

One morning, two months into our stay, a list of members of the new cabinet was published, who had assumed office until the country at large was stable enough to conduct elections. It exceeded my worst fears. Elena had been appointed Junior Minister of the Interior, serving under the erstwhile commander of the royalist paramilitary wing who'd murdered so many of our comrades in the camps of the north. And a few lines below I found Marc, poet as he was, perfectly ensconced as Minister for Information and Culture.

Perhaps it was an act of mercy that the list shredded to bits any last attempts at self-deception, yet for days after that a fire blazed inside my head and every vein in my face felt like it must explode. During the first few weeks I'd clung to hoping, against all sense, that Elena, for motives of love, friendship, loyalty and reason, would trace me to the hotel and write to explain. I even assured myself I was staying here just so she could reach me. Yet, long after that threadbare effort to maintain my illusions had crumbled, I'd refused to move or act, passive, indecisive and cowardly.

It actually made for something of a spectacle, to witness my own disintegration even as I was enduring it – the complete collapse of my beliefs, my dreams, and now evidently, my very self. Countless times each day, in our room, at my desk, or out on a job pacing the streets of E., I would confront myself with the same question: would I have preferred to be captured in outright defeat, even if it had meant torture and death? And each time I grew surer of my response – because it would have meant all of us going together, rather than being dismembered by this hollow agony in which nothing worthwhile had survived. Our deaths would have been recalled and commemorated elsewhere: our efforts would have set an example. Wouldn't it be better even now to be betrayed by one of Paul's friends and arrested, then taken away and executed by the secret police on the outskirts of E.? Why had I ever feared such an outcome? Wasn't it in fact what I secretly hoped for, and the reason I still kept sharing my stories? I could make sure to insist to my captors that I had met Paul only after the war had ended. After all, who lived merely to draw breath? What parody of existence was I prolonging now, on the other side from friends and love, in the aftermath of belief and the absence of the future?

Eugene's face exploding before my eyes, Elena's body never again to lie intertwined in sleep with mine, the years, the forests, the barns, caves and huts, the thrills, the jokes and the victories, the scores of dead friends and thousands of slaughtered countrymen, and here I was choosing each day to outlive them all. After being forced to participate in the gigantic bonfire of betrayal that had engulfed my country, I was casting into the flames a little more of myself every day at this post, negating with my work in three months everything we'd striven for the past three years. Fleeing had accomplished nothing: the enemy had me exactly where they wanted, recruited amongst the lowest of their ranks, to run their filthiest, most degrading errands, pimping my own younger sisters each night. This was all I had to look forward to, or worse. No explanations, no justice, no stunning reversal or awakening, or announcement that it was all a giant strategic hoax, were forthcoming.

This was how I felt, repetitively and uselessly, on the eve of Elena's return into my life, late at night, manning my desk, while unknown to me, she was already inside the building, in one of the top-floor suites, probably conducting some of the many unorthodox, unofficial consultations for which The Bristol was renowned.

Or, it could well have been that she was here in her new official role as our junior Minister of the Interior.

Either way, of course, Franz already knew of her arrival.

3

A story from my diary, that arose out of a dream I noted down shortly before my re-encounter with Elena.

It is the spring of '46, three years ago, and Elena and I are visiting the mausoleum of our revolutionary leader, legendary even to you foreigners, the one whose ideals have been so spectacularly twisted in the twenty years since his death, and whose name still somehow binds us together. It is blackly funny how both parties in our upcoming election swear to be abiding by his principles and fighting solely to perpetuate his legacy. How can all of us be telling the truth? Anyhow, on this bright day, when the naked sun makes the marble platform blaze and sparkle, and the tip-over into outright hostilities is still a cancelled election and a coup d'état away, we are mere citizens, unsuspected as yet although seething within from secret subversion, enjoying our weekday unemployment along with off-duty soldiers, numerous school-groups, retirees, and vendors of beer, American cold drinks, and smuggled cigarettes.

Suddenly screams arise from behind us, loud and shrill, clearly originating among the large group of schoolgirls on the steps leading to the 'eternal flame'. I rush towards them, forgetting to release Elena's hand, and dragging her behind me. Soldiers are arriving from two other directions, but at this precise moment, Elena and I have nothing to fear, and besides, curiosity has overcome us all.

It is a sight the horror of which can never wane, no matter how long we live. At the heart of their group, in a clearing formed by the retreating girls, how shall I phrase it, one of them lies *fizzing* in the noonday sun, as if the marble is frying her. There is no clearer way to express what we see. In fact, it is a wonder the girls are only screaming instead of fleeing for their lives. Grown men are bellowing at the tops of their lungs, soldiers are fainting, shuddering, possibly surrendering control of their bodily functions.

Clinically speaking, before our eyes, solid flesh is bubbling, cooking, and gradually vaporising into a gagging stench. The eyes have exploded, every last hair is thoroughly singed, the face is being eaten away at an inconceivable rate, and boiling blood is streaming out of the holes that are being burned through her tunic. The entire process is accompanied by hissing and crackling, as when you sprinkle water over coals in a sauna, although mercifully she has lost her capacity to shriek long ago.

And yet we watch, mesmerised, completely overruling for a moment our own imperative to survive: time resumes only with another heart-rending scream in the portion of the circle opposite us. Another schoolgirl, somehow standing as we turn towards her, who then crashes to the floor, is losing her arm, once again to the same invisible inner acid, with identical symptoms, melting skin and heated blood sizzling upon the marble in globs.

The second victim breaks our trance, and I shout to whoever can still comprehend language to cover their mouths and eyes and run. With one hand firmly clenching Elena's, the other covering most of my face, I dash towards the long alleys of the old city to the right of us. It is as we are descending the steps a hundred metres away that the first shots are fired, but we don't pause to confirm who they were intended for. I only wonder if a soldier was courageously putting the second girl out of her misery.

Rumour flies swifter than bullets, and the street we race through – that should have been full of stalls and barrows conducting brisk, midday trade, and visitors from the provinces refreshing themselves in and around the taverns and squares – is already deserted. Only the things remain, as if for once, the terror of such an awful fate has overcome everyone's obsession with their property.

After we've passed three or four alleys, Elena begs me to stop: she is desperate to use a bathroom. My heart breaks imagining her nausea even as I admire her fortitude. There is an open café at the corner and I wait for her outside. More shots can be heard, unmistakable, although how they hope to quell this crisis with gunfire is beyond me. Elena would point out that it is the typically barbaric response of those trained bloodhounds, conditioned only to kill in any circumstance. Yet I have glimpsed how this illness consumes its victims, and perhaps in this case *pity* is the appropriate explanation for the firing. At this point, the only causes that occur to me are some dreadful agents that have been released into the air or the water, and could be breeding inside all of us already, or the contamination from some horrendous accident in the American base just beyond our border, where we know they stockpile the world's deadliest weapons, always with the implicit approval of both neighbouring governments.

By the time I realise how long Elena is taking, she has disappeared. The café owner, who emerges fearfully from the kitchen when I threaten to smash his counters, confesses she'd fled through the back door. Truly, of everything that has occurred on this stunning day, nothing mystifies me more. I can conceive of no reason we had to part. Had she spotted danger: was she leading someone away from me? Had war been declared in this unprecedented, deadly and devious way? But who is the enemy? How did so many people know they should flee? Had more incidents been reported elsewhere?

Within the next five minutes I receive one possible answer. After I stagger out of the café continuing in the direction away from the mausoleum, I am arrested by military police in the heart of Cinélandia, who seem not to be picking me up as a stray, rather as an intended target. Why couldn't Elena have warned me? The war has been launched in this underhanded manner. A pretext has been conjured up. We would be blamed for the destroyed children, and not one tear would be shed over our purge, neither at home nor abroad.

It is a wrecked man they line up to shoot the following morning, a man corroding within from the same questions all night. How could she have left me to die? How could she have left me to die? She was much more crucial to the struggle than I ever would be, but what about our love? Did that count for nothing? Then how was it that *my* first thought was for her safety? How could she have left me to die?

The one who crumples beside me was a scientist. The soldiers have kicked him around as though he were scum, but their officer has treated him with a surprising degree of respect, never forgetting to address him as Dr Shtrum, always preparing him for the next stage and excusing himself along the way. Straight afterwards I am shot in the chest and stomach, and fall to the ground aware I am dying. 'This is that moment,' I think, 'and nothing has come to fruition. It's all ending now, and none of it's been worth anything.' I see, taste and touch my blood as it wastes itself amid the grass.

Elena is in the van beside me when I return to life. She is holding my hand, weeping silently, in the same golden dress of the morning, only it is streaked with grease and ripped in many places. Instantly I forgive her, even before I understand what I'm doing. It is my first instinct upon awakening. The films are right about this, I realise: one does arrive into consciousness seeing everything as a blur, as if surfacing from underwater. But as soon I'm awake, I must have screamed hellishly, because between my neck and my legs everything is on fire. Then I cannot see, think, or speak any further. I must be damaged beyond repair. In terror of the future I scream, unaware of everything else, until mercifully, the world vanishes once more.

The next time I'm awake it is as though I were a mummy. Elena is nowhere to be seen, I'm bandaged and numb, but I feel like I have no body. I'm a head with some toes and fingers I can move. A boy asks me if I need water. I decline. He assures me we're over the border and I have nothing more to fear, since I'm out of danger and we're on our way to a hospital. I stare at him, and can sense he knows what is wrong with me, because I can sense his fear. He is afraid of being trapped with a corpse. So he babbles incessantly. This time I can comprehend. He informs me there are hitchhikers everywhere in this country, sitting on the grassy banks of the highway. Everyone wants a ride to E., the capital. He says there are men in office suits, chefs, circus performers, chorus girls who sign for us to stop by standing in a line on their toes to wave, and even painters with easels working furiously to capture the rush of the road. The more desperate ones scramble down right in front of us and don't flinch until we're almost upon them. Our odd neighbours, living in the 'American way'.

His final words are to reassure me we've arrived, and to convey his impressions of the hospital. He is startled by its size: he describes a gigantic estate of treeless lawns through which we drive, with distant towers in both directions. Towers as in the movies and *Life* magazine. The awe is followed by an optimistic grin. Suddenly Paul (he mentioned his name before) cheers up, since it has occurred to him that from towers such as these I can only emerge good as new. According to him, I'm already healed. And although I've seen nothing thus far of this country, its roads or its towers, although I know organs of my body must have been removed forever for me to feel so numb, although I've no idea why Paul is accompanying me instead of Elena, I know suddenly that I believe him.

Elena

IT HAPPENED JUST LIKE THAT, unheralded, and I almost failed to see it coming. With a smile hovering on his lips that I noted at the time but forgot afterwards to think about, Franz dispatched me to Suite 703; apparently I had been specially requested.

'I've caught a glimpse of her myself,' he grinned, 'and it made me wish I was thirty years younger, fit and ready to run like you, and provide anything else that she might desire. But then she called and asked for you by name, so obviously she must have walked past while you were at the desk, and liked what she had seen.

'Young man, by now you're aware I won't let you down in any matter involving delicacy, so go forth with a blameless heart and enjoy the first fruits of this position that have fallen into your lap. And as a bonus, I want you to take your time, you've been reliable for me, and today in your hour of need, I'll stand by you. Take a couple of hours off if you want to, but please her as much as you please yourself. Remember, that is what we aim for, we pride ourselves on pleasing and providing. And it's never going to be as easy as this.'

I puzzled over his words as I rode the lift: how could he be granting me a licence to commit what was strenuously forbidden to any member of staff within the guest-rooms of the Dowager? Who could this exception be that would cause Franz to giggle like a schoolboy? What if somebody questioned my absence or noticed how long I'd remained in her suite? Was it imperative that I obey and perform? Was he certain that was what she wanted? How dare he assume I'd step up and consent? Part of me sickened even further at falling to this new low, with full official sanction, and so far, not as much as a murmur of dissent from me. Indeed, my inner disintegration must have been complete. In a world I couldn't read at all, I was finally unrecognisable to myself.

And then, with my fingers poised to knock, as impossibly unseeing as ever, I understood who was behind that door, and the reason for Franz's incongruous cheer. In that moment I felt more dread than hope, washed over by a surge of premonition that hurled me against the wall, as though I were an animal very close to danger, about to step fatally beyond its element. This would be our first meeting alone since the nightmare commenced; it was also the long-awaited opportunity for the one in me craving answers, the all-encompassing explanation that would cover Eugene's slaughter, Elena's betrayal, our country's downfall and my own exile. Yet suddenly those answers seemed fearsome; like a child I was now convinced of her dark powers, and even more terrifying was the prospect of seeing her again, as though she were a witch or a sorceress.

Everything unfolded calmly at first. She was transformed in appearance – instead of fatigues she now wore a slim grey dress with a row of buttons in front. She'd left her hair up, and I suddenly flashed back to the hours I'd spent inhaling its fragrance and covering her neck with kisses, and then clasping her tightly, our bodies perfectly complementary, listening to her heartbeat while she spoke, with my head upon her chest. But here she was inviting me to take a seat, and as usual I obeyed without thinking, walking into the well of the living room and taking the sofa opposite her. Then she was already uttering her first words, even before I'd had a chance to grasp anything. It was all so characteristic of her, from the very first afternoon when she handed me her house key, never failing to seize the moment, never failing to realise that she was in the present, and it was there to be made, and whoever leapt in first had first chance to shape the future.

'Are you calmer?' she asked. 'You've had a lot of time to calm down.'

I didn't know how to reply, and stayed still.

'I wanted to begin by congratulating you for landing on your feet so well. This is a fine position you've found for yourself.'

'Don't you think it's me who should step forward with the compliments? I should be praising *your* agility. After all, not a single detail have you overlooked, from arranging this job for me, to keeping all the killings out of the papers.'

She seemed genuinely surprised when she asked what killings.

'Come on, Eugene couldn't have been the only one. Just as I wasn't the only one who needed to be removed by other means. There must have been thousands like us, in every town, village and forest, surely in the capital itself, who would have been too inconvenient with their shouts of dissent and their awkward memories of yesterday on that glorious 'day zero'. And yet, not a mention anywhere of their fates. How did you manage this great conjuring trick? Oh wait, I'm forgetting you specialise in such magic. After all, you somehow forced an entire country to alter the direction of its history overnight, and the whole world seems hypnotised by this spell, so disposing of a few thousand bodies would have been child's play for you.'

She started laughing even before I'd finished, with no trace of seeming disturbed. In our years together, despite coming through numerous life-threatening emergencies, I never saw her approach panic, fear or hysteria.

'Ivan, you give me so much credit. I'm impressed. You really think I can redirect history, order mass slaughters and then make the corpses vanish, hypnotise people so they won't notice anyone's missing? But most of all, I feel delighted that you should deem me responsible for your presence here, and believe that my tentacles could spread so far. You know, I would hate to disappoint you. Even I feel proud of my supposed accomplishments when I listen to you list them like that. I would like to be that person, at least in your eyes. So, whatever you wish to believe is all right by me.

'There is just one idea of yours I will contradict. Why don't you return and take a little tour of the country before you judge whether people are indeed hypnotised, or we are forced to kill them in order to ensure their silence, and whether or not they are happy that the war is over, and the factories are opening again, and those who live near the border can once more come over three times a week with their produce to E.? We're good Communists, aren't we? So why don't you return and actually ask the people how they are?'

I didn't move from my place as I replied (she had leaned back, across the coffee table from me, and crossed her legs), and gave no sign of noticing her mockery. 'As always you've begun playing games with me, the child who never knows any of the rules. It doesn't matter what you say. You're a master, all of you, Robert and Marc and all the other ministers in the new government. I'm just a kid you allowed into your team, because you needed someone to dig the trenches, and amuse you during those long nights with my baby-talk.'

Now she got up and spoke with her back to me, as she moved towards the bar on the sideboard. 'Ah, so that is it. Drink, Ivan? No? They have a very good selection of schnapps, and real whisky too. Sure? Then I'll make just one. Yes, of course, the baby. You always saw yourself as the baby, didn't you? It's such an easy role to play. Everything that happens is the fault of the grown-ups. What does the baby understand? He only knows how to throw grenades into marketplaces and operate a machine gun. He only knows how to terrorise entire villages and force them to lynch supposed informants. Another game he learnt was to blow up trains, and yet another was to torture captured soldiers. But then just like any baby, tired after his play, he wanted to come home to Mamma in the evening, enjoy a full meal, and be played with a little bit before his bedtime. And each night, like a baby, you slept unbrokenly, peacefully, in order to wake up fresh for the killings of the morning, for which, if I recall correctly, you always prepared with a shave and a careful brush of your hair, and right through the war you wore your good clothes on the days when there wouldn't be any fighting.'

Despite myself I was awestruck, at how, within not more than ten minutes, she'd turned the conversation I'd intended to have upon its head. For the first time, I felt the full, stunning force of her enmity, the very force which had once propelled me – emboldened, convinced, inspired me – to commit all the acts she'd listed. No means was off limits for her, and yet, as I knew, throughout the war, she had never personally borne arms. She didn't need to.

She returned to her sofa, her drink in a crystal glass in her left hand. It occurred to me, as the light from the lamp to her left briefly caught her face, that she had begun wearing make-up. That was why she looked different. During the war, when I slept all those nights with my face buried in her hair, there had never been any question in the morning of her, or any of our women fighters, applying make-up. But of course, how foolish of me not to have guessed, the junior Minister of the Interior of a newly constituted sovereign government, visiting a prestigious Western establishment such as The Bristol, could not appear in public without make-up.

'Yes, Ivan,' she continued, placing the glass on the table between us, 'it's an unusual defence for someone with your track record, this plea of innocence. You were one of our most reliable instruments of war, whatever was required. Information, assassination, terror. Remember those days, your enthusiasm and your readiness. No wonder you feel so out of place at any prospect of peace. You must be missing your vocation.'

When my voice finally emerged, it sounded strangulated, and I felt grateful to be seated, or else I would have been unable to bear my own weight. At that moment, the furthest thing in the universe was that I'd ever been in love with her, this creature who could not be human, whose soul contained nothing that I recognised.

'But you ordered everything, from the beginning you ordered everything. Whatever Marc and Eugene and anyone else commanded, I always checked with you. And each time you assured me it was necessary.'

Now she laughed harshly, triumphant, irritated and bored at the same time. 'No, that was what you told yourself. There were many occasions when I was elsewhere, remember? Who guaranteed for you then that each action was necessary? Every last shot that you fired into crowds, every bomb you detonated, was I present by your side, pressing your hand? This is another fairytale you've told yourself, just as you believe you sold me your soul. When we met you, you were already a young man with big ideas. Come on, let's be really honest if you mean to go all the way back. Why were you in the tram that first afternoon? Hadn't your royalist great-uncle instructed you to watch us? And if I truly was your fairy godmother, the keeper of your spotless conscience, how is it you never confessed that tiny detail to me before?'

She paused to lean forward and pick up her drink, then sipped it before she concluded.

'Ivan, I forgave you that long ago. I haven't brought it up to accuse you. All I want you to accept is, I wasn't responsible for you then, and I'm not responsible for whatever you feel and believe now.'

'What are you saying? How can you not remember? When we met, I wanted to leave all that behind to be with you. Didn't I beg you to escape many times even after the fighting began? Didn't I suggest that we flee here, and from here try and get to a Western country, while our borders were still open? You forced me to stay, convinced me of the arguments, told me why it would be necessary for a while to harden our hearts and kill until we achieved our aims.'

She was a study in stone while I squeaked and prattled. She was in no hurry to contradict me, and her powdered face barely registered a reaction until I'd finished.

'*You* elected to join me in love, leaving your great-uncle's job behind, and you elected to share our aims, and participate in whatever needed to be done. And, when things turned out a certain way, you found the new realities unpalatable. So you made your way to the exit, and here we are today, catching up like old friends. It's not me that led you here. I've never led you to anything. I'll tell you the only thing I *have* done for you. Far from ordering any new killing sprees, I made sure that your name does not appear on the lists of those the Americans want for wartime massacres. Like Nuremberg, you remember? They want a trial, all sides included. It is one of their more comic rituals. They have a free press at home to satisfy.

'Look, it didn't hurt me that you chose to abandon us on our day of victory. I know how you felt about Eugene, and about the war. And if you'd ever decided to return, if you *still* decide to return, there will always be a place at home for you.

Unpersecuted, without conditions, free to resume normal life. But let's be clear once and for all, it'll be your choice, as it has always been – everything, this, us, and whatever has gone before. *Your* choice.'

I remember noticing she hadn't left her sofa through any of this, as if showing her refusal to indulge any pointless drama. I thought about that, but I also thought about the other Elena whom I used to listen to for nights on end, as she would explain to me why even our love could not eclipse the urgencies of our struggle, why we had to endure the separations and the distractions, why we *had to* risk losing ourselves, and more, each other, in the service of this 'higher cause'.

While I watched the creature before me, I remembered the occasions when that Elena, overcome by some particular tragedy or injustice she was recalling, could be reduced to tears out of helpless empathy for the unknown many who had suffered. These were the only times she lost her composure, we were always alone, and I remembered my marvel at someone's ability to feel so deeply for something far outside their own skin, a trait I had hitherto never possessed, and how it had made me love her even more, not just as the woman I felt sure was my personal destiny, but also as my only hero.

All these irrelevant reflections expressed themselves that night through a few last words.

'I have one final question. Is there anything at all you consider yourself responsible for?'

'Of course,' she replied without a moment's hesitation. 'I'm responsible for everything I have ever done. I know that, and it doesn't trouble me in the least. At each instant, a set of choices faces me, and I utilise all my powers to decide, as any wakeful adult would. What I'm not responsible for, what no one person can ever be held accountable for, is the big picture, and how it alters constantly, and how, if we wish to stay alive, we're enslaved by its whims and requirements. That is the cap on my freedom, as well as on my responsibility.

'I fought for things I considered to be important when the circumstances favoured us. I wanted that world as badly as you or Eugene whilst we struggled for it. Remember, I was with you, ahead of you, in each and every challenge we faced. But then things changed, and the only alternatives facing me were to adapt or die. Those above us, including dear Cagney, had already struck a deal. All this Marc told me while adding that I had *one night* in which to decide my own future: yes, Marc, who before this war had spent two years fighting the Germans. I learnt that several meetings between our representatives, Marc among them, and those of the government had taken place, with the Americans in attendance, and with sanction from Stalin. You know where, just out of curiosity? In a suite down the hall, *here*, where by an incredible coincidence, you have so successfully landed. How's that for a historical comedy?

'What I'm trying to explain is, the war was over and the new plan decided upon even before they asked me. What do you think my options were? They knew what Eugene would have chosen, so they settled matters on his behalf. Who would I have served by being dead?

'Ivan, I've always been aware of what I have done. I've not blamed it on God or the leader, or fate, just as I don't blame you for your actions during the war. I understand, I was with you, and I would never have brought up the past today. I also knew the Americans wouldn't see it that way, so in order to give you a fresh lease of life, I requested some friends to erase your name from certain lists. Look, the world changes every day. The only way to cope with that, to remain alive, is to realise your own freedom to change yourself. Nothing is set in stone, least of all your right to live. I have no family to protect me. Everybody is gone. I accept the way things change beyond our powers, and simply use the only freedom I possess, that of revising myself from day to day. Improvisation and flexibility, those are all people like me have in the fight to survive.'

There was no point in prolonging this. She had come thoroughly prepared for this encounter. Anything I countered with would only sound immature and hysterical. Without another word, I left. I had no thoughts to collect, no dissent to express. I forgot about Franz and mechanically descended all the way down the service stairs to our room. It was only when I was lying on my back, staring at the gleam from the streetlamp visible through the air-vent, that I realised not a word had been exchanged about our love.

Down to Experience

1

Everything changed again within the next few days. I revealed nothing to Franz about the details of my reunion with Elena, and from his relentless teasing about the superior quality of the beds in our suites, I realised she too had allowed him to perpetuate his own impressions. The very next weekend, Paul and I had our first few days off, after working four months non-stop. When I suggested a break in the countryside just to see a bit of the world outside E., Paul readily accepted. But it was his idea to hitchhike, since he wanted to recreate the carefree way in which we'd entered the country and begun our new lives, not knowing or worrying about what lay ahead. This was how he recalled those dreamlike twenty-four hours.

In fact, we found ourselves a like-minded lorry driver, who was heading for the town of Borda, and soon proved to be just as impulsive and artless as Paul. An hour into our journey, we were overtaken by another lorry, one with an unusual cargo. Three women in brightly coloured dresses, gypsies most certainly, waved energetically at us as they drove past, blew us kisses, and wiggled their hips. As far as Paul and Gabriel the driver were concerned, three on three was a match made in heaven. With barely a nod between them, they decided this was an invitation impossible to refuse, and soon we were driving south from E., and Borda seemed the furthest thing on their minds. It didn't matter to me where we went, so I remained silent, puzzling the others with my lack of enthusiasm. They even picked out girls for themselves, leaving me with the one neither wanted, Gabriel claiming by way of apology that I appeared to be indifferent anyway.

Our following them seemed to please the women, since their gestures of enticement grew ever bolder. Paul could hardly stay still in his seat, and there were moments when I was worried Gabriel would drive right off the road. At one point, as we were passing through dense woods, the unthinkable happened and the girls lifted their blouses together on cue. Even I was jolted into life by this, and Gabriel (counter-intuitively, since what we needed was to draw near) slammed on the brake. Our heads nearly went through the glass, delighting the girls, who still had their blouses up. And thus it continued for over a minute, as we re-started and got closer. Paul hadn't seen anything like it, and Gabriel was simply shrieking in delight. After a while, I realised I too was smiling, not least because I'd noticed that the girl arbitrarily assigned to me was as firm and youthful as the others, and not a little larger. The boys had made their choices simply because they seemed younger, and suddenly, even though it was the first time Iw feebly felt a stake in the proceedings, I decided I was quite satisfied with the allocations.

Shortly after sunset their driver stopped to let them off at a village square, and disappeared straight after dropping them, an occurrence that brought great pleasure to my companions (we soon learnt the girls were still some thirty kilometres from their destination, but that the lorry was going a different way). With this removal of the last possible obstacle, and in the absence of any competition, Paul and Gabriel linked up with their preferred choices as naturally as if they'd all discussed it en route. My own partner was as voluble and cheerful as the other girls, one of whom was her younger sister. They were travelling performers, renowned in these parts: their troupe had pitched camp in the neighbouring province, and they planned to continue their journey in the morning. Apparently they too had examined us with some thought during the ride, and were equally contented with the offerings of fortune.

Aishe was the first woman I'd touched since meeting Elena nearly four years ago. And throughout that night, every time we embraced one another, I felt certain I wanted to see her again. I knew that for each of the other four, this was most likely some harmless fun, an episode with no weight or sequel. Perhaps it was so even for Aishe, who seemed as free-spirited as the rest. But it was different for me, and I attained this clear yet surprising recognition through every reaction of my body, in the ways it drew breath and strove, in how it touched as well as rested, most of all in the unprecedented manner in which it attempted to slow down time itself, so that every instant could be fully inhabited, extended and explored. For the first time in years, there was nothing to rush towards, and no one in the surroundings to fear. And although that night we spoke about none of this, and I had no idea of her circumstances, I understood that I wanted this again and again, insatiably, not only now, but for as long as we could be together.

It was a promising sign that during our private leave-taking the next morning, before stepping outside to rejoin the others, she readily divulged the name of the village where they were camping. I confessed I dearly wanted to see her again, if she would have me. She kissed me full and long upon the mouth, and asked me to come and find her within the next fortnight. Then we would see where things went. There would be competition, she cautioned with a grin, all of this happened without any warning, you can't just make the rest of your life vanish like that, but her eyes seemed to be assuring me not to worry.

Later that morning it was time to say goodbye to Gabriel, although he knew now where to look for us the next time he was in E.. The boys both appeared to have had fantastic nights, and bid their companions very affectionate farewells, but things were clearly much more light-hearted between them: they were delighted with what they'd unexpectedly found, and were each fully confident they'd chance upon such wayside joys time and again. None of them would have considered this a significant parting.

Paul decided we should begin our holiday walking in the woods we'd driven through last afternoon. The nights were perfect for sleeping outdoors, and moreover, the owner of our tavern had told him there was a river running through the valley parallel to the road that had been dammed a few months before, and it would be a beautiful spot for a picnic. The ideal recovery from our nightlong exertions, the inn-keeper had winked and teased, while his wife made up a basket for our lunch. I noted at the time how ironic it was that all the plans that suited me so well were being suggested by Paul.

The forest was in full leaf, and the spring sunlight brought forth the freshness and sparkle in its young foliage. We soon left the path that followed the top of the ridge and walked between the trees, leaping over streams with single strides, and then rushing downhill at Paul's insistence, winding exhilaratingly at high speeds in between the trunks, branches and stumps, all the while heading towards the river at the bottom of the valley that at points gleamed like gold on fire, and in which we longed to plunge.

It seems amazing now that none of this – not the lorry-ride with Gabriel, nor the marvellous events of the previous night, nor the shockingly cool tingle of leaping into the water and thereafter settling in without fear or hurry just as I had with Aishe, to make each moment as long and lovely as it could be

– ever distracted me from my purpose that weekend. It feels incredible that rage can be so icy. Over an hour later, after drying off in the sun, we reluctantly put on our pants and continued along another tiny, rocky path that led downriver, until we arrived above the sink of the dam, looking down thirty metres at the crash of the falls, and further ahead, at the large unsightly barrage beyond which the forest continued.

It was the perfect spot. Also, it wouldn't feel quite as right after lunch. And so, although I had to raise my voice because of the unceasing thunder below us, although we were both enjoying being freshly beaded all over our shirtless bodies by its fine spray, I opened finally the real business of the morning.

'Paul, I want you to listen carefully. I don't know how much you know about me, but if you do, you shouldn't have any trouble believing what I am about to promise. Which is that I'll throw you without any hesitation into the water and against those rocks if you utter a single lie today. Are we clear?'

Despite looking stunned, as though he were witnessing a ghost, or perhaps it was the cold conviction in my voice that I intended to leave here having ended his young life, he managed a nod. I was unmoved by his shock, although I do remember feeling that I must have worn exactly the same expression as Eugene's head was shot off in front of me four months ago, on the bank of another river. But there was no question of sympathy. I had had to deal with the facts of betrayal and death, and so would Paul. He shouldn't have been here if he wasn't fully aware of the risks. It was his choice that had led him here today, and ignorance or immaturity was no excuse. That was what Elena had taught me.

'Were you assigned to report to Franz every last thing I said in your presence, and everywhere we went together?'

He couldn't face me anymore, but nodded. I could make out the shame that had crept into his face, mixed with the fear.

'And it was Franz's idea for you to urge me to open up and tell everyone my war-stories?'

This time he didn't look up.

'And everything else you told me was a lie, about being chased out of your school, about arriving in E. by chance, and Marlene being an aunt of yours who fortunately had these jobs available?'

'The school story was true,' he finally spoke in a voice that was unrecognisably halting. 'Every word of it. It happened last year, and I did run away. Only I joined up with our forces, outside my town in the hills. That's how they picked me for this job. I already belonged to our side, as a spy and a courier. They sent me into other towns to talk to people and find out things, and report back to our divisions.'

'Who explained what you had to do with me?'

'Someone. I don't know. He claimed to be an old friend of yours, who said you were about to face grave danger so we had to smuggle you out. He didn't tell me anything about you except that you'd been a loyal ally, but now with things about to change your enemies would seek their revenge. Then I was told exactly what to do, and made to memorise the sequence of what was to happen that day we crossed the border, all the way from the field where we were deposited at the feast, to the cart that drove us into E., to the fat lady who would be visible to us as soon as we approached The Bristol, ready to pick up the part of my aunt.'

Now I was looking directly at him, while he had fixed his gaze on the opposite bank of the river. 'Paul, remember, I said no lies. You're asking for trouble. Your story doesn't add up. You must see that for yourself. If someone is an ally, you don't spy on him. You don't watch him, follow him, fill him with lies.'

'Yes, yes, I thought that as soon as Franz called me in the first night, and explained I had to report everything to him. I even asked him who you really were. He said he didn't know for sure, and that was the point of the whole exercise. With all the changes at home, people weren't sure what you really thought or what you'd do next. It was our job to find out. But he assured me you were both important and dangerous, and so I had to follow each order to the letter. We had to keep you safe until we knew whether you were a friend or not. That's why he said I should encourage you to talk.'

'Believe me, Ivan,' he turned towards me to plead, 'I've now told you everything I know. That was the sum of my duties. I never brought any harm upon you. I never even had to fake liking you. I enjoyed our life together. I was proud that you were my friend. Our good times were all absolutely genuine. I had no idea my information would cause you harm.'

'Did you read my diary?'

He gazed downwards once more without speaking.

'And Gabriel and the girls? You knew we would come across them, didn't you?' I had asked this last question from within a trance, with no preparation or previous insight, unaware until I spoke the words that they had formed inside me.

'Franz introduced me to Gabriel three days ago, and told me his lorry would stop for us.'

'And?'

'And which girl to leave for you.'

Like Paul, I took my time before speaking again. I motioned to him to sit down. Then I drew closer to loom upon him. The moment to end this mock trial had arrived. I'd allowed the defendant to present his case, and it was now the hour of the verdict.

'Look, Paul, nothing in my life has been genuine the last few months. Perhaps not even the last few years, throughout that bastard war. Everything has crumbled into lies. You're not to blame for any of that. In fact, your role in it is very small.

It's just that I have to begin cleaning up somewhere. I have to reclaim my life at some point. I was always someone who acted. Since coming here, as you know, I've been too confused to do anything. Punishing you will by no means square the account, and it's a long way to go to the very top if I want justice from everyone who wronged me, but it's a bad beginning if I let you off alive. I'm sorry. We're both part of something bigger than ourselves, and we've both been its victims. I'm sure sooner or later they'll catch up with me to finish me off, if I don't take care of that myself, but today, my friend, it's your turn.'

My voice was as reasonable as my words. There was no flame to douse, nothing to cool down. I could see the panic in his eyes, but I also knew he wouldn't fight back. I was going to get down, place my knee upon his chest, and strangle him. I also held a knife in reserve in my bag.

I knelt. My knee curved just short of his throat. He began a high-pitched wail punctuated by shrieks and breathless yelps. I gazed fully into his eyes once more before reaching for his throat. In that moment, I saw Aishe first of all. But she too had been part of this. I saw Paul himself, asleep at the back of the truck with his head on my lap, our first morning together. That had been a pretence. I saw Elena, whom I despised too much even for revenge. And then I watched myself, as if on a screen on Paul's face, during the long war, firing my rifle, biting off the rings from grenades, shooting Masek in the head after an interrogation. These were scenes I'd hitherto never witnessed, even though I'd played the central role in every one of them. They hadn't been *my* killings: I had never imagined them before or afterwards, or borne their full weight.

The film flickered and a hole appeared where my face was, as though the reel had caught fire. It was actually the tears in my eyes. Elena was right about at least one thing, I'd never allowed myself to see my own choices. I was about to choose again in a moment, but once more, magically, someone else, other forces, would be held responsible. What did I hope would end with Paul's death? Who could I fool with that answer again?

Paul hadn't stopped squealing while staring fixedly at me. I was back to where Aishe had taken me, to where Paul and I were a little while ago floating in the water, in a pocket of free time concealed snugly within the present, the instant right before any action. Nothing had been forced yet, and the future lay open in every direction. A few seconds later, and all but one path would remain. To the right of us, within my field of awareness, the sun had climbed to its midday high, and blazed directly upon the meeting of the wall and the water.

Incongruously I stretched out my arms. I was already aware of what my decision entailed. I could conduct myself freely just now, but as soon as this was over, a future would have to be fashioned, and filled somehow with purpose, activity, and trust. Moreover, simultaneously, the past would come crashing upon me without mercy, in all its vengefulness for being so long ignored. There would be countless ghosts to stare down. None would ever forgive me. There would be no Elena, no alibi, no defence. Such loneliness was what that future promised before it allowed me anything new, the price it demanded for letting me proceed further.

I stepped off Paul, and sank to the ground beside him. I told him he was free to run away at any time. I wanted to ask him to stay, because I would need him, I would miss him, I would be so alone without him, once he disappeared through those trees. But all I did was repeat to him he could run away.

He seemed too tired to respond. Without climbing to his feet, he turned around and sat up, facing the waterfall with me. Time crashed down before us, flowed on a bit further and pooled into a giant calm. Paul couldn't stop weeping, head between his knees, howling loudly, crying as if for both of us.

Acknowledgements

I'd like to thank Nandita Aggarwal and Rohan Chhetri at Hachette India for supporting this book from the start. Especial thanks go to Rohan for his edits, and for suggesting the cover image. I'm also very grateful to the photographer, Pol Úbeda Hervàs.

For taking the time to share their thoughts on several of these stories at different points, I want to thank Sasha, Ma, Baba, Ankur, Chloë, Tess and Tony. Thank you also to Renuka Chatterjee and V K Karthika, who read and commented on earlier drafts of the novella.

My gratitude to the *Istanbul Review*, *Turbine*, *Tehelka*, the *Sunday Star-Times* and the *Edinburgh Review* for publishing some of the stories in this collection.

Thank you to Doug and Ann, and to everyone in my family for their constant support and affection. And finally to Ma, Baba, Didi, Kishoreda, Sasha and Leela – my amazing presences. Never lost when I think of you.